T0129305

New Spun Yarns From Across the Big Divide

More Ghost Writings of
Charles M. Russell

With an Introduction by the Late Nancy Russell

Richard Bird Baker

iUniverse, Inc.
Bloomington

New Spun Yarns From Across the Big Divide
More Ghost Writings of Charles M. Russell

iUniverse books may be ordered through booksellers or by contacting:

iUniverse
1663 Liberty Drive
Bloomington, IN 47403
www.iuniverse.com
1-800-Authors (1-800-288-4677)

Because of the dynamic nature of the Internet, any web addresses or links contained in this book may have changed since publication and may no longer be valid.

The views expressed in this work are solely those of the author and do not necessarily reflect the views of the publisher, and the publisher hereby disclaims any responsibility for them.

This is a work of fiction. All of the characters, names, incidents, organizations, and dialogue in this novel are either the products of the author's imagination or are used fictitiously.

ISBN: 978-1-4759-9542-8 (sc)
ISBN: 978-1-4759-9543-5 (e)

Printed in the United States of America.

iUniverse rev. date: 6/21/2013

Dedications

This book is dedicated to the neighborhood children who were fortunate enough to sit on the floor of Charlie Russell's cabin and listen to him tell stories as he painted with one hand and sculpted animals with the other. These kids include George Fisher, Neddy Lincoln, Jack Russell, Jeanette Willis, Charles Bartelt, Chuck Johnson, Don Johnson, Harland Menti, Howard Brovan, Bill Bertsche, Carl Snyder II, Howard Baker, Norman Wenner, Bruce Wilkins, Elton Good, Doug DeCew, Anna DeCew, Larry Conklin, Steve Swanberg, Emil Erickson, Helen Strain, Florence Bondy, Viginia Bondy, Betty Kaufman, Charlie Wynn, Evelyn Fisher, Beth Fisher, Marge Fisher, and many others.

It is also dedicated to the bartenders who kept Charlie's glass full until he quick drinking in 1908, including Bill Rance, Sid Willis, Fred Piper, Al Trigg, Cut Bank Brown, Shorty Young, and Charlie Green.

It is also dedicated to the business persons on the corner of Great Falls' Fifth Avenue North and Thirteenth Street who served the Russells, including Carl Snyder I, druggist, Bill DeCew, grocer, Frank Sherer, cobbler, and Mabel Green, beauty shop owner.

It is also dedicated to the firemen of the North

Side Fire Station, and to the memory of the building itself, which was located on the south-west side of the corner enumerated above. These men pitched a lot of horseshoes and swapped a lot of yarns with Charlie.

It is also dedicated to my great-grandfather, George Washington Bird, and my grandmother, Stella Willard Baker Tuman, two centenarians and early Great Falls settlers who knew Charlie, and to Doctor Edward Edwin, who accompanied Russell to the Rochester Clinic and to whom Charlie spoke his last words as he trailed out across the Big Divide.

Finally, this book is dedicated to all of Charlie's Great Falls neighbors, especially those who were still living in the neighborhood when I was a child. An extensive list of their names is written in the Author's introduction of my book *Letters from Across the Big Divide.*

Acknowledgements

I'd like to express my thanks to Tara Cabarett for illustrating this book's front cover. Thanks to Brian Morger for the sketch on the back cover, the water color of the cowboy cooking dinner, and the oil painting of Russell's house and cabin. Thanks to Don Nicklen for permission to print the Brian Morger painting of Russell's home. Thanks to Jessica Damyanovich for the sketch of Russell painting a clay statue of a rattlesnake. Thanks to Diane Stinger, Lonnie Baker, Don and Diana Hartman, Suzie McIntyre and Jacque Balyeat for helping me with the infuriating technology involved in writing and submitting a manuscript. Thank you to the Great Falls Public Library staff and the volunteers in its Montana Room for assisting me with the research involved in producing this book. Thanks to the members of the Great Falls writers' group W. O. W. (Writing Our Way) for listening to me read excerpts from this book's rough drafts and offering constructive criticism. Thanks to Louis Guttenberg, Diane Stinger, Lonnie Baker, and Dianna Hartman for donating to me the used computer components I used in polishing these writings for submission. Thanks to Diane Stinger and Lonnie Baker for your wonderful proof-reading. Thanks to everybody willing to give this book a fair shake.

"The West is dead my friend
But writers hold the seed
And what they sow
Will live and grow
Again to those who read"

Charles M. Russell
Great Falls, Montana
1917

"The lady I trotted in double harness with was the best booster and pardner a man ever had. She could convince anybody I was the greatest artist in the world, and that makes a feller work harder. Ya jes' can't disappoint a person like that, so I done my best work for her. If it hadn't been for Mame, I wouldn't have a roof over my head."

Charles M. Russell
Great Falls, Montana
1926

Table of Contents

Great Falls, Montana

The Great Falls —Photo by Kool.

Author's Introduction

During the late Nineteenth Century and early Twentieth Century, a fiction style utilizing a narrator was quite popular. It differed from first-person writing in that the narrator was never the protagonist and was seldom a main character. The narrator's attitude toward his characters and their events was usually obvious. That attitude, together with the narrator's dialect, gave the writing much of its tone.

Of course, Charles M. Russell is much more famous for his paintings than for his writings, but in the early nineteen twenties, he published two delightful short volumes of yarns, his *Rawhide Rawlins* books. They were printed in Great Falls, Montana and sold for a dollar a copy. After Charlie died, Nancy Russell sold the publication rights to Doubleday, who combined the two volumes under the title *Trails Plowed Under.*

Charlie's narrator was a seasoned, old cowpuncher named Rawhide Rawlins, telling Russell's favorite yarns in a relaxed, meandering style utilizing colorful cowboy lingo. Rawhide Rawlins set a tone that was humorous yet subtly nostalgic. The ninety years that have passed since their original publication have taken nothing away from the stories' humor, wit, wisdom, and universality.

This book represents the third volume of writings I've published utilizing Charles M. Russell, story teller extraordinaire, as my narrator. My first volume, *Letters from Across the Big Divide, i*s a collection of over eighty letters I wrote depicting Charlie Russell commenting about today's events, issues, and trends in Will Rogers-styled editorials. My second volume, *Corral Dust from Across the Big Divide,* depicts Charlie telling cowboy yarns, some of which were true events but many of which were "corral dust." This volume, *New Spun Yarns from Across the Big Divide,* continues with Will Rogers' favorite story teller, Kid Russell, spinning more yarns filled with Charlie's attitudes and philosophy.

As in my last two volumes, I have attempted to imitate Russell's linguistics, originally a Missouri dialect that soon became highly embellished with metaphors from the cow camps, saloons, and card tables of Central Montana. Charlie also adopted many colorful phrases from the Blood Indians, and I've utilized a generous sample of them in these yarns. All "mistakes" in grammar and usage are intentional, used to make the tone of these yarns more in accordance with Russell's delivery. For clarity, I've chosen to use conventional punctuation and capitalization, two entities Charlie often ignored. However, I have maintained a few of his common misspellings for literary flavor.

This volume presents Charlie giving us his interpretation of more actual historical events than did my last volume, *Corral Dust*. These historical events include Judge Pray's yarn, the Texas cowboy strike, the 1894 march on Washington, Hogan's Army, Big Nose George, John B. Stetson, Kid Curry, Rattlesnake Jake, Charlie Fallon, the murder of Sheriff Jim Webb, Charlie Bowlegs, and the flying machine incident in Glendive.

Some of these yarns tell of incidents that actually occurred to Charlie and his friends, while others are obviously tall tales. Some of these occurrences were written in the memoirs of Russell's old friends, including Teddy Blue Abbott, Kid Amby Cheney, Con Price, Kicking Bob Keenan, Patrick (Tommy) Tucker, and Frank Bird Linderman. Others are yarns that circulated throughout the cattle-raising West and found their way into more than one cowboy's memoirs.

Three of these yarns are exceptions to the samples listed in the two preceding paragraphs. "Lying Fishermen of Fort Benton" is adapted from a scene in the novel *Three Men in a Boat*, published by Jerome K. Jerome in 1889. "The Demise of Wild Wolf Willy" and "The Hanging of Stu Green" are adapted from yarns in Alfred Henry Lewis' *Wolfville*, published in 1897.

Although some of these events actually occurred and some of the people involved actually existed, the book in general should be regarded as a work of fiction. Keep in mind I've taken advantage of "artistic license" in expanding, romanticizing, and fictionalizing many of these accounts. That's a fancy way of admitting I've coated them with corral dust.

In my introduction to *Letters from Across the Big Divide,* I described some of my childhood memories of growing up near Charlie's cabin and living among many of his former neighbors. I won't subject you to that again, but allow me to reiterate I am not an authority on Russell's life, his art, or his writings. Nevertheless, I couldn't resist writing another volume of yarns using Will Roger's favorite story teller, Charlie Russell, as the honored narrator. Whether or not Charlie actually told many of these yarns himself isn't my concern. My concern is whether or not I can do justice to Charlie Russell's dry wit, humor, and story-telling techniques as I utilize him as the story teller. The readers will be the best judges of that.

These yarns are presented in the order they were written, but they don't need to be read in any particular order. In fact, it might be best to read a few of the shortest yarns first to become acclimated to the late-nineteenth-century cowboy lingo. My favorite is "The Dragon in the Silver Dollar," allegedly a true account. Of course, it's best to read Nancy Russell's introduction first.

I will be happy to read and answer any questions, comments, or objections concerning this book sent E mail to richardbakerbird@yahoo.com. Thank you for reading this collection.

Richard Bird Baker

An Introduction by the
Late Nancy Russell

It was not without considerable reluctance that I submitted to writing an introduction to a book written by a Great Falls author. Although I was strongly inclined to deny his request, I ultimately agreed to the task out of respect for Charles. I decided he'd have been proud to be chosen narrator of a publication written by the great-grandson of the late George Washington Bird.

I was but a young sprout of sixteen when I met Charles in '95. I was working as a cook and child tender for Ben and Lela Roberts in Cascade. Ben had known Charles for several years, and he had periodically helped Charles sell his artwork. Charles had quit working for the cattle outfits two years prior, and he was now living and painting in a shack on Mr. Roberts' land. The Roberts children had renamed me Mamie by then, and Charles called me Mame ever after.

I won't burden you with all the bleak details of my tragic youth in Kentucky. Let's simply say I came from a broken family—very broken. My father left my mother while she was still carrying me, and my stepfather refused to accept me, causing me to live much of my childhood with my grandparents. Finally, my mother and my stepfather brought my half sister and me with them when they fled to Helena, Montana, seeking a better life.

The depression of '93 hit us hard. My stepfather was out of work, and my mother tried to feed the family by taking in sewing. Finally, my stepfather went to work in the mines of Idaho, promising he'd send for us soon. Before he could, my mother died of consumption. When my stepfather returned to take my half sister Ella with him back to Idaho, he declared that since I was not his blood relative, he would not be burdened with me. I was left alone in Helena to fend for myself at the age of fifteen.

My luck finally took a turn for the better when Mr. and Mrs. Roberts came to Helena to hire a live-in maid for their home in Cascade. On the way home, they told me about a promising, talented, young cowboy artist painting and living in their cabin, and I anxiously anticipated meeting the man. When we finally met, I sensed immediately that this was a man unlike anyone I'd ever known.

Never had I felt such a strong radiance of charisma from a man. He seemed like a cowboy, certainly, but so unlike any cowboy I'd ever met. I felt strongly that God had created Charles for the purpose of leaving a legacy and that I had been created to play a vital role in it. Yes, Charles and I seemed created for each other.

Many people, including Mrs. Roberts, warned me not to become too fond of Charles and not to let him court me. They said he drank too much, lacked ambition, and would never own a ranch or even become a cattle foreman. They said that whenever Charles sold a painting, he and his cowboy pals would spend every cent it earned on a good time. Besides, I was still a child of sixteen, and Charles was thirty-one, and he'd known the society of the "painted cats" of the saloons and the "girls of the line." But I knew somehow that Charles was bound for greatness. All he needed was a good wife and a determined business agent. I was soon to become both.

Charles courted me for almost a year before he asked me, "Mame, would you like to throw in with me?"

That was the first time I ever became angry with Charles, thinking he was inviting me to live with him out of wedlock. He calmed me down by saying, "Mame, I was talkin' about us marryin'."

We married in September of '96, and we tried hard to survive in Cascade by selling his paintings, but as Charles said, "The grass wasn't so good." I convinced him the grass would be greener in Great Falls, a larger and busier town than Cascade with more potential art buyers passing through on the trains. Besides, Great Falls had just acquired electric lights, streetcars, and even telephones, things that Cascade would lack for two or three more decades. In April of '97, we rented a small house on Great Falls' lower north side.

Shortly after we moved to the "Electric City," Charles Schlatzlein, a Butte shop keeper who occasionally sold Charles' art, persuaded my husband to make me his business agent. Charles said, "That's just fine with me. You sell the pictures; I'll just paint." Once we reached that agreement, Charles' work would never again be traded for a round of drinks, a few dollars, or a sack of groceries, as Charles and his friends had been doing for so many years.

The worst quarrel we ever had was early in our marriage when I demanded seventy-five dollars for a painting Charles was about to sell for five. He always insisted I was charging "dead-man's prices" for his work and I'd never sell anything. People soon began to refer to me as "Nancy the Robber," "Nancy the Road Agent," "Russell's Slave Driver," "that damned woman," and a few other names I'd never say, let alone print. But I knew from the start Charles was a genius and his work was worth many, many times more than he and his friends ever realized.

In 1900, Charles received a small inheritance from his mother, who'd died shortly before we met. We used it for a down payment on the house at 1219 Fourth Avenue North—the one pictured at the beginning of this introduction—and the two city lots to the west. For three years, Charles painted in our dining room, which suited him just fine. After all, it was a much better place to work than he was used to. Most of his work had been done in saloons or in shacks full of noisy, unemployed, hard-drinking cowhands. But I knew he could do his best work in his own private studio, so in 1903, I purchased a large load of surplus telephone poles and hired a contractor to build his famous cabin studio he named "The Medicine Tipi." In there he did his greatest work, including the masterpiece of his life, the mural that still hangs behind the Speaker's Station in the House of Representatives in Helena.

For a long time, it was very difficult to sell Charles' art. Many large museums, including the one in Charles' home town of St. Louis, displayed Remington's work, but they wouldn't hang Charles'. After all, Mr. Remington had studied art abroad, and he lived in prestigious New York City. It was known that Charles had very little education and was simply a self-taught artist, to say nothing of his background as a Montana cowboy. The museum operators believed that Charles was an illustrator, not a true artist.

In 1903, I spent weeks knocking on the doors of

publishers and art venders in New York City with almost no sales. A year later, I knocked on all those doors again with a little more success. But it wasn't until 1911 that I succeeded in gaining Charles' first one-man showing in New York, a city Charles thoroughly dreaded.

I was always painfully aware of the fact that many people in Great Falls disliked me. Charles' old cowboy friends resented the way I always tried to convert Charles to a gentleman. Of course, I was never very successful with those attempts. His pals resented me for often coming between them and my husband, depriving them of much of the time they wanted to spend with Charles. I felt sorry it was necessary for me to do that, but if Charles had continued to waste most of his time drinking and horsing around with displaced cowboys, he would never have left his great legacy. Charles needed to be taught creative discipline.

Of course, I didn't want to shut off his fun completely, so Charles and I reached a compromise. We agreed he'd spend every morning and early afternoon painting. Mid and late afternoons and early evenings were his to spend with his wild friends, as long as he was home by dark. If his friends arrived for him before his work day was over, they'd have to wait on a bench near the cabin door the cowboys called "Death Row."

I well realized that many Great Falls citizens disliked me because they thought I was too obsessed with earning money from Charles' art. I can't deny

I always sought financial security. As a child, I was so deprived I often found myself sucking on rocks to forget my hunger. When you bear memories like that, you do what you have to do to never return to such horrible poverty.

At the peak of his career, Charles enjoyed more success than most artists ever achieve in a lifetime. Nevertheless, neither of us was ever totally accepted by Great Falls' elite society. Charles was excluded because of his lack of education, his cowboy lingo, his clothes, and his choice of friends. Although he quit drinking in 1908, many Great Falls residents preferred to believe he died a drunkard. I was excluded from high society because of my Kentucky mountain background and speech.

This exclusion never bothered Charles, who strongly preferred the society of what he called "regular men" to that of high-society socialites. I must admit, it deeply troubled me. I did all I could to become socially accepted. I learned to dress in the formal, modern style of successful men's wives, but Charles stuck with his riding boots, Stetson hat, and half-breed sash. Josephine Trigg worked with me at acquiring formal English grammar and pronunciation, and I joined the Meadowlark Country Club where I took up golf and learned to dance. Charles refused to play golf, but he took a few dancing lessons with me.

In spite of all those efforts, we were continually shunned by the snobs of Great Falls. I didn't realize it then, but my resentment from this shunning caused me to try to become wealthier than all of my neighbors on Great Falls' prestigious Fourth Avenue North. Success and wealth became my obsession and my revenge, causing me to become more and more disliked by the "regular" people who knew and loved Charles.

I finally became so disgusted with Great Falls' self-righteous cliques that I decided I no longer wanted to live there. Charles wished to remain there because he loved his cabin studio, and so many of his old friends from the cow camps remained in the area. Again we reached a compromise. We agreed to spend our winters in Pasadena and our summers at our cabin on Lake McDonald, a place Charles loved and named Bull Head Lodge. We'd still live in Great Falls during the spring and the fall. We were in the process of having a house built in Pasadena when Charles passed away.

When I left Great Falls for good in 1928, that corrupt town deceived me in another way. I sold the town our house, Charles' enlarged cabin, and the two empty adjacent lots to the west for twenty thousand dollars with one stipulation: the expanded cabin would serve as the Charles M. Russell Museum and that no modern structure would be built on the property. The land around the cabin was to serve as a small city park. Today, any visitor to the Charles M. Russell Museum can see how drastically the city officials broke their word.

By now, almost a dozen scholars and writers have written biographies about Charles. Considerable disagreement has existed among his biographers, and a reader can become confused as to which authors to believe. My advice to you is this: believe the written words of people who actually knew Charles, people like Austin Russell, Frank Bird Linderman, and Frederick Renner. Above all, believe the words in the biography published by Homer Britzman and Ramon Adams. Allow me to explain why.

After Charles' death, I spent several weeks dictating the details of his life to a former "Great Falls Tribune" writer named Daniel Conway. The biography we produced was titled *Child of the Frontier*. Since the Doubleday Publishing Company had already published a compilation of Charles' letters under the title *Good Medicine*, as well as a collection of his short stories titled *Trails Plowed Under*, I expected them to eagerly accept our new book. However, the depression had recently arrived, and neither biographies nor western non-fiction was selling. The book was rejected.

When I left this world to join Charles in 1940, Homer Britzman bought my Pasadena home, including most of its furnishings. In a filing cabinet, he found the manuscript Mr. Conway and I had produced, and after World War II, he hired Ramon Adams, a well known western writer, to rewrite it in Adams' words. They renamed it *Charles M. Russell, the Cowboy Artist*, and it was printed listing Britzman and Adams as the co-authors. No credit whatsoever was given to Daniel Conway or me for the original manuscript. In my mind, Homer Britzman was a thief and a felon. However, this book still stands out as being the most accurate of Charles' biographies simply because I provided its information.

In addition to being the greatest western artist ever to live, Charles was considered by many, including our friend Will Rogers, to be the best cowboy story teller of all times. Richard Bird Baker's attempt to keep his style and vocabulary alive by using Charles as his narrator is nothing short of complimentary to my husband. I hope these writings can almost live up to Charles' story-telling talents.

The Late Nancy Cooper Russell

The *W. B. Dance* at the Fort Benton levee, the head of navigation on the Missouri River.

2011 in the moon the berries are ripe

Lying Fishermen of Fort Benton

I've said it before, and I'll chew it finer. The Old West could put in its claim for more liars than any place under the sun. When a man came west, he took lessons in lyin' from the prairies, where Ma Nature herself seems to lie. Sometimes ranges of mountains a hundred miles away look close enough to hit with a Winchester, and streams appear to run uphill. But these old-timers weren't vicious liars. It was a lack of readin' matter, a love of romance, and a wish to entertain that caused them to stretch the blanket when they hatched up yarns.

When I crossed the skyline for the land beyond the Big Divide in '26, the Old West was deader than a can of corned beef. Most of the grassland and the old buffalo trails were plowed under, and dirt roads, railroad tracks, telegraph lines, and bob wire crisscrossed the land like a surgeon's stitches. Man's inventions had thrown a lariat around the corpse of the Old West and tied it to the East. But the old western habit of stringin' a whizzer—what the Red man called "spreadin' buffalo chips"—still rode the great ranges of Montana.

Maybe the first great liar of the Old West was Jim Bridger, the mountain man and trapper who discovered the land they later branded Yellowstone Park. He was huntin' elk one day and spotted one that looked maybe forty paces away. He fired his front loader, but the shot hit nowhere near the elk. He stepped a dozen paces closer, reloaded, cocked, and fired again, but the elk didn't move.

"Something's amiss with my flintlock," Jim tells himself. "I'll have to club the critter." He grips the rifle by the barrel, rushes toward the elk, and lams into a glass wall, knockin' him on his back. But Jim don't stay down for the count. He bounds to his feet and sees before him a glass mountain. When the sun's three or four fingers from bein' straight up, the glass works as a telescopic lens. That darn elk was a good twenty-five miles away.

Jim found a huge mountain that a Crow medicine man had long ago put a curse on. Everything on it was petrified: the trees, the grass, the birds, the antelope, the elk, the bear, and even the streams. That medicine man had even petrified the gravity. Bridger rode his hoss across a canyon without fallin' in once.

Jim liked to rise just before sunrise to get the jump on his huntin' or fishin'. But often he overslept and woke after the critters were finished feedin'. Jim soon learnt that if he hollered "Get up!" at the mountains at bed time, the echo of them two syllables would wake him just before dawn.

Jim said once a seven-foot snowfall trapped and froze a big herd of buffalo. He rolled them up in a big snowball and rolled them down a hill and into one of them pools of steamin' water. He said he fed boiled buffalo meat to the Indians all winter.

Jim said the mosquitoes there were so big they had to be swatted with tree boughs. Then they'd fly to a hillside and throw rocks at him. He said he had to sleep under a big iron kettle to keep the blood-suckin' rascals off him, but the buggers finally drilled through that kettle. These episodes are just a small scatterin' of the passel of buffalo chips Jim Bridger spread.

Jim might have been the king of the liars in his time, but Jim and all the other great liars of the Old West, liars like Old Man Babcock, Old Man Patrick, X Biedler, Buckskin Williams, and Milt Crowthers didn't hold openers to the fishermen I knew the decade before I crossed the Big Divide. In the short time it takes to down three drinks, I heard the best in the West once in Fort Benton.

If my memory's still sittin' square in the saddle—and I ain't none too sure it is—it was durin' that war with the Kaiser when this misdeal foots up. Me and Teddy Blue and Bill Skelton found ourselves in Fort Benton where the Stockgrowers Association was holdin' their annual roundup of themselves. Three decades had passed since I'd wrangled hosses or roped a steer, but I still kept afoot of the ropin's and wranglin's of the stockgrowers.

It was between confabs that me and Bill and Teddy Blue leaked out of the scenery and ducked into the Overland Bar to oil our tonsils. I hadn't downed a snort of likker in nine years—and I'll whoop the man who says I died a drunkard—so I told the barkeep to deal me a glass of mineral water as he sloshed out forty drops of nosepaint for my two old trail pals. We paid for our drinks and camped at a table near the fireplace. From the jump, we took to eyeballin' a giant stuffed rainbow trout in a glass case above the mantel.

"I'll be a prohibitionist if that ain't the biggest rainbow trout I ever beheld," Bill puts up.

"And the most colorful, too," Teddy stacks in. "It's as radiant as any rainbow the Maker ever painted in the sky."

"I wonder who caught it?" I chip in.

"I'm the wrinkle-horned mossback who pulled that whale out of the river," answers a grizzled old freighter camped nearby.

"When?" Teddy asks him.

"Sixteen years ago, come the third of next month."

"Where?" shoots Bill.

"Not fifty rods from where you gents are seated, just below the Geraldine Bridge."

"What did you use for bait?" I ask him.

"I baited my hook with a minnow," he shoots back. "It took me three summers to snare him. I'd heard he was in there for years, and I swore some day I'd rope him in. He weighed a whoppin' eighteen and a half pounds."

Our eyes were still admirin' the mammoth fish when the old wagoner sauntered out of the saloon. In less time than it took for the barkeep to slop us out another round, an aging sodbuster shuffled up to our table.

"I notice you stockmen have been sizin' up that trout hangin' over the fireplace. I surmise none of you were here in Fort Benton when it was caught."

"Can't say we were," Teddy answers. "None of us are from here."

"'Twas five years ago I caught it," he boasts, "just below the Great Falls of the Missouri one chilly sunset in June. The remarkable thing was I caught it with a thin line and a fly, even though the giant weighed twenty-six pounds. And I snagged her my first time out, and on my first darn cast."

"That was a mighty lucky first cast," I ante up.

"Weren't nothin' lucky about it," he snaps. "It's

know-how, all in the flick of the wrist." With those boastful words, the sod buster plowed his way out of the saloon. Our eyes were still sizin' up that trout when the town barber comes ambulatin' into the saloon to wet his whistle.

"I couldn't help noticin' your eyes stackin' up that stuffed trout above the fireplace, cattlemen. I don't suppose anybody's ever unfolded on your ears the story of how it was caught."

"No, we're not from here," Bill stacks in.

"Where'd you catch it?" I chip in. "And what did you use for bait?"

"Who told you I caught it?" the barber shoots back.

"Nobody. I just somehow savvied it was you," I humor him.

"Well, you're quite right. I caught it with a worm early one morning up on the Marias River. And I'll tell you cattlemen, nary a locoed steer, a wild bronc, or even a bear ever put up such a fight as that fish. It took me over an hour to land it, and it broke my stoutest fishing pole. That fish weighed in at not one ounce less than thirty-four pounds."

As soon as the barber trailed out of the saloon, the barkeep ambled up to refill our glasses. "I couldn't help overhearin' the fish stories them three peddlers of loads unloaded on you gents," he antes up. "I hear fish tales like those every time a stranger's in town. As one former cow puncher to another, let me tell you, they're all feedin' you a bushel of Mexican oats. I caught that fish myself."

Of course, the questions "where, when, and how" followed, sure as a remuda follows a bell mare.

"I caught it up on the Milk River years ago when I was a boy. I'll never forget that day. I played hooky from school one fall morning and rode my roan to my favorite fishin' hole. Our family was possum poor, so poor, in fact, when the wolf came to our door, he packed a lunch, so we didn't own no fishin' tackle. Danged if I didn't catch it with a string tied to a tree. My bait was a grasshopper on a bent nail."

In two flicks of a lamb's tail, the barkeep was back behind the bar caperin' to his manly duties.

"Let's sneak a closer look at that mammoth fish," Teddy Blue whispers to us the first time the barkeep turns to face the back bar. He scoots a chair up next to the wall, steps up on it, and lifts the trophy fish from the glass case above the fireplace. Quick as a horse bucks, the front legs of that chair buckle, slammin' Teddy against the floor like a rider thrown from a bronc, the trophy fish landin' beneath him. He lays there still as a corpse for about as long as it takes a man to deal four poker hands.

"You didn't hurt that fish, did ya?" bellows the barkeep as he prances over to Teddy, who's still in partial eclipse on the hardwood floor. Me and Bill pull Teddy to his feet, and there on the floor we see the fish in hundreds of pieces—pieces of plaster of Paris.

Ride easy and save the best of your mount for the trail that crosses the Big Divide.

Your friend, C M. Russell

2011 in the moon the leaves turn color

Three More Yarns
of Fort Benton

Fort Benton has as colorful a history as any camp on the Missouri. She was founded several decades before most Montana towns as an army fort, a trading post, and a steamboat landing. Every brand of man and woman the Maker ever created passed through Fort Benton. Over the years, many a good yarn brewed in that camp. One of my favorites touched on a hangin' bee that fetched loose back when I was still a wobbly colt in Missouri.

One day in August of '68, William Hynson came

amblin' down Front Street near the post office, and he happed up on some members of the local vigilance committee buildin' a wooden scaffold in the street. One of the citizens hollered, "Say, Bill, could you lend us a hand?"

"What are you gents riggin' up?" Bill antes up.

"It's a scaffold for a necktie party," they stack in.

"And who's the guest of honor at this necktie social?" Bill raises 'em.

"You'll soon see. There's no time to talk now. The vigilance committee chairman and the hangman will be here any time. Take this saw and start cuttin' these boards to size, Bill."

"I'm proud to, if it means I can watch a hangin'," Bill puts up as he rolls up his sleeves, spits on his hands, and takes to sawin' like a man possessed. "It's been months since I've seen a good hangin'."

When all the boards are cut to size, they hand him a hammer and a small keg of nails and say, "Start nailin' these boards to the frame, Bill."

"I'm glad to, just for the privilege of watchin' a good hangin'," Bill tells 'em again. "Now who did you say we're hangin'?"

"You'll see soon enough, Bill. There's no time to talk now. We need you to climb up on this ladder and nail down the gallows pole."

This being done, Bill climbs down the ladder to the floor. "Who is it we're hangin'?" he nudges 'em again.

"You'll know soon, Bill. Right now we need you

to climb to the top of this ladder again, and we'll toss you the end of this rope."

Bill does as directed, and then he's told, "Tie it around the gallows pole, Bill. Fasten it good and tight."

Bill does as he's told, and when both his hooves are back down on the floor, he asks the man tyin' the noose at the other end of the rope, "Who did you say it is we're hangin'?"

"Here come the chairman and the hangman now!" one of the vigilantes hollers.

The chairman, formerly a Civil War officer, tall, stalwart, and dignified, asks, "Is everything ready?"

"Yes, sir. We've tested the noose and the trap door, and they seem to work just fine."

"Then bring the felon up on the scaffold," he orders.

Quick as dry gun powder, three strong vigilantes seize hold of Bill, tie his hands behind his back, lift him up on the trap door, and slip the noose around his neck. The roundup boss of the vigilantes announces, "William Hynson, you are hereby charged with the following felonies: one count of stealing a rifle, valued by its owner at twenty-four dollars; one count of robbing a freighter of seven furs, valued by their owner at forty-two dollars; and one count of killing a Chinese servant, valued by his employer at four hundred dollars. Do you have any last words before we swing you off?"

It was a howlin' shame William Hynson couldn't

have seen this hangin' from the view of the audience. Folks who watched it said it was as good as any. It came off without a hitch, the cash-in bein' quick and quiet.

Of course, the tradin' post at Fort Benton always drew a good many Indians, swappin' furs for firearms and trade whiskey. This oft times caused some of the white town folk to feel nervous as a cat in a room full of rockin' chairs. One day shortly after the Sioux trumped General Custer, the commander of the fort decided to show the Indians some muscle. He heralded the demonstration of a Howitzer would cut itself loose on the parade ground just outside the fort's walls. An old broken-down supply wagon was dragged to the center of the parade ground to serve as a target, and all the town folk, soldiers, and Indians about Fort Benton flocked in like dry cattle to a waterin' hole to watch the explosion.

A Howitzer was a small cannon built to be fired from the back of a mule. It seems the mule chosen for this feat that day was a green hand who'd never in its life packed a cannon. With the Howitzer saddled on the mule's back and the muzzle aimed over its rump at the target, the commander ordered, "Stand back!" and lit the fuse.

Somebody should have told that commander the sizzlin' of a burnin' fuse is more than enough to spook a green mule. The big critter took to spinnin' in circles, first this way and then that, now and then kickin' up its hind legs for general effect. Anybody who's ever had a speaking acquaintance with a mule can tell you once they get a notion bored into their heads, you can't shoot it out with a buffalo gun. Nor can any soldier stop a mule from spinnin' without being kicked to glory. The mule kept whirlin' as the fuse burned shorter and shorter. When the critter finally stood still for a heartbeat, that cannon was aimin' straight at a company of cavalry.

"Hit the ground!" the commander orders, and all the soldiers in the formation fall flat as wet leaves, coverin' their heads with their arms. The fuse keeps hissin' like forty snakes, and the mule again becomes uncorked and takes to windmillin' like a fence-wormin' hoss. When he stops for another heartbeat, his rump and that cannon are aimed straight at a herd of civilian spectators.

"Everybody take cover!" the mayor bellows, and the crowd commences to scatter like a flock of blackbirds, divin' under wagons and tables and hidin' behind trees and walls. This sets the mule to churnin' once more, and when the fuse finally touches off the powder, the cannon fires straight at a large band of Blackfeet. They hit the ground like they've been thrown off a wagon, and the cannon ball flies not more than two feet over their heads and explodes on the ground maybe thirty paces from where they lay.

Some of the younger warriors take this fiasco to be a low-down army play at reducin' the population of Indians, and they knock their arrows to their bowstrings and cock their firearms. But the army played in luck that day. Some of the tribe's wiser elders savvied it was an accident, and they held onto the reins of the young bucks' tempers. The important thing is nobody was hurt in the misdeal.

My cowboy friend Kickin' Bob Keenan unloaded this last yarn on me, and it's true as preachin'. I won't tip anybody's hand by tellin' you the name of the gent this fate fell to, 'cause his descendents still dwell in Fort Benton. Let's just say he was one of the town's most wealthy business sharps, and he'd never been married. He was gettin' on in years, and he well savvied if he was ever gonna get hitched, it was none too soon.

Finally, an unmarried school marm steamboats into town, and our merchant aims from the jump to slap his brand on her. In a few short months, he has her roped, throwed, and hogtied for matrimony. No cowboys were invited to the ceremony, but just the same, every cowhand in Choteau County who wasn't in jail tracked in, just to have a shot at kissin' the bride and eatin' the wedding cake.

In the old days, it was the custom in Fort Benton for the groom to take all the single men to McGraw's Saloon after the weddin' ceremony and pay for all the drinks they could down. Now this particular wealthy groom was known to be such a tightwad he was a model to Scotchmen, so the cowboys and barkeep Johnny McGraw cooked up a scheme. McGraw agreed to have plenty of good, pricey whiskey on hand for the boys. They allowed that if they got the groom well soaked with champagne, he'd be more prone to pay for everybody's drinks.

The wedding came off without a hitch, and after all the cowboys kissed the bride and ate up the wedding cake, they retired to McGraw's Saloon to await the lucky groom. But the groom didn't track in. Bein' cowhands, none of the riders had enough dust to pay for many drinks, and it was a cinch that if the eminent groom didn't trail in soon, it would surely put a damper on the joy of the occasion. So a delegation of cowhands was sent to the groom's house to convince the tightwad to come to McGraw's to host the party.

The delegation was greeted by the cheapskate's voice from behind a locked door saying, "I didn't invite you wild buckeroos to my wedding, and I didn't plan on any party. Now make tracks from here before I sick the law on you."

Quiet as shadows, the cowhands cat-footed into the groom's back yard where they soaked an empty gunny sack in a rain barrel and hoisted Kickin' Bob up on the groom's roof. Bob stuffed that wet sack into the stovepipe, and in less time than it takes to down a drink, the bride and groom came boilin' out of the smoky house like ants from a burnin' log.

The cowboys snared a rope around them both and led them up the street. They marched the groom into McGraw's Saloon and surrounded him like magpies around a dead steer to cut off his chances of escape. He gave in a little and laid a five-spot on the bar to pay for their first round of drinks. In the meantime, the bride was taken to a café to wait for her new groom, because, of course, ladies weren't allowed in Montana's distinguished drinkin' establishments.

Somehow, they encouraged Mr. Groom to down a few cow swallows of champagne with them. Of course, that five-spot our groom had laid on the bar didn't last as long as a pint of whiskey at a four-handed poker game, but the groom refused to pay for any more likker.

"Where's my wife?" he demanded of his herders.

"We won't tell you until we've drunk our fill and you finish your bottle of champagne," they answered.

Maybe it was partly that threat, and maybe it was partly the champagne, but whatever the cause, the groom began to loosen his purse strings. The horseplay and the laughter grew louder and louder, and the likker bill grew bigger and bigger. To be safe, McGraw made our groom pay up from time to time in case he managed to fetch loose.

For a time, this wild bunch played their hand well at keepin' the groom close-herded, cuttin' off any chance he had to make a break from the herd. But after ridin' a half dozen drinks down the trail, the cowhands waxed a little loose-reined, leavin' the groom with his first opening. He bolts out the door like greased lightning and races up the street toward his house, passin' all the jack rabbits on the trail like they was turtles. But ol' Kickin' Bob runs him down on hoss back, catches him in the loop of his lariat, and leads him back to the saloon like an ornery steer, the groom cussin' like a stuck bullwhacker.

It fell out that the saloon had a large ice house attached to it to keep the beer cold. Three hardy riders seize hold of the honored groom and escort him into the ice house, promisin' to cut him loose as soon as it's time for him to pay the bar tab. Trouble is, the barkeep soon joined in on the libations, causin' him to plumb forget about collecting the groom's tab. The more joy juice everybody downed, the less they remembered the groom.

At four in the morning, McGraw chased everybody out of the saloon, locked the door, and went home to sleep off the whiskey. Three hours later, he was awakened by a poundin' on his door and the voice of an angry school marm demandin' to know where her new husband was.

"Last I seen him, Kickin' Bob Keenan had him in the loop of his catch rope," the barkeep recollected.

She learnt quick that Bob was hibernatin' in the Grand Union Hotel. She found his room and darn near beat down his door. Bob was still none too sober, but somehow he calmed her down and sent his soggy memory backtrackin' the muddy, hazy trails of the past night. Finally his memory trailed up on the ice house.

"Holy snakes, the ice house!" he recalled. "Follow me!"

The bride chased Bob to the icehouse, where he unbolted the door and packed out the forgotten groom like a frozen side of beef. Bob said the groom's limbs were soon moveable, but his mustache stayed frozen stiff for two hours. So were all the cuss words he tried to shoot at Bob.

When you cross the Big Divide, watch for the smoke of my campfire. The latch string's out for you.

Your friend, C. M. Russell

2011 in the moon the leaves fall

The Dragon in the Silver Dollar

Now if I was within shootin' distance of your jaw, you'd be pointin' at me like I'm a rattlesnake and sayin', "Russell, your yarn about that plaster fish is a pile of corral dust if I ever rode up on one. Any sculptor or painter—even an old cowboy like you—can tell a real stuffed trout from a replica."

And I'd be tellin' you them words don't stack up true every roll of the dice. And it ain't just 'cause Old Dad Time traded me wrinkles for some of my eyesight. The injun truth is that oft times good sculptors and painters sure enough *can* turn a statue out of the chute that can fool us into thinkin' it's a live critter, sometimes even without the aid of likker. Some of your best artists could sculpt a statue of a cow that could fool a keen-eyed bull.

I was never one of your best painters or sculptors, but there were some worse. But if my memory's dealin' a square game—and I'm never sure it is—I can fasten a lariat on at least two times my God-given talent churned up such a statue. Oh, the first one ain't worth blowin' about much, 'cause it was only used to fool a drunk sheepherder. Take any sheepherder to one of them assayers in Butte, and they'd tell you the sheepherder didn't quite assay two ounces of sense to the ton, even when he was sober. But the second critter I sculpted fooled the mayor, the town council, some peace officers, and most every man in Great Falls who wasn't in jail.

Before I begin to hit the trail of them memories, let me slop out a little ink for the folks around Great Falls who'd tell you the first art studio I ever had was a storeroom in the back of Albert Trigg's Brunswick Saloon. The good luck that dealt me that studio crossed my trail in '93, and it *was* my first studio in Great Falls. But my first art studio ever was in the back storeroom of the Utica Saloon in '85. It belonged to one of the best barkeeps ever to pop a cork and drain a bottle, my friend Jim Shelton.

For five days and nights, Sheepherder Sam had been pesterin' around the Utica Saloon, paintin' his nose with trade likker. He'd been cut out of the herd of gamblers two days prior, havin' too often reached for the jackpot with a pair of low cards, convinced by the rot gut whiskey he was holdin' four of a kind. Then his attempts to "baaa" like a sheep along with the piano on every song caused the piano player to fold up his box and stop dealin' his game. When Sam finally fell into the habit of smashin' the likker glass on the floor by way of roundin' off each drink, barkeep Jim Shelton allowed it was time for Sam to hibernate in another den.

Oh, sure, Jim could've sent Sam soarin' through his swingin' doors all sprawled out like the card sharps had done two days prior, but there's funnier ways to rid yourself of drunk sheepherders. As I remarked prior, Jim was supplyin' me with an art studio in the back of his Utica Saloon. On the fifth eve of Sam's drunken jag, Jim asked me to prance back there and sculpt and paint him a rattlesnake. I was none too steady on my hooves, bein' a pint or two down the trail myself, but I shuffled up some clay and sloshed up some water colors, and I hatched up the best serpent my blurred vision could fancy. It was coiled like a lariat and looked ready to strike, its beady, evil eyes glarin' at you with a devilish grin exposin' three-inch fangs.

Two cowhands turn Sam's attention while Jim injuns up and sets that snake on the bar just within striking distance of our sheepherder. When Sam turns and beholds that clay rattler, his eyes bug out like a tromped-on snail's. But I'll have to hand it to the sheep tender, he keeps his sand up. He sits still as if he himself was a clay statue and he whispers, "Gents, I can't make any sudden moves, but if somebody would kindly pull your revolver and split that snake's skull, I'll buy the next round."

"Do what, Sam?" Jim asks.

"Kindly take your lead pusher and send that serpent to the realms of light where the wicked cease from troublin' folks."

"What serpent, Sam?"

"That big rattler on the bar who's fixin' to stake a claim on my neck. Shoot him."

"There's nothing on the bar but your glass, Sam."

"By the grave of Moses, can't you inebriates see them big fangs at my throat?"

We all assured him there was no snake on the bar that wasn't brought on by the aid of likker. Jim tells him, "Sam, the man who sold me this trade likker said if folks start seein' snakes, cut 'em plumb off, or they'll blink out and never wake up. You've had enough scamper juice, Sam."

Weavin' like a boat that lost its rudder, Sheepherder Sam somehow found the door. As he trundled out, he swore, "I'm never gonna touch that trade whiskey again."

And he never did.

The cowboy never lived who didn't enjoy pullin' a prank or two on a sheepherder. One time in a Cascade Saloon, a sheepherder surrounded too much joy juice and fell asleep sittin' on an empty wooden beer keg. He was wearin' a pair of them Scotch-bottom shoes, with rubber soles stickin' out a half inch or more past the leather. While the sheepherder was sound asleep as a tree, I nailed his soles to the floor. Then I lit a corn shuck on fire in front of that sheepherder and I yelled, "Fire!"

That sheepherder wakes up spooked as a yearling steer, springs to his feet, and makes a play at stampedin' for the door. But his feet are stuck like a hog in a bog, so he shrugs, camps back down on that beer keg, and takes a few more tugs on his bottle.

Later, another sheepherder a dozen drinks down the trail fell asleep sittin' on a keg. This time, I thought I'd see what would come of nailin' his pants to the keg. When I lit a corn shuck and whooped, "Fire!" the sheep wrangler springs to his feet and stampedes out the door wearin' that keg behind him.

Then there was the time I tracked up on four sheepherders passed out in a saloon sittin' around a small table. I pranced out to my hoss Grey Eagle and fetched my catch rope from the saddle horn. I whirled a big loop around that herd of sheepherders and my pals helped me hogtie them all together. Then I lit a shuck and shouted, "The saloon's on fire!" As that tangle of sheep wranglers tried to scramble out of range, they knocked over the wood stove. That saloon sorta *did* catch fire that day.

One Thanksgiving day in Cascade, an old woodsman known by the handle of Old Yank took on an overload of jig juice and passed out behind the saloon. It was a warm day for November, by reason of a chinook blowin' through the Wolf Creek Canyon, and Old Yank was wearin' a coat, so everybody decided to let him lay there and sleep it off.

Now could Old Man Fate deal a prank lover a better hand? The saloon owner was fixin' to roast four Thanksgiving turkeys for his patrons. I took the entrails from all them turkeys and layed them right beside Old Yank's mouth. Then I repaired to the saloon to await developments and maybe see who might be buyin' the next round.

It ain't more than two or three drinks later when Old Yank trundles into the saloon and croaks, "I'll buy the next round, boys. I want to share my last drink with you."

"What do you mean, your last drink, Yank?" we ask him. "Are you goin' away?"

"I'm goin' to ride that range beyond the sky."

"Why do you say that, Yank?"

"A man can't live long without his guts, and all mine are layin' out back on the ground."

Anyway, that rodeo with Sheepherder Sam and the clay rattlesnake was funny enough to make a cow laugh, but I'd say any fool could take some clay and watercolors and hatch up a rattlesnake fit to fool a drunk sheepherder. But if I may brand my own hide, I'll declare it takes more than a green hand to sculpt and paint a dragon that can fool sober policemen, business sharps, and political sharps. But that's just what I did one day in the Silver Dollar Saloon.

Where was the Silver Dollar? Why, there's nary a man alive today who remembers that waterin' hole first hand. It stood across the street from the Mint on Great Falls' Central Avenue. It was owned by my old friend from the cow camps, Bill Rance, the best barkeep ever to slop out a round of drinks or wave a bar rag. I sloshed around in that saloon as much as I did in the Mint, and just as many of my paintings were tacked on its walls. Bill had helped me over some pretty boggy crossings when we were wild young bucks, so I was proud as a cock partridge to help Bill hit pay dirt, as I'm about to unfold.

But first, allow me to steer you away from the main trail of this yarn long enough to explain why the Mint is remembered so much more than the Silver Dollar. When the prohibitionists made outlaws of good, drinkin' men, Bill Rance sold most of his paintings to the Mint. The he laid down his cards and folded his game, and his distinguished waterin' hole became the Silver Dollar Barber Shop.

My friend Sid Willis kept the Mint alive by sellin' Coca-Colas and maple nut sundaes until Roosevelt restored our inalienable right to drink, and he stayed in business until he bore the weight of seventy-eight winters. I hear tell a wealthy Texan roped onto all my paintings from the Mint, branded 'em "The Mint Collection," and corralled them in the Amon Carter Museum in Fort Worth. That's the long and the short of why folks still talk about the Mint and not the Silver Dollar.

But I'm ridin' too far away from the herd. Let me trail back to my yarn. Here's how the cards fell. One day shortly before that war with the Kaiser, Bill Rance roped onto a picture of a big lizard called a gila monster, big as a groundhog and ugly as a black widow. He takes me aside and says, "Charlie, I want to commission you to secretly sculpt and paint one of these dragons."

My hoss Neenah was saddled and hitched outside, and as I was no longer a drinkin' man, we hit only a few high spots in the topography as we sprang back to my cabin on Fourth Avenue North. I could see with one eye this prank might be more fun than a barrel of money. Usin' Bill's picture as my guide, I sculpted the dragon from wax and painted his scales orange, black, and pink. If you can allow me to shoot off my mouth a second, I'll say that noble reptile looked real enough to fool most drinkin' men—and a lot of tea-totalers to boot.

Bill corralled the critter in one of these here glass boxes learned men call an aquarium, and he set it on the back bar where every gent could eye it from the brass rail—of course, women weren't allowed to enter Great Falls' distinguished drinkin' establishments. The Mint, the Silver Dollar, the Brunswick, and the Maverick all hung collections of my paintings on their walls. They'd all shut down their bars for a couple hours a week so the ladies could come in a take a squint at my smoke-covered water colors and oils.

Bill told everybody the gila monster sleeps all day and eats just before dawn. The saloon's regular old bunch would watch Bill set an egg in the box at about fifth drink time every evening, and at second drink time every morning, they'd watch him clean the egg shells out. Every now and again, some fellow a half dozen drinks down the trail would want to pet the critter, but Bill would always head 'em off, warnin' 'em the lizard's bite was more poison than any rattlesnake's. To keep the men from sizin' up the dragon too close, Bill told 'em even its breath was so poison, a strong man could wax plumb sick from breathin' near it.

"You'll feel like you swallowed a bull snake," Bill warned 'em. "It'll make you heave up everything but your socks."

You can bet a new hat most gents covered their mouths and noses when they eyeballed the lizard. Many even refused to drink within a few rods of it. Some even declared they sure as shootin' *did* feel sick and they had to repair to the Mint or the Maverick to restore their health.

Bill's hay ride with that lizard went lopin' along at a smooth road gait for a few weeks, but when the mayor and the city council finally caught wind of the poison-breathed dragon, they weren't slow to declare the beast a health hazard. They ordered Bill to destroy the reptile or they'd board up his saloon.

"Please give us until tomorrow," we pleaded,

"to get used to this cruel decree. That lizard's our favorite pet; we've grown dang fond of the critter. This will be as sad as if we were ordered to destroy Mose Kaufman."

The next day, that late-afternoon newspaper— they branded it the "Great Falls Leader"—heralded the cowboy artist would send a gila monster over the jump in the Silver Dollar that evening at third drink time sharp. It printed the mayor, the city council, and some peace officers would adorn the saloon to make sure the execution comes off without a hitch.

If my memory's keepin' its feet, every gent who wasn't in jail tracked into that saloon to see what a gila monster was, packed thicker than hoss thieves in hell. When I arrived and squeezed my way to the back bar, they grew still as graven images. They watched like hen hawks as I hefted that big wax dragon out of the glass box. Chokin' back tears, I hugged our scaled side-kick for a few heartbeats, just to help mix the medicine.

"I'm sorry, dear old pal," I sobbed to the lizard, loud enough for every gent in that silent crowd to hear. "I hate to do this to you, but the honorable mayor has decreed it."

Quick and loud as a rifle shot, I snapped that dragon in half over my knee and handed the top half to the mayor. The politician let fly the yelp of a scared pup and hopped backward like I was handin' him a hissin' rattlesnake. The applause that cut loose was louder than forty cattle stampedes.

Richard Bird Baker

That waterin' hole raked in over eight hundred round, heavy silver dollars that night, a new record for all Great Falls saloons. Them dollars were soon planted in the sidewalk for all drinkin' men to see, just outside the front door of Bill Rance's Silver Dollar Saloon.

When you drift my way, watch for the smoke of my camp. A robe is spread and a pipe is lit for you.

Your friend, C. M. Russell

2011 in the moon the geese fly south

The 1894 March on Washington

On this side of the Maker's Big Divide, we don't keep tabs on the numbers you folks hang on the days. Nor do we pay much heed to the numbers and names you hang on the years and months. But a few new pilgrims to this range tell me this is the moon the geese fly south in the year of our Lord two thousand and 'leven.

Natur'ly, I always ask these pilgrims how events are stackin' up on your side of the Big Divide. Most of what I hear still ruffles my feathers. Man is still playin' his inventions to the limit, and by now, man's inventions have almost backed him plumb off the board. History will remember your years as the century people destroyed the Creator's world to keep man's inventions churnin'. Do you know the saddest part of all? Man's inventions still ain't made him no better.

I recall warnin' people about them inventions ninety winters past, but everybody said it was just the brayin' of a conservative old fool opposed to progress. That's also what they called me when I cussed at men for shearin' our forests. I'm told people who called me a conservative old fool ninety winters past would call me a tree-huggin' liberal today.

The new pilgrims to my range say that in many big American cities, hundreds of folks are floodin' in and campin' downtown. The pilgrims say these migrants are there to nail down a point: big companies, bigger than folks of my time could fathom, have corralled America's pot of blue chips. Many pilgrims say they're sore at your last president for stackin' the deck so them big companies don't have to ante up their fair share of taxes. They tell me the police have been ordered to take cards in the game and arrest the campers who won't leave. As I write these words, these campin' folks are plannin' a march on Washington.

It's no secret I never had much schoolin'. I don't pack much savvy of tax loop holes, big businesses, politics, and other crimes. But sometimes horse sense shoots farther and truer than book learnin', so let me shoot you this: could these big companies have corralled all your chips if you folks hadn't kept fallin' for all their inventions like a bevy of sheepherders? So blame yourselves. When you're in a hole, stop diggin'. You don't have to play every card dealt you. Stop buyin' every new invention dangled before you.

Even under spurs and quirt, my memory can't lope back to more than one march on Washington that cut loose durin' my short ride through Montana. If my memory ain't pulled its picket pin and drifted plumb astray, it came to pass about a year after I hung up my spurs and lariat and quit singin' to the cattle for good. It was when Al Trigg gave me my first Great Falls studio in the back room of his Brunswick Saloon, maybe she was eighteen ninety-four. That must be right; it bobbed up on the hocks of the Panic of '93.

What was the Panic of '93? Somebody should have told ya. It was the worst spell of depression ever to hit this land. I don't savvy as much about these economic wranglings as a cross-eyed steer, but they say that when President Cleveland shot down the Sherman Silver Purchase Act, whatever that was, the bottom fell out of silver mining. The whole city of Butte—and it was a big city in '93—went belly up, and the whole state of Montana followed suit. I'll tell a man, it was dang hard to peddle paintings for a few years, and if it weren't for them eastern suckers passin' through town on James Hill's trains, I'd never have sold enough to keep me and the bunch in likker.

This depression that ran over Montana like a baggage wagon didn't just pitch camp in Montana.

It spread across the whole nation like the grace of heaven through a camp meetin', and hard workin', hard drinkin' men were out of work everywhere. Folks began ropin' at Mr. Cleveland and the congress to play a hand at puttin' these hungry and thirsty gents back to work.

Finally, an old fireball in Ohio named General Jacob Coxey took hold of the reins of reform for these out-of-work fellers. Now let me tell you what the odd card in that deck was. As you go lopin' through the pages of history, you can see plain as plowed ground most reformers weren't your wealthy folks. They were mostly plain folks, even poor folks, people with nothin' to lose but their poverty. And that's true today with these folks campin' out in your big cities. These out-of-work and out-of-cash parties are disgruntled about seein' one percent of the country's people corrallin' most of its wampum, I'm told. But Coxey had more money than most folks have hay or straw.

General Jacob Coxey owned a rock quarry in Ohio, and it's said he had a stack of chips higher than two hundred grand. Now that may not sound like much of a roll today, when many folks on your side of the divide round up that many chips every year, but in '93, that was a bigger stack of loot than a cord of wood. Yet Coxey was a reformer who threw in with the People's Party, kind of a socialist outfit. He was such an odd duck he named his son Legal Tender Coxey, and he branded his army "The Commonwealth of Christ." No, he wasn't a Civil War veteran or a leader of any military outfit that would merit callin' him a general. He hung that brand on himself when he rounded up his army of discarded workers, the fate of which I'll unload on you directly.

The first thing our good General Coxey did was to write up what he branded the "Good Roads Bill." It roped at congress to ante up five hundred million blue chips to hire out-of-work folks for a buck and a half a day, dang good wages then, to build roads throughout the land. Then he roped his congressman into unloadin' this bill before the House of Representatives. Now remember, this was a good fifteen years before we saw any horseless carriages—I still call them skunkwagons—flitterin' hither and thither throughout the scenery, so them congressmen didn't see no sense in wastin' all that dinero on roads. Congress tossed that card in the discard pile.

Never a quitter, General Coxey decided to lead a huge march of disgruntled, unemployed folks from all over the land through Washington, D.C. They'd tread from the Capitol to the White House and back to the Capitol, callin' on the political herd there to do something to put these ragged folks back to work. He put ads in all the country's big newspapers callin' for recruits, and he declared he expected to see nothin' shy of a hundred thousand marchers throwin' in with his army in the capitol city.

Meanwhile, back in Montana, things were growin' dimmer than the old buffalo trails. Many mines were shuttin' down, and the shopkeepers who supplied the miners were goin' belly up. Scores of banks were layin' down their cards and foldin', and twenty thousand Montana workers were out on the streets. Finally, a fiery young unemployed teamster who went by the handle of William Hogan was spurred by Coxey into roundin' up a herd of out-of-work Butte miners and linin' out for Washington D. C. to throw in with the march.

Hogan had already made a name for himself as a reformer in Butte. He'd thrown in with the trade unions in buckin' against hiring Chinese workers and against allowin' foreigners to buy local property. He'd already been ropin' at Montana's governor to hire out-of-work folks to build irrigation canals throughout the state. Early in '94, he branded himself General William Hogan, and he gathered in an army of over five hundred out-of-work silver and copper miners. Then he roped at the mayor of Butte and the city commissioners to help pay the cost of transportin' his troops to Washington.

The mayor and the commissioners thought this was the biggest tomfoolery they'd heard of, and they laughed it off. Then the young general roped at the local Northern Pacific Railroad station to haul him and his men east, and to everybody's surprise, the Butte station master agreed to let them ride a freight train to the east end of their trail, which was on one of them Great Lakes. The station master even agreed to send a wire to some eastern railroads askin' them to haul this ragamuffin army to Washington.

But the Butte railroad station's offer was soon trumped. Somebody higher up on the Northern Pacific totem pole feared this ragged herd would mix themselves into a stew in some other state, or even in the capitol city, and cast a dark shadow on the Northern Pacific. They wired the station in Butte to tell these wild folks their hand is played out.

Hogan's army was camped near the railroad yards when the Butte station master tracked in and unloaded the Northern Pacific corral boss' message. Hogan thanked the gent for tryin', and he and his men broke camp and pretended to trail out. But four hours before daylight, they broke into the station's roundhouse and manned a locomotive. They shoveled in the coal, fired up the boiler, and chugged that engine out of the roundhouse just as Marshal Bill McDermott rode up and told Hogan he was under arrest.

Before the bold marshal could unlimber his six-shooter, a quartet of husky silver miners seized hold of him, snatched away his pistol, and locked him in a boxcar not otherwise employed. They coupled one boxcar and six coal cars to their borrowed locomotive, and all five hundred of them piled aboard wherever they could fit. I heard it said a streak of lightning played second fiddle to the speed that train streaked from Butte to Bozeman.

It was only five-thirty in the morning when the breathing of that engine was heard slowin' itself into Bozeman. Everybody at the Bozeman station and in the train yard treated them like fellow union workers and allowed them to swap the coal cars they were luggin' for a few more boxcars. The whole army squeezed into those boxcars as Hogan fired up that big black locomotive, and they streaked out of town like greased lightning, headin' east toward Livingston.

Meanwhile, Marshal McDermott was turned loose from that boxcar, and he set about tryin' to deputize men to help him chase down Hogan's army. But only a hatful of men around Butte would throw in with him; they all stacked their chips with Hogan. So he wires the Yellowstone County Sheriff statin', "Blockade the tracks near Columbus and arrest the ragged army who stole a train."

The sheriff wasn't in town that morning, so the delivery boy handed the telegram to a deputy. The deputy laughed and told another, "This is one of the best pranks dealt us yet, but they can't job me."

The deputy hot foots it over to the telegraph office and returns a prank wire to Marshall McDermott: "County Attorney and Sheriff out in Bull Mountains laying out additions to Billings. All able-bodied men busy selling real estate. Arrest the army yourself in Livingston."

Marshall McDermott now savvies he won't convince the Yellowstone County Sheriff's Department of what's afoot unless he goes to them himself. He orders the Butte station master to fire up his fastest locomotive to pack him and a small band of deputies up the track to arrest Hogan and his ring leaders. They say a comet is slow as cold molasses compared to the speed that engine stormed out on Hogan's trail.

It was a quarter to five that afternoon when the Hoganites chugged into Livingston. By now, all the town's citizens had heard that Hogan's army was approachin' in a stolen train, bound fer the great march on Washington, and a crowd was waitin' to cheer them on. Hogan's men filled the boilers with water, misappropriated some coal, and pointed that train east—until they came to a spot where somebody had dynamited a hillside to cause a rockslide onto the track. But if you have an army, you can move a rock pile quick as you can lead a few cows to pasture. They cleared the track, moved the train forward two dozen rods, stacked the rocks back on the track, and hot-footed east.

Hogan's army camped that night near Columbus. As they were breakin' camp in the morning, Marshal McDermott trails up with sixty-five mounted men he's deputized along the way. He demands that Hogan surrender, but having five hundred men to back his play, Hogan refuses and orders his men aboard the train. McDermott and his men saddle up and trail that train to Billings.

In Billings, Hogan's heroes were so well received they picked up a hundred more volunteers. But McDermott picked up more men too, and he once again got up the sand to try to arrest Hogan. The fracas that followed looked like a Mexican revolution. One Billings deputy was creased in the battle, and a dozen men on both sides were wounded. The deputies finally scattered, and Hogan's army was back on velvet, stormin' east like they were late for a dance.

Meanwhile, Governor John Richards, allowin' there ain't enough lawmen in Montana to corral Hogan's army, wires President Cleveland. The president wires the U. S. Cavalry at Fort Keogh— that's over by Miles City—and the next morning, an army of bluecoats track up on the Hoganites breakin' camp near Forsyth.

Now it's one thing for a passel of out-of-work miners to *call* themselves an army, but it's a whole different proposition to *be* an army. Against a few companies of thoroughbred soldiers, Hogan's army had no more show than a stump-tail bull in fly season. Some of Hogan's men scattered off into the hills, and the rest were captured and railroaded off to Helena to be tried by a Federal Court. Hogan was sent up for six months, and forty of his ringleaders got thirty days. The rest were cut loose on promises to desist from stealin' trains.

But four hundred of them miners stayed in the game. They marched from Helena to Fort Benton in five days and loaded themselves on flat barges headed for St. Louis, the camp of my childhood. They allowed they'd rope at a railroad in St. Louie to haul them to Washington, but by the time they arrived, the march on Washington had already been played out.

Here's how the cards fell at that famous march. When General Coaxy blew into Washington to meet his army, he didn't quite find the hundred thousand head of cattle he'd counted on. There was scarcely a hundred men waitin' to join him. They waited a week until their ranks swelled to some five hundred, and then they lit out on their march from the White House to the Capitol. But before they reached that hive of lawmakers and law breakers, Coaxy was arrested for walkin' on the grass. While he was corralled in jail, all five hundred members of his Commonwealth for Christ seeped out of town.

And now you savvy all there is to know about the '94 March on Washington. I'm all in now, so I guess I'll turn up the box and close the deal. Give my regards to the bunch.

Your friend, C. M. Russell

2011 in the Moon of the First Snows

The Chapping of Sheepherder Bill

There was a saying in the Old West, "There's nothin' dumber than sheep except the man who herds them." Cowboys and sheepherders seldom mingled. In many cases, they plumb didn't care for each other's society. Said lack of friendship stemmed from the lack of affection between the critters themselves.

The injun truth is most cattle would rather die of hunger or thirst than graze or water where sheep have been. And by the time the stockmen's range wars began, those dirty little buggers had been almost everywhere, most often takin' the best waterin' and grazin' spots. In some states, both breeds of stockmen took to expressin' their views with their guns, and more often than not, the sheep raisers took second money. There was a practice among cattlemen called "cookin' mutton," which meant settin' fire to a sheep-grazin' range to drive out a sheep outfit.

Let's saddle our imaginations for a short ride and fancy that cattle and sheep honest to John *did* enjoy each other's company. Wouldn't we still see as much difference between the two breeds of stockmen as we see between cattle and sheep? Cowboys always rode the best horses their roll could buy, but sheepherders mostly traveled on foot. A cowboy would almost rather herd sheep than be caught afoot. But then again, sheepherders didn't travel much. They couldn't leave their sheep to fall prey to wolves, coyotes, bears, lions, renegades, and low-down sheep rustlers.

A few times a year, the owner of a sheep outfit would give a sheepherder a day or two off if he could find another man feeble-minded enough to guard the sheep. The sheepherder would walk to town with his dog and drink in whatever saloon would allow his dog to enter. For a long time, sheep dogs were more welcome than their masters in most saloons, but by now, town laws began to ban dogs from these distinguished drinkin' establishments. So a few saloon owners, probably former sheepherders, built sheds out back for sheepherders' dogs.

When cowboys hit town after weeks of roundin'

up or drivin' cattle, they weren't slow to find a saloon with poker games and the society of the gals they called "painted cats." But most sheepherders would seek a quieter saloon and drink alone—except for the society of their dogs when welcome—until their roll was gone. Then they'd sleep off their drunk and return to the companionship of their sheep for a few more months.

Of course, there were always a few sheepherders who *did* seek the society of a painted cat, but such a rendezvous was as risky to a sheepherder as ridin' a green bronc. Often the barkeeps were in cahoots with them painted cats. They'd slip a drug into every sheepherder's drink to make 'em fall dead asleep quick as the painted cats could lure 'em upstairs, and while their lights were out, said painted cats would lift their roll. Sometimes a sheepherder would lose a few months' pay in the hold-up.

Sheepherder Bill had lost his roll in this fashion more than once, but he still wouldn't quit them painted cats. He allowed the way to side-step a sheepherder's fate was to disguise himself as a cowboy. The next time he walked to Billings, he tracked into the Montgomery Wards store and bought him a ten-gallon hat, ridin' boots, California-made cowboy trousers, a flannel western shirt, an orange vest, a blue bandana, and a pair of crooked-shank spurs. Dressed as a mail order catalog on a spree, he pointed his muzzle into a waterin' hole called Bob Nix's Saloon.

Bearcat Williams, foreman for the N Bar outfit,

had just blown into Nix's fresh off the trail with his herd of gritty riders when Sheepherder Bill trundled in and ordered a round for the house. Bill told everybody he'd just ridden down from Alberta where he'd been ridin' brand for an open-range cattle outfit. Of course, any thoroughbred Montana cowboy can tell a true rider and roper from a Monkey Ward cowboy at forty paces. Besides, they well savvied a cowboy smells like a cowboy and a sheepherder smells like a sheepherder, same as a horse smells like a horse and a sheep smells like a sheep.

"Some deck must be shy a joker," a rider told Bearcat.

"This Alberta joker smells like a sheepherder to me," another chipped in as Sheepherder Bill ordered a second round for the house.

"I could see wool around his eyes the second he ambled in," another rider stacked in.

"It's a cinch he's a sheepherder masqueradin' as a cowhand," Bearcat agreed. "But as long as he's payin' for our drinks, let him play out his hand."

After Bill's paid for three or four rounds, in blows Lou Hankins, trail boss for the Bird Head outfit. Bearcat tells him, "This here's Alberta Bill. He's been ridin' brand for an outfit across the border."

Bearcat throws Hankins a wink to tip him off that everybody's ridin' this Monkey Ward cowboy to rope onto free drinks. But somehow Hankins don't see that wink, and he puts up, "It's a load of corral dust he's been feedin' you, Bearcat. This four-flusher is one of Charlie Bair's sheepherders."

"No, that can't be so," bluffs Bearcat.

"I reckon it is, sure as the hills," Hankins stacks in. "I've seen him herdin' every time I've rode out there to scare old man Bair."

"Impersonatin' a cowboy is a hangin' offense in Yellowstone County, Mr. Sheepherder," a rider antes up.

"Let's stretch his neck from the rafters of this ceiling," another chips in.

"I'll trail out and fetch my lariat," another raises him. "You punchers fetch hold of him and heft him on top of a stool."

"Wait a minute!" Bearcat orders 'em. "Before we swing him off, this man gets a gambler's chance for his ante. We're no lynch mob here. Let's conduct ourselves like a fair and just vigilance committee and hold a trial. Barkeep, the cards fall to you to appoint a judge, a nine-man jury, two lawyers, and two bailiffs."

The barkeep wasn't slow to appoint Bearcat to be judge. The cattle boss camped in a chair behind a card table and hammered on the table with the butt of his Peacemaker.

"Order! It's time to shuffle, deal, and open this game. Bailiffs, bring forth the accused."

Two stalwart young bronc busters hefted Bill by the upper arms and planted him in front of the judge. Bearcat opened the game with, "Sheepherder Bill, you are hereby accused of impersonatin' your betters. How do you plead?"

For a moment, Bill said nothin'. Bearcat broke the silence with, "In this court, silence is a plea of guilty. If that's your choice, I'll send for a lariat."

"Innocent, Your Honor," the accused decided to plead.

The judge dealt, "The chief witness for the prosecution will start the bettin'. Lou Hankins, the play is to you."

Hankins bowlegs up to the jury and puts up, "Three times I've had to ride out to Bair's spread to warn him about waterin' sheep upstream from our cattle. Every time, I've seen this man tendin' Bair's sheep."

"Now the play is to the defense to place its bets," deals Judge Williams.

Sheepherder Bill's lawyer antes up, "I'd like to cross examine the witness, Your Honor."

"Permission granted."

The lawyer leads with, "Mr. Hankins, are you sure you ain't mistakin' Alberta Bill for some sheepherder who favors him?"

"It was this man, I tell ya. I'd know his ashes in a March wind."

"Then you must have stacked him up very close as you rode past."

"You betcha'."

"Why did you want to size him up so close?"

"I had a feelin' he'd need hangin' some day."

"I see," said the lawyer as he stepped closer to Hankins. He planted himself in front of Hankins so Lou couldn't see the sheepherder and said, "Since you eyed the accused so thoroughly, surely you noticed the mole on his face. Can you tell us where it is?"

"I didn't see no mole," Hankins snorted back.

The lawyer raised the bet with, "Gentlemen of the jury, it's a cinch this witness didn't make a good enough roundup of that sheepherder's face. His testimony must be thrown out. If you don't mind, I'll return to my stool and my whiskey."

"The play is to the prosecution again," the judge dealt.

The lawyer for the prosecution left his stool and called every member of the jury to come forth, one at a time, and take a whiff of Alberta Bill. Then he urged the jury, "You all know the smell of a cowboy and the smell of a sheepherder. If you think the accused smells like a sheepherder, then you owe every Montana cowboy and Teddy Roosevelt a verdict of guilty. If he smells like a cowboy, cut him loose." That said, he retired to his perch at the bar.

"The defense now has the chance to see the bet, raise it, or fold," the judge told the court.

The defense lawyer slid off his bar stool and again took the floor. "Good men of the jury," he crooned, "if you sense Cowboy Bill reeks slightly, it's because he just rode in from The Good Shepherd's Saloon in Roundup. Last night, he engaged in a long poker game with half a dozen sheepherders with the hope of winnin' a roll big enough to pay for our drinks."

Then the honored judge asked the prosecution, "Don't you want to cross examine the accused?"

"Yes, Your Honor."

"Then wade in and roll your game. This is your last chance to play out your hand."

"Alberta Bill," the lawyer anted up as he slid from his perch, "how long have you worked cattle?"

"Since I was a just a colt," anted up Alberta Bill.

"Have you ever branded cattle on the open range?" the lawyer put up.

"Thousands of times," Bill saw and raised him.

"Then I assume you've roped a lot of steers for brandin'," the lawyer raised him back.

"Forty million steers," the accused upped the bet.

Here's where the lawyer took the bull by the horns and bumped the bet with, "Are you a dally-welter man or a tie-on man?"

Bill looked like he'd been slapped. He fell silent as a shadow for another moment until the judge barked, "I'll remind you just one more time; silence is an admission of guilt. Now play out your hand before I send for that rope."

"Counselor, could you kindly repeat that question?" Bill asked.

"Are you a dally-welter man or a tie-on man?"

"I can't remember which is which," folded the sheepherder.

The prosecuting lawyer poured himself another

drink and stacked in, "Alberta Bill's hand has been played down to the turn. Any man who don't know what a dally-welter man or a tie-on man is ain't no cowboy, no more than a saddled hog is a cow pony. I rest my case."

"The defense has one last chance to play out its hand," the judge deals.

The lawyer for the defense slides from his perch and steps up to the jury. He lays down the bluff, "Gentlemen of the jury, due to his surroundin' too much scatter juice, Alberta Bill's memory ain't keepin' its feet…"

"Bull feathers!" Judge Williams busts in. "Every one of us has been a heap sight drunker than Alberta Bill. We've all been too drunk to remember the name of the brand we rode for or the way back to our roundup camp. We've been too drunk to hit the ground with our hats. But no cowboy is ever too drunk—even if he passes out—to remember what a tie-on or a dally is. Take your seat, Counselor."

The lawyer for the accused gladly retired to his stool and his whiskey. The judged trailed on with, "Every card has been played and this trial has come down to the turn. You men of the jury gather around that table and combine wits—that should give you about a wit and a half—and see how fast you can lope to a verdict while I send an hombre for the rope."

It's a cinch I'll need to stray from the main trail of this yarn long enough to teach folks the difference between a dally-welter roper and a tie-on roper. A tie-on roper ties the end of his catch rope to his saddle horn. He figgers it's easier on the cattle and makes for less rope burn on his hands. Trouble is, once in a while, a darn strong steer can pull a hoss plumb over onto its side, causing your tie-on roper to break limbs. Or that steer might fight hard enough to bust your saddle cinches and scamper off draggin' your saddle across the prairie, maybe with your foot stuck in a stirrup.

A dally-welter roper don't tie his lariat to his saddle horn. As soon as he whirls his loop around a dogie's neck, he takes the loose end of the lariat and winds it a few turns around the saddle horn. Them turns are called dally-welters or dallies. That name comes from the Mexican words *dar la vuelta*, which mean "go around." If a dally roper fastens onto a cow or steer that's too ornery and strong to handle, he can unwind them dallies from his saddle horn before his cinches snap or his hoss is pulled over.

But there ain't no safe way to rope cattle. Your dally-welter roper has his bad days too. He might lose his lariat if the steer he unwinds scatters across the prairie and out of sight. More often, he chases the critter down on foot and cuts the lariat off the outlaw's neck near the noose, shortening his catch rope by a few feet. But losin' a lariat ain't the dally-welter roper's biggest worry. Many a roper has gotten a finger or two caught in them dallies as the steer pulls that rope tighter than a fiddle string. When you see an old cowboy missin' a finger or two, figger more than like he was an old-time dally-welter roper.

But we're ridin' away from the herd. Ropin', throwin', and tyin' down a verdict took the jury less time than it takes to down a drink. They all agreed on "Guilty, Your Honor."

Judge Williams rapped the butt of his six-shooter on the table and announced, "Sheepherder Bill, this trial has come down to the turn. You've been out played, out bet, and out held, and found guilty of impersonatin' your betters. Normally, a hangin' is too good for a four-flusher like you, but since you bought us a few rounds, I reckon I'll let you off with just a chappin'. I hereby sentence you to a chappin' of forty lashes." As Bearcat reeled out that sentence, Sheepherder Bill noticed for the first time the judge's left front paw was shy its trigger finger.

Now I couldn't expect most modern folks to pack a splinter of an idea what a chappin' is. Here's how it falls out. First, ya roll an empty wooden whiskey barrel into the saloon. Then you lay your sheepherder across it spread eagle and belly down. You'll need four strong cowboys to hold the sheepherder's arms and legs still. Then you appoint a greenhorn cowboy to pull down the sheepherder's ragged britches and apply ridin' chaps to the sheepherder's bare rump with cowboy vigor.

If no greenhorns were in the saloon, you'd have to send a rep to find one in another waterin' hole. Most green cowhands were game as hornets to oblige. In Yellowstone County, no tenderfoot cowboy was reckoned a true cattleman until he gave a sheepherder a chappin'.

In addition to that chappin', the judge fined Sheepherder Bill three more rounds for the house. He took his chappin' like a man, and he laughed at himself like a cowboy. He bought everybody drinks until his roll was gone, and then the jury members took turns buyin' him drinks until he passed out in a corner. This was the only time he ever slept in a saloon without his dog at his side. But never again did he dare to dawn the harness of a cowboy.

When you cross the skyline, look for the smoke of my campfire in the Shadowy Hills.

Your friend, C. M. Russell

2012 in the moon of the shortest days

The Murder of Sheriff Jim Webb

Like Sheepherder Bill, most sheepherders could take a prank, same as most cowboys. Most were easy goin' and not prone to churn up much dust. But just like there's a bad apple in every barrel, once in a long spell you'd ride up on a bad sheepherder, and no man is worse than a bad sheepherder. As my memory prances back over trails plowed under, it can't ride up on a sheepherder more ornery than William Bickford.

I ain't referin' to Sheepherder Bill, the Monkey Ward cowboy who was sentenced to a chappin' in

Nix's Saloon. Will Bickford hailed from somewhere in Canada where he once wore the brand of the Royal Mounted Police. Somewhere along the trail, he'd fallen out of favor with the Dominion law, maybe for stealin' hosses. He blew into Montana just one jump ahead of the Mounties and found work herdin' sheep for the Wolford and Richardson outfit on the Musselshell River. But he never quite shook loose of his past, which followed him like a dark shadow.

The Sheriff of Yellowstone County was a seasoned cowpuncher named Jim Webb. He'd rode many years for the 79 Cattle Outfit and was well respected as a roper and a rider and later a cattle foreman. At the turn of the century, he was appointed stock inspector, and he earned a good reputation playin' that hand until1906 when he ran for sheriff.

There was a custom in Yellowstone County that Jim Webb refused to abide. A candidate runnin' for sheriff or any other office was expected to track into the saloons from time to time and buy every man a drink—of course, ladies weren't allowed to enter Montana's distinguished drinkin' establishments or even vote. But Jim didn't drink, and he didn't enter saloons except in the line of duty. Often drinkin' men would ask him, "When are you gonna stop by the saloon to buy us all a drink, Jim?"

His answer was always straight as a wagon tongue. "I may win this election or I may lose. Win or lose, I never want it said I bought votes with likker."

But Jim won that election and became as good a

sheriff as he was a cattleman. It was said he had more guts than you could hang on a fence. When a tough job needed to be done, Jim would saddle up and rope after it without the help of deputies.

One day, the judge handed Sheriff Webb a warrant to arrest Will Bickford for horse stealin'. When Jim rode out to the sheep camp, the first man he tracked up on was old man Richardson, owner of the outfit.

"I've come to arrest your man Bickford for horse stealin'," the sheriff told him.

"I think it would be easier to arrest a grizzly. Are you sure you want to draw cards in this game alone?"

"Just show me where he is," Sheriff Webb answered.

Richardson told the sheriff to hop in his wagon and he hauled him out to Bickford's camp. They found the wanted sheepherder outside his sheep wagon, doin' something you seldom see a sheepherder do, washin' clothes in a wood tub. Jim Webb greeted him calmly and then added, "I have a warrant for your arrest."

"What's the charge?"

"Horse stealin'."

"It's a big mistake," Bickford put up. "I can prove I'm innocent."

"You'll have a shot at provin' it to the judge and jury," the sheriff trumped him.

"Can I go into my sheep wagon and change clothes before we leave?" Bickford asked the sheriff.

Jim gave him permission and Bickford stepped

into the sheep wagon. In two shakes of a lamb's tail, Bickford stepped back out from the wagon sportin' a Winchester .30-30. "Hands up, both of you," he growled, shootin' a bullet between them to punctuate his command. Richardson wasn't slow to reach for the stars, but Webb just stood lookin' at the man he'd come to arrest, calm as an Indian.

"I said get 'em up," Bickford ordered again.

Nobody knows what happened next. Richardson didn't see if Webb went for his Peace Maker or if Bickford shot him in cold blood for not raisin' his hands. One thing was clear: Bickford's Winchester fired again, droppin' the sheriff deader than a six-card poker hand.

Why Bickford didn't shoot Richardson is another conundrum that's never been understood, but Bickford cut him loose after threatenin' to blow his lamp out if he ever leaked one word of what he saw. As soon as the dust settled from Richardson's departure, Bickford hid Webb's corpse in a coulee. He didn't suspect Richardson had left his wagon long enough to sneak back on foot and watch him cache the corpse.

Lightning played second fiddle to the speed Richardson's wagon clattered to the nearest stage station. He sent a wire to the sheriff's office in Billings tellin' of Sheriff Webb's demise and where his corpse was cached. It fell to Deputy Jack Hereford to rope up a posse and lead them to the Musselshell at the mouth of Willow Creek. They followed the crick up to the sheep outfit and tugged on their bridles when they came to the first sheep wagon. An aging sheep herder was perchin' on his wagon hitch smokin' a corn-cob pipe.

"Can you tell us where Will Bickford's wagon is?" the deputy asked him.

"You might need a bigger posse, Deputy, if you want to rope and tie down Bickford. Don't start a war dance with him."

"The dance has already cut loose. Where's his wagon?"

"It's the fourth one up the valley, maybe she's two miles."

The posse didn't try to approach Bickford with a friendly greeting and a formal arrest like Webb. Quiet as shadows, they surrounded the wagon, stood behind cover, and yelled, "Come out of there, Bickford, or we'll set your sheep wagon on fire!"

When Bickford opened the door, the posse thought at first glance he was fixin' to lay down his cards and fold. But don't ya think it. He pointed his Winchester out the door, fired a shot in the direction of the voice for general effect, and slammed the door shut.

In all of a buck, the air was full of lead as a bag of bullets. The posse shot that canvas too full of holes to hold hay. When they kicked the sheepherder's door open, they found him face down like a newly-dealt card, too dead to skin.

It had always been customary for lawmen to bury an outlaw on the plains when they creased him far from a cemetery. Trouble was, in their rush to reach

Bickford's wagon before he pulled up camp, nobody in the posse had remembered to pack a shovel.

"We don't need to dig no hole," one rider recalled. "I know of a hole already dug. There's a dried-up, abandoned old well a short ride from here."

They lay Bickford across the lower back of a rider's hoss like a bag of bran and packed his murderin' bones to the abandoned dry well. As I remarked prior, there was no shovel to dump dirt on the corpse once it was dropped down the well. But the wolf hunts with what teeth it's got. The next best thing was to gather in the biggest rocks in sight and to keep droppin' 'em down the hole until the corpse was covered with a few feet of stone. When that hand was finally played out, the posse brought the news of the sheepherder's justice back to Billings.

In the eyes of most Yellowstone County citizens, Deputy Jack Hereford was now a hero. But in the eyes of the Yellowstone County Coroner, Hereford overplayed his hand.

"You had no right to bury that corpse," the coroner scolded him. "We've begun the Twentieth Century now. We don't bury our fugitives out on the lone prairie any more, not even sheepherders. The coroner always has to inspect the corpse. We have laws to abide by nowadays."

Deputy Hereford explained how they'd piled a few feet of rocks atop of that corpse, and it would take a heap of work to uncover Bickford's remains.

"Work or no work, I must inspect that corpse. Go uncover it and bring it to me."

Hereford and three other deputies loaded a buckboard with ladders, buckets, ropes, boards, and pulleys, and lit out for the abandoned dry well. They found the work went fastest by havin' two men down in the well loadin' the buckets with rocks, and two men at the top of the hole pullin' up the buckets with ropes and pulleys. Every hour or so, the fellows in the hole would come out and take a turn at hoistin' the buckets, and the bucket hoisters would take their turn down in the hole. In four or five hours, they had Bickford in the buckboard, lookin' about the same as he'd always looked herdin' sheep.

Of course, no hoss thief was ever granted a funeral or a marked grave, so history has likely forgotten where Bickford was planted. But Billings sure did it up proud for Sheriff Webb. Yellowstone County couldn't have put on more style if they'd been plantin' Teddy Roosevelt. The court house and all businesses—even the saloons—were closed for two hours. The procession to the grave yard was led by Deputy Hereford on horseback leadin' the sheriff's bay horse sportin' an empty saddle. It was followed by marchin' bands, formations of lawmen, church choirs, and all manner of cattlemen, sod busters, merchants, and even sheep herders. There were railroad men, freighters, school marms, girls of the line, barkeeps, gamblers, Indians, and a hold-up man or two.

Shortly after plantin' Sheriff Webb, a stone

monument about seven feet tall and five feet wide was erected to his memory near the Yellowstone County Court House in Billings on Second Avenue North and Twenty-Seventh Street. Instead of a statue, the monument held a fountain from which passers-by could drink, water their hoss, or wash their face. Friends who've recently crossed the Big Divide tell me the monument still stands, but water no longer flows from the fountain. Carved into the monument are these words:

James T. Webb, Sheriff of Yellowstone County
Sealed Duty with His Life
On
March 24, 1908
A Community's Tribute to Faithfulness

2012 in the moon the river freezes

Rattlesnake Jake and Charlie Fallon

Sad though the murder of Jim Webb was, don't it do our hides proud to hear of men like Jim who had the sand to face men who needed their rope shortened? Heroes like that must always be remembered. But one thing I can't fathom is why historians bother to remember men—some of them dang brave men—who made themselves famous by pourin' lead in the direction of good people.

Human understanding has its limits, same as the range of a rifle. It'll sometimes shoot far enough to understand man's will, but it can't shoot far enough to understand the will of our Creator. His reasons for pullin' off certain odd tasks, such as grantin' courage to men who use it to murder, are beyond the throw of our ropes. But that's the kind of men He sculpted when He created Rattlesnake Jake and Charlie Fallon, brave men who put their courage to the devil's use.

Eighteen hundred and eighty-four was a harsh, cruel year in the Judith. It carved some trails in my memory that time can't grass over. Big gangs of rustlers were thick as hoss thieves in Hell, stealin' cattle, horses, even sheep, and anything else they could pull up. They'd kill any man who tried to defend his livestock. What little law the territory had could do little more than stand by helpless as a frozen snake. Finally, Granville Stuart was spurred into formin' the famous vigilance committee known as Stuart's Stranglers.

Now don't get the notion I'm talkin' about a lynch mob. The difference? Why, a lynch mob is blood thirsty as a pack of wolves and has no more conscience than longhorn cattle in a stampede. But a vigilance committee backs the play of a square leader and hangs only those who deserve the honor. They give every outlaw a square chance for his ante before swingin' him off. And Granville Stuart was the most honest and respected vigilante leader ever to drop a noose around a hoss thief's neck.

Granville Stuart was one of the biggest cattle bosses in the Judith and probably the most learned book sharp in the whole Montana territory. Every cowhand wanted to work for him because he treated his riders square and paid them better than most outfits. Unlike most cattle bosses, Stuart allowed his hands to start their own herds while workin' for him. Later in life, he became a state senator and a lecturer, and he wrote some scholarly books about the days I'm jawin' about. But in '84, he was roundup boss of the grittiest herd of vigilantes ever to ride the west.

I never had much stomach for shootin' or hangin' men, even rustlers, to say nothing of bein' shot at, so I reckon I played in luck to be wranglin' for the Judith Basin Cattle Pool and not workin' for Stuart when he rounded up his Stranglers and lit out on the trail of them horse thieves and cattle rustlers. In twenty days, they ran the devil's brand on some twenty-seven outlaws. The saying was, "They all bucked out from lead poison and hemp fever." The rustlers who escaped the Stranglers' noose disappeared like a pint of likker at a four-handed poker game. These hangings were followed by those peaceful, honest days when no man owned a key except the key that wound his clock.

It was while scoutin' for rustlers that Granville Stuart and his Stranglers rode up on the camp of the two meanest, orneriest looking men ever to steal a horse. You could smell trouble off these two devils like you can smell a storm approachin'. A one-eyed bat could see they were nothin' but two-bit hoss thieves who somehow missed their turn at bein' hung years ago. It's a cinch they didn't deserve to go down in history as famous outlaws like they did. And let me say from the jump, these polecats would never have been remembered like Jesse James, Billy the Kid, Cole Younger, or Kid Curry if it hadn't been for the way the cards fell from the deck on Independence Day of '84. Pace by pace, I'm trailin' up to that day.

This pair of mean-eyed outlaws went down in history as Rattlesnake Jake and Long Haired Owen, sometimes referred to by history sharps as Charlie Owen. If you hear tell or read about Long Haired Owen, remember, recorders of history got the two miscreants' names wrong. Granville Stuart was likely the first party to mistake their names. Or maybe these two misguided drifters didn't make themselves clear when Stuart demanded, "Who are you?"

Charlie Owen was the true birth name of Rattlesnake Jake, although nobody'd called him Charlie in twenty years. He was maybe just a little bigger than average, and his hair was black as a chuckwagon skillet and long and thick as a pony's mane. He had a peaked nose, a cruel smile, and shifty, grayish-green eyes. When you're lookin' at the meanest, orneriest sidewinder you've ever beheld, it's sorta' tough to guess his age, but Stuart reckoned he'd been raisin' hell on earth for thirty-five or forty years. On his gun belt hung two long-barreled .45 revolvers and two knives in sheaves.

His sidekick, the outlaw who went down in history for over a century as Long Haired Owen, was truly named Charlie Fallon. Some folks who crossed the divide in recent years tell me it's been only two decades since historical sharps have gotten that confusion untangled. He was about the size of Rattlesnake Jake, probably just a few years younger, almost as evil lookin', and his brown hair was long and thick enough to afford nests to forty flyin' squirrels. He didn't pack a revolver, but he always kept a Winchester handy and wore a Bowie knife.

As I heretofore mentioned, the Stranglers at first glance sized the two up as hoss thieves and holdups who need hangin' every minute. But the Stranglers—an honorable vigilance committee, remember, not a lynch mob—never hung a man out of suspicion. If they'd caught these two hoss thieves with stolen stock, it would have meant a quick trial and a suspended sentence—in the Old West, that meant a sure-enough hangin'. But Stuart was a just and honest leader. He asked the two varmints a passel of questions, and they proved themselves top hands at coverin' their tracks. The Stranglers came up with nothing a vigilance committee could fasten a rope on.

A day or two later when the vigilantes rode up to a stage station, Stuart sent telegrams to lawmen around the West, asking if anybody could offer him a reasonable excuse to hang the snake and his sidekick. He didn't receive an answer for a week or two, and by then, a hangin' wasn't needed. The telegram Stuart finally received was from a law man in Buffalo, Wyoming. It read the two outlaws had wintered in Buffalo, gamblin', drinkin', and racin' horses. Come spring time, they stole some horses from the remuda of a cattle outfit and traded them to some Crow Indians for some horses they sold in Montana. After they left Wyoming, the Buffalo law man learnt Jake was wanted for murder in Louisiana and Fallon was wanted in New Mexico for shootin' up a ranch and burnin' it to the ground.

But our noble vigilantes didn't know about these crimes yet, so they trailed out lookin' for rustlers with stolen stock. The dust of their departure had barely settled when the Rattlesnake and Charlie beheld a few riders leadin' a string of race horses. When Rattlesnake asked them where they were headin', they answered they were trottin' to Reed's Fort—now they call it Lewistown—to run their horses in the Independence Day races.

"I bet this Indian cavayo I'm ridin' could beat any horse in your string," Rattlesnake boasted. "He's the fastest horse ever to look through a bridle."

A man named Ben Cline answered, "I'm ready to take that bet." He and Rattlesnake both put up a stack of chips and Cline's race hoss promptly proceeded to show Jake and Charlie how a true race horse runs. His thoroughbred left Jake's pinto behind like a jack rabbit would leave a sow pig. That racer hit only a few high spots in the topography and was halfway to the finish line before Jake's mount found its stride. Cline proudly collected his winnings and he and his racin' friends lit out for Reed's Fort.

The next day, the two sidewinders decided to pull

their freight for Reed's Fort. They knew people would be comin' to town from as far away as a hundred miles, bringin' in a passel of money for bettin' on the races. It was a day and a half ride from the Judith in good weather, so by the time they trailed in the next day, the Independence Day celebration was almost played out except for the races.

The festivities had begun about third drink time that morning. The local vigilantes, under the leadership of chairman Andrew Fergus, began celebratin' the patriotic day by decoratin' a cottonwood tree with two hoss thieves. Oh, yes, the vigilantes of Fergus County had been almost as busy lately as the Stranglers. If fact, two days prior, they'd swung the famous outlaw Sam McKenzie over the jump. A parade followed the public hangin', and then a picnic was held, which included kegs of hard cider and grog for all the vigilantes. A hog callin' contest and some trick ropin' and ridin' came on the heels of the picnic, after which most of the gents repaired to the saloons to partake of a little more inspiration before bettin' on the horse races.

By fifth drink time in the afternoon, most of the vigilantes had trailed out of town, at least those who could ride without fallin' out of the saddle. The horse races were about to begin and men were already placin' bets on the first race as Rattlesnake Jake and Charlie Fallon blew in. Jake and Charlie weren't slow about layin' some money down on the first four or five races, which left them deficient about half their roll. Said lack of luck may have contributed some to their growin' orneriness. At this point, our gamblers decided to repair to a saloon to wash the trail dust down their throats. Downin' a few drinks led them to feel the odds were good their luck would start rollin' better. They decided to place most of what was left of their roll on a few more races.

When they returned to the race track, a small herd of gents was already millin' about, waitin' for the races to start. Our two miscreants noted from the jump that two men were arguin' about something, the devil knows what, slingin' harsh words back and forth like men a few drinks down the trail sometimes do. It was within the Code of the Old West that all quarrels are private matters, but Rattlesnake went bargin' into the fracas like they were talkin' about him.

Bob Jackson, one of the quarrelin' parties, reminds Rattlesnake, "This here dispute is a private game, one you're not entitled to take cards in."

Quick as the rattlesnake he was named for, Jake snatches one of his .45's and shuts Jackson's mouth with the side of its long barrel. Jackson wasn't armed. When he saw the snake was coiled to strike again, he lit out afoot on a high lope. The horse thieves chased him up the street, caught him, knocked him around awhile, and wound up the dance by partin' Jackson's hair with the barrel of a pistol.

"Let's restore ourselves in the saloon before placin' any more bets," Rattlesnake decides.

Now here's where they dropped their watermelon. While trailin' back to the saloon, they let fly some drunken words about how easy they could take over the whole dang town and by golly, maybe they would, just to show everybody they could. But I'll tell ya true as preachin', territorial Montanans were a tough game, and don't ya think the men who overheard that boastin' didn't begin shufflin' to deal the hand I'm fixin' to unfold.

As you'd guess, a few more drinks made them wax even meaner. When they tracked out of the saloon to return to the races, they passed a cow puncher named John Doan. Mind you, Doan didn't say a word to these snakes or even look at 'em cross ways. Jake just didn't like his looks. He pulled out both his revolvers and unbuckled in the sport of burnin' the ground around Doan's feet and orderin' him to dance.

Before I crossed the Big Divide, western story book writers were always writin' about trigger-happy bullies who made dudes dance. But in the real West, that seldom happened, probably because of our tendency to shoot back. But sure as the hills, the snake tried to play the risky card of givin' John a dancin' lesson. But unlike Jackson, Doan *was* armed, and you can shove in your stack of blue chips and bet he didn't wear that Peacemaker as an ornament. About the third time Rattlesnake was spittin' out the one-word sentence "Dance," John drew that pistol and fired without aimin'. His first shot carried off half of Jake's trigger finger. From this point on until the end of his short life, Jake shot left handed.

In all of a buck like a buckin' bronco, the air was

full of lead as a bag of bullets. Charlie Fallon leaped into the saddle and pranced up and down the street, firin' his Winchester at anybody in sight—until he was shot through the guts and fell forward on his saddle horn. After heavin' a groan of seven sinners, he sat up straight, spurred his hoss, and tore out of town fast as an antelope.

Charlie was a quarter of a mile out of town when something strange pounced on him. He turned that hoss around and raced back into the heart of town to throw in with the Rattlesnake, who by now was down on one knee, fightin' hard with six bullets in his hide, shootin' left handed at everybody he could see. Fallon dismounted next to Jake, dropped to his knees, and began shootin' at anything that moved. He even downed poor old Ben Smith who'd taken no hand in the fightin' and was just tryin' to scamper out of range.

They say Rattlesnake Jake had nine holes in his hide before he died from lead poison to the skull, puttin' an end to his hoss stealin' and killin' for all times eternal. Fallon bucked out with eleven holes in his hide. Nobody could say they were quitters.

That dreadful day left the story of these two hoss thieves branded on the pages of Montana's history, a fame they didn't deserve. Although they weren't the first or the last outlaws to shoot their names into history by gunnin' down good men, they fast became Montana's most remembered. No doubt these two marauders packed a barrel of courage, but I can't fathom a bigger waste of it.

When outlaws like these two opened a play on territorial Montanans, they found us a tough breed to scare. Let's hope spirited Montanans will always remain too tough to bluff. Keep your feet in the stirrups and keep lookin' ahead, and never let go of the reins.

Your friend, Charles M. Russell

Granville Stuart

Granville Stuart, pioneer and chronicler. Courtesy of the Montana Historical Society

2012 in the moon of the deep snow

Skunkwagons

It's no secret I didn't cotton to that new invention called the automobile. I was over forty when I first saw one, and I savvied from the jump I'd sooner be seen stealin' chickens than jockeyin' a horseless carriage. Of course, by then, I was sorta set in my ways, and I couldn't stomach nothin' more modern than an egg beater. But there was a bigger reason I didn't want skunkwagons hankerin' around, and I'll unload that on you directly.

As long as I lived, I refused to own a horseless carriage and I never learned to ride herd on one. I called 'em "skunkwagons" 'cause to me, their exhaust smelled worse than forty skunks. What's worse, I swore they were the most dangerous things alive to ride.

I tried to become a bronc buster when I was a young buck, but I wasn't a good enough rider, so I remained a horse wrangler. In the process, I was thrown from many a snaky range horse. But many years later, I held that ridin' a pitchin' bronc is safer than throttlin' a skunkwagon. In 1918, I made that clear in a letter I wrote to a friend who was ponderin' buyin' one. Remember, in 1918, horseless carriages had been sold in Montana's biggest towns for only nine or ten years, and you didn't see many flitterin' about the scenery quite yet. A lot of people felt like me and wanted to stick with their horses. I wrote this paragraph in that letter of 1918:

"I never saw a gentle automobile. If you're stuck to take chances, why don't you try bulldoggin' big steers? It ain't so dangerous, and there's more glory in it. Of course, an automobile is easier to throw than a steer, but it falls so hard, the human generally takes second money. His prize is a wooden overcoat and lots of flowers."

In about 1914, my old friend from the cow-camp years Pete Vann owned a splinter of a bank he and some others cattlemen had started. Another rancher wanted to buy out Pete's stake in that bank, and offered him a 1914 Model T and a bull for it. Pete was startin' a cattle ranch at the time, so he figgered he could use the bull, and he'd been curious to try out a skunkwagon, so he took the swap. My advice to Pete was, "If I was playin' your hand, I'd ride the bull and put the skunkwagon out to pasture."

Today my memory is trailin' back to a calm afternoon in 1904. I ambled into the Maverick Saloon where my old friend Sid Willis was tendin' bar. I'd just returned from visitin' my relations back in St. Louis. I tried my best to describe to everybody a new-fangled invention I saw back there called a horseless carriage. I can't claim I had much luck paintin' a word picture of the contrivance, but they all told me they'd heard of the invention already. But to them, skunkwagons were just some fool experiment back east somewhere. It wasn't until 1908 when we began to see a few grindin' hither and thither around Great Falls.

By the summer of 1909, nobody had seen a skunkwagon yet in the Judith Basin. One day, Pat O'Hara, camp finder and mayor of Geyser, announced, "I've decided to try out a horseless carriage. The nearest place to buy one is in Great Falls, so I'll catch the train in the morning."

The next afternoon, everybody in the Judith stood waitin' on Main Street in Geyser for their first view of this new invention. Finally, they sized up a cloud of dust approachin' from the west, two or three miles away. They stared with eyes big as stove lids and soon heard the growin' sound of a steady growl.

"Sounds like somebody's teasin' a grizzly," a sod buster gasped.

The horseless contraption growled through Geyser without stoppin' or even slowin' down. Pat O'Hara waved to his wife and friends from the driver's seat and sputtered east on the road to Billings. He and his Model T didn't stop until they were near Greybull, Wyoming, plumb out of that new fuel called gasoline. O'Hara said, "They taught me how to start the dang contraption, but they didn't have time to show me how to stop it." And that's a true story.

A lot of us early Montanans hated horseless carriages because they spooked our horses, causin' 'em to unload riders and run off with empty saddles. Horses pullin' buggies, wagons, or carts would also spook and run off the road, often dumpin' out the cargo and the riders. Of course, most horseless carriage owners were good men who didn't mean any harm. But every now and again, you'd ride up on a prankster who was fond of unloadin' riders.

Let me unload on you a true episode of such a prankster. One day, two top hand ropers and riders named Stu and Tanglefoot were on horseback west of Lewistown. This prankster in a Tin Lizzie rides up on 'em and causes his engine to snarl louder than forty cougars. Both of them range horses come uncorked and unbend in a debauch of pitchin' and buckin' that would have thrown anybody but a top rider. But these top hands stayed in the middle, and the skunkwagon jockey roared off toward town laughin' like a loon.

Two days later, these two cowpunchers were ridin' fence near the road when they beheld the same prankster makin' that skunkwagon growl like a cow camp cook, thereby unloadin' a gent from a one-horse buggy. Stu and Tanglefoot grabbed their lariats from their saddle horns, built a loop, and went prancin' after that laughin' sidewinder.

Now if you've ever been to a rodeo and seen team ropin', or if you've ever watched an open-range brandin', you can fancy what happened next. Stu hollers, "I'll rope the head and you heel it!"

The prankster looks over his shoulder and beholds the two ropers spurrin' their hosses, twirlin' their lariats, and chasin' his horseless carriage like he owes 'em money. The rocky road is wrinkled as a washboard, so the prankster can't throttle his skunkwagon much faster. Stu's poor hoss is rollin' his eyes and snortin' in fear of that growlin' machine, but he's more afraid of Stu than the model T, so he comes abreast of the contrivance while Stu throws his loop. It sails over the left front wheel and fastens around the axel. Stu takes a few dallies around the saddle horn as Tanglefoot tosses his loop over the rear right wheel. As it fastens around the axel, Tanglefoot takes his turns around the saddle horn.

Stu points his horse north and Tanglefoot points his south, just like they've done hundreds of times stretchin' out steers to brand. This jerks the horseless carriage half way around, and it goes skiddin' down the road sideways. The cowboys unwind the turns from their saddle horns and watch the horseless contrivance quit the road and slam into a cottonwood tree.

"We can rope the critter easy enough," Tanglefoot brags to Stu, "but how do you hogtie it?"

The ropers couldn't see any way to hogtie the invention, but brand me if they didn't rope, stretch out, and hogtie the driver.

I was a horse wrangler for the big cattle outfits for eleven years, and before that, I was sorta one for my father and uncle's hosses in Missouri. And you can bet a yearling pinto I sure loved horses. My friends always said they never knew a man who savvied hosses like me. That's the straight goods. They swore I spoke their language. They said my genius with hosses was a rare gift from God, same as my gift with paint brushes.

I don't know how true them praises might ring, but I know this, sure as the hills: the biggest reason I hated the automobile is because I feared it would replace the horse. I wrote this paragraph in a letter in about 1919:

"It will take a million years for the gas wagon to catch up with the horse in what he's done for man. There's not a city in the world the horse did not help build. The horse took man from the caves. He carried settlers across the plains and mountains. He helped build every railroad in the world. Now he builds roads for the automobiles that threaten his existence."

I couldn't help feelin' a tad bit betrayed by my friends who bought skunkwagons. But soon everybody wanted one, even my wife. Everybody called her Nancy the Robber because she charged dead man's prices for my paintings, even years before I crossed the divide. She earned our money; I just painted. I always told her she had more right than I had to decide how to spend it. Trouble was, in 1916, she insisted on ownin' a skunkwagon.

Now if she'd wanted any other darn thing, I'd have told her sure, go buy it. But we fired hot words at each other for weeks over her hankerin' for a skunkwagon. I finally gave in and told her, "All right, you can have your dang skunkwagon. I'm willin' to water the critter for ya, but don't ask me to do anything else with it. I'm stickin' with my hoss. We understand each other better."

Trouble was, Nancy had an expensive taste in horseless carriages, same as her taste in clothes. Her first one was called a Pierce Arrow. In 1923, she bought a Cadillac Roadster, and after I crossed the skyline, she bought a Lincoln Roadster. But she never learned to drive. In those days, drivin' a skunkwagon wasn't held to be lady like. She always hired a chauffeur.

In '26, after Doc Edwin told me my old pump would soon quit, I told my wife, "I don't want no skunkwagons in my funeral procession, Mame." My dear pardner and booster kindly abided. By then, horse-drawn hearses were almost extinct. We had to advertise for one, and we found one in Cascade in time for my cash-in. My old friend Ed Vance, a former stage coach driver, held the reins from the driver's seat of the hearse with the mortician seated beside him and me snug behind them in the coffin.

My old cowboy friends who were still livin' and

not in jail for makin' prohibited likker trailed the procession from the Episcopal Church to the cemetery on horseback. Then half the town trailed them on horseback and in all manner of buggies and carriages. By the time I cashed in, I no longer owned a horse, so a borrowed horse named Dexter, led by cowboy artist Charlie Beil, carried my empty saddle. From the saddle horn hung my six-gun, my lariat, my chaps, and my spurs. That's how my friends who trailed me across the Big Divide described my send-off.

Pilgrims new to my range tell me my funeral is still the biggest one ever to fetch loose in Great Falls, and they say I should be proud as a peacock. I can't say my old hide doesn't swell up with pride to hear that, but I'm much prouder to say I wasn't carried to my rest in a skunkwagon.

May you always ride a good hoss and may you never get your spurs tangled up.

Your friend, C. M. Russell

A COPPER MINE AT BUTTE

2012 in the moon of the hawk winds

The Ghost of Cross-eyed Pete

The house Mame and I owned on Fourth Avenue North was branded 1217. Behind the house stood my small horse barn and my corral, and across the alley we owned a cottage. I usually rented it cheap to some unmarried old cowboy friend. If my memory ain't dealin' me a cold hand, Charlie McCardle was still campin' in there when I crossed the Maker's Big Divide in '26.

I shot you this historical trivia because, if my memory ain't ridin' a lame hoss, it was Charlie McCardle who unloaded this yarn on me. He swore it was true as preachin', but you know how old cowboys are when we tell yarns. He said he once took the train to Butte to throw in with some Irish-bred miners who were holdin' a wake for a countryman who cashed in his chips while asleep.

By the time I ranged on your side of the Big Divide, a wake had long before become another excuse for them Irishmen to go rioting off on a drunken debauch. I heard it said the only difference between an Irish wedding and an Irish wake is at the wake, there's one less drunk. But Charlie McCardle told me that long ago, likker was no more a part of a wake than cuss words were part of a sermon. A wake meant sittin' awake all night with a newly deceased corpse.

Like as not, you're wonderin', "What a strange custom. Why would any fool do that?"

In the old times, once or twice every generation, somebody's body parts would bluff and feign bein' dead, probably to rest up before ridin' new trails. When them body parts go on strike in said fashion, you have what the medical sharps came to call a catatonic state. So when a livin' person graduated to the ranks of a corpse, it was an Irish custom to have some kinfolks take turns watchin' the cadaver all day and all night, maybe for as long as three days. If the watchers caught wind of any motion on the part of the corpse, their hopes would rise that the grim reaper was just bluffin'. Then folks would hold off on the burial for a couple days, hopin' the deceased would soon rise and return to ridin' his old roundups. Of course, if the corpse was someone nobody liked, the watchers probably didn't overwork themselves lookin' for signs of life.

As you can fathom, a corpse don't always make the best company to sit up with until dawn. Folks began to realize it's easier to accept the night-long society of a cadaver with the aid of likker. This became the practice more and more until them wakes evolved into the debauches of likker they are known for to this day. Even the corpse is often fed enough drinks to float a keelboat.

The funeral Charlie McCardle blessed with his society began at second drink time in the afternoon. These rites were over by fourth drink time, and no time was wasted in turnin' the wake out of the chute. Somehow, word had gotten around town there'd be Irish whiskey instead of Butte's usual rot-gut at this wake, so more mourners trailed in than expected. For many hours, joy held the top hand and drink drowned all gloom, but shortly before midnight, the mourners ran plum out of whiskey. They quickly decided to continue their wakeful libations in Con Peoples' Saloon.

"Wait a minute," one mourner remembered. "Who's gonna stay and sit up with the honored corpse? That's what a wake is for, after all."

Nobody volunteered. Somebody finally asked, "Can't we just bring him along?"

Nobody could ante up a good reason why they couldn't fetch the corpse along. As luck held it, the deceased was thin and of average height. His two arms were flopped over the shoulders of two strong miners, Pat and Dan, and they packed him off to the saloon, his toes draggin' in the dirt. Nobody seemed to notice they were transportin' a corpse. It looked like they were just haulin' home the average Irishman who'd surrounded too much likker.

When Pat and Dan and the corpse blew into the saloon, the two living miners propped the deceased miner up against the bar between them. This was one of them old-time saloons with no bar stools. You'd just put one foot on the brass rail and stand there drinkin' like a man. Of course, ladies weren't allowed to enter Montana's distinguished drinking establishments.

Pat ordered a bottle of rot gut and three glasses. He poured himself and Dan a drink and poured one down the corpse's throat. After repeatin' this ritual four or five times, they heard a voice rumblin' from across the saloon.

"Pat! Dan! Let's see if you two paddies pack the nerve to try me and McBride out in a game of billiards. Let's say we wager a day's wages."

Pat and Dan couldn't decline this challenge, no more than they could decline free drinks. "Get your money out and get ready to lose it," Pat answered as they left their cadaver of a sidekick leaning against the bar and picked up cue sticks.

While Pat and Dan are shootin' their game, the corpse's posture takes to slumpin' like a lazy sheepherder's. Soon his head and shoulders are almost touchin' the bar.

"You can't pass out in here, Mick!" the barkeep barks at him. "You'd best mosey along."

Of course, Mr. Corpse don't make any great effort to remove himself from the mahogany. He don't even have the respect to answer the barkeep.

"You heard me. Now trot along!" the barkeep growls again.

Again the rude corpse refuses to answer.

"This is the last time I'll say this, immigrant. Pull your freight!"

Now the barkeep's big as a haystack, strong as a bronco, and mean as a one-eyed mountain cat, and he has the reputation of bein' fond of giving drunk Irish miners the old heave-ho. When the corpse doesn't move after that third warning, the barkeep scrambles out from behind the mahogany, seizes the cadaver by his collar and the seat of his pants, and sends him headfirst through the swingin' doors.

When Pat and Dan catch a glimpse of their deceased sidekick soarin' through the swingin' doors all sprawled out like an ejected drunk cowpuncher, they chase the lifeless figure out into the street. They scoop the cadaver up from the dirt and tote it back into the saloon.

"Now you've done it, Blackjack," Pat accuses him.

"Done what?" the barkeep wonders.

"You got too rough with this paddy, Blackjack. You blew his lamp out."

"That can't be," the barkeep puts up. "I only gave him a normal shove."

"You shoved him across the Big Divide, Blackjack. Feel his pulse."

The barkeep takes hold of the corpse's wrist and finds it has no more pulse than stone walls or steel bars.

"Already he feels cold as a snake," Pat puts up.

"He aint' breathin', and his heart ain't beatin'," Dan chips in.

"When you tossed him out into the street, you shipped him to the realms of light, Blackjack. Dan, you'd better go fetch the law."

"Please," begged the barkeep. "You fellas know I sure didn't mean to turn this card. I'll tell ya what. If you would carry your friend home like he's too drunk to walk, put him to bed, and tomorrow let everybody think he trailed out in his sleep, I'll make it worth your while."

"How worthwhile, Blackjack?"

"Any time you track into this saloon, all your drinks are on me."

"And we'll need a few quarts to take with us now," Dan raised him.

"Take 'em."

"And we want one more thing, Blackjack," Pat raised him again. "Swear you'll never toss another Irishman through them swingin' doors, no matter how sloppy he waxes."

"I swear it."

Dan and Pat each flopped one of the corpse's arms over a shoulder and toted him out in the same fashion they'd hauled him in. They walked him back to the hall where the wake had cut loose and returned the cadaver to his coffin. Then they sat up surroundin' the whiskey and watchin' the corpse until dawn, but they saw no twitch of life return to it. They were hopin' that once the corpse sobered up, it might up and take to carryin' on like a live Irish miner, but that wasn't in the deck. The deceased was buried two days later.

In my time, most country doctors were better at doctorin' horses than people. They couldn't always tell a corpse from a fellow whose innards had chosen to render him catatonic for a spell. I've heard tell there were a few cases of catatonic folks bein' buried before the Maker was ready to send for 'em. Undertakers didn't drain a corpse's blood and pump it full of this here embalming fluid I hear they use nowadays.

Even under spurs and quirt, my memory can't gallop back to more than one time a catatonic party was buried before he was called across the Big Divide. This strange burial fetched loose in Billings. The folks in Billings never forgot the day they planted Cross-eyed Pete.

In his younger days, Cross-eyed Pete had been a prospector, and he'd scouted Indians for Uncle Sam's Army. Even though he was cross-eyed as a crow, he once was as good a shot with a pistol as any man beneath Montana's big sky. But by now, he spent his days wearin' thin his boot soles on the brass rails of the saloons around Billings.

Of course, bein' cross-eyed meant Pete was the butt of many jokes. "Which eye is lookin' at me, Pete?" was a common one. In his younger years, he might have taken a man's scalp for such words, but by now, the whiskey and the years had rendered him good natured, so he always laughed along and poured the jokers more whiskey.

The only sign of wealth Pete had to show for his long life was in the form of a big diamond ring he wore on the pinky of his shootin' hand. He was proud as a peacock of that jewel, which looked almost the size of a mule's ear, so he always polished it shiny as the sun at high noon and wore it in plain sight for all to see.

One of Cross-eyed Pete's many drinkin' friends was Jed Tombs, the gravedigger for the town cemetery. He had buried the remains of so many drunken gunfighters that the sight of dead bodies didn't bother him no more than the sight of dead leaves. It was sometimes rumored around Billings that Tombs wasn't above stealin' from the dead. Remember, back then, people often buried the deceased with their favorite gems, guns, watches, all manner of jewelry, and even silver and gold coins.

Gravedigger Tombs had long before set his eye on that big diamond, and he coveted it like a weasel covets baby chickens. While downin' drinks in a saloon with Pete, Tombs had more than once been heard to say, "When you die, I'll lift that ring off your frozen finger."

Pete was always heard to answer, "If you do, I'll haunt you until I see you in your grave." Then they'd unbuckle in hearty laughter, slap each other on the back, and resume their daily libations.

After too many rounds of nose paint for too many years, Cross-eyed Pete finally took powerful sick and tracked into the doctor's office above the hardware store. The doc laid him on a cot, findin' him too sick to perch on a stool. When it appeared that Pete had given up on his efforts to breathe and pump blood, the doc pronounced him deader than a can of fish. Cross-eyed Pete was planted the next day in a pine coffin. The town folks stood by his grave readin' psalms and singin' hymns as Jed Tombs lowered him down and covered his casket with dirt.

Late that night, Tombs crept back into the cemetery with a shovel, a pickax, and a lantern, and went to work like horses refreshed diggin' up Cross-eyed Pete. It took three hours to uncover the corpse, but all that diggin' was holiday fun compared to fightin' that ring off the corpse's finger. Pete had worn that ring so many years that by now, flesh had grown up on both sides of the ring, sorta like moss growing on the side of a tree. Tombs wished he'd brought his bowie knife along to cut the finger off and save himself a lot of work, but he'd forgotten it. He just had to keep pullin', twistin', and spittin' on that finger until the ring was finally pried off. Grinnin' at that jewel like a tomcat grins at a nest of baby field mice, the gravedigger slid the ring onto his own finger.

Now whether all that jerkin' on his finger helped cause the revival of Cross-eyed Pete, or whether his catatonic innards decided to climb back into the saddle and ride, one can't say. Whatever the cause, Pete sat up, wonderin' where he was. In the light of Tombs' lantern, he saw his diamond ring glowin' on the gravedigger's pinky. He waxes madder than a teased hornet and hollers, "You stole my diamond, you horse thief! Give me back that ring!"

That gravedigger lets fly the screech of forty Apaches and riots off like his rear's afire. Pete seizes hold of the pick ax and hot-foots after him. Lightning plays second fiddle to the speed Tombs scatters across the graveyard. But as fate plays out its hand, our grave robber stumbles over a headstone and falls to the ground flat as a wet leaf. Before he can rise, he beholds what he surmises is the ghost of Cross-eyed Pete, standin' over him brandishin' the pick ax.

"You stole my ring like you said you'd do!" bellows Cross-eyed Pete. "Burn me if I'm not inclined to claim you with this pick!"

"Please don't kill me, kind spirit," Tombs begs. "I swear I'll never steal from a grave again!"

"Gimme that ring, you sidewinder!"

Tombs returned the ring, and Cross-eyed Pete returned to crookin' his elbow and paintin' his nose in the Billings saloons. Everybody said the good gravedigger, Jed Tombs, was broken of his habit of robbin' the dead for good and all. And now you savvy all there is to know about the ghost of Cross-eyed Pete.

I'm hopin' sickness don't locate your camp and health rides herd on you.

Your friend, C. M. Russell

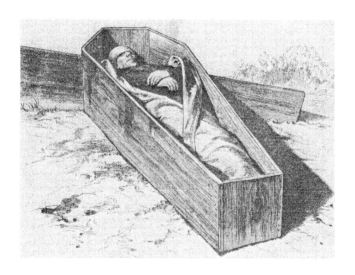

2012 in the moon the ice breaks

More Yarns of Cranky, Cussing, Cow Camp Cooks

Just north of the Bear Paw Mountains, out on the flats they call Sun Prairie, the Bear Paw Cattle Pool had a roundup camp in the spring of 1890, or maybe it was '91. We'd just finished spring roundup, and many of our riders would soon be drivin' a herd of longhorns to the railroad corrals of Malta to be shipped east.

Although it was only late June, the weather had already turned hotter than the hinges of hell. It was hot enough to wither a fence post or to fry meat on a stone. If there'd been any farmers near by, they'd've had to feed their chickens cracked ice to keep 'em from layin' hard boiled eggs. The heat would've popped their fields of corn, and their cows would've given evaporated milk. If their dog had chased a cat, they both would've walked. But we played in luck, for no sodbusters had yet taken a plow to that stretch of the prairie.

Trouble was, there were no trees on that range, and the few scrawny shrubs we saw didn't give no more shade than a bob wire fence. Now that was rather a boggy ford for me and Kid Amby Cheney—we were the nighthawks who night-herded the remuda—and for the two night riders who circled the bedded herd. How could us night hands sleep without shade during days that were hotter than a two dollar pistol?

Today, my memory is combin' the ranges of trails plowed under tryin' to ride up on the reason the camp cook let the four of us sleep in the cook's tent that day. No camp cook was ever known to allow another party, man or beast, inside the cook's tent. Every man knew that was the cook's domain, and any cook would fight like a bear if a rider tried to drag his spurs inside.

But for some reason my memory can't fasten a loop on, us four had permission to flop down on the ground in the cook's tent to try to sleep. Maybe it was because the old cook knew he wouldn't have to feed us young whippersnappers much longer. Maybe the roundup boss had asked him for that favor—and even the bosses respected the kingdom of the cook's tent.

For whatever reason, I was layin' on my back in that tent that morning, sound asleep as a tree, havin' been up wranglin' horses all night. The bottoms of the tent flaps were fastened about a foot off the ground to let in a breeze. My three friends were still awake, sharin' a little chin talk, and the cook was puttin' away a bevy of utensils. All of a buck, that cook gasped like he'd just turned around to face a grizzly. The cook motioned for everybody to be silent, and he pointed at a fat, six-foot rattlesnake not two feet away from me. They knew if I woke up spooked, that viper would be none too slow about sinkin' his fangs into me. They knew if they shot the diamondback and it didn't die fast, it would bite me again and again until one of us cashed in. The only thing to do was to stand still as graven images and let the snake play out its hand.

I'm glad I wasn't awake to watch the snake's meanderings, because it crawled over my belly and out the other side of the tent. I woke to the sound of two shots fired from a .45 and a passel of war hoops, and then I beheld Kid Cheney blowin' into the tent, holdin' high a dead serpent that's longer than he is tall.

Of course, I couldn't swallow their story that the snake had crawled over my belly, no more than I could fathom a buffalo had tromped over my belly. Would you believe some prank-lovin' cowboys if they told you a snake the size of a stovepipe crawled over you in your sleep without wakin' you? But when the cook finally chipped in, vouchin' piously for their words, I turned my disbelief out to pasture. There was a saying in the Old West, "Only a fool would argue with a skunk, a mule, or a cook."

Cow camp cooks were always known to be "techy." That means they were cranky as a sore-headed bear. And why were they such a crusty brand of cattle? I reckoned it's 'cause they could no longer do the work they deemed themselves created for. Most of them were former cowpunchers who'd grown too stove up to ride herd on longhorns all day. By now, the cowboy life was all they knew, so the cattle outfits kept 'em on as cooks. After all, *somebody* had to cook for us ingrates, and cookin' for a passel of young whippersnappers who always kick about the meals can't improve an aging man's disposition none. Cattle hands were called cowboys because most us *were* still boys when we threw in with our first cattle outfit. To these older cooks, we were just a passel of silly kids. Their patience for young men's pranks and stunts became thin ice after years of tough sleddin' on the range.

The cattle outfits paid their riders somewhere between twenty and thirty-five bucks a month, depending on the cowboy's skill and his number of seasons with the outfit. The cook was paid five or ten bucks more a month than the best riders, but nobody doubted he earned it. He was the first man up and at work every morning, and he was the last one workin' every evening. His duties, besides cookin', included gatherin' fuel, be it wood or cow chips, fetchin' water, washin' dishes and forks, scrubbin' pots and pans, and peelin' potatoes. He was always expected to have a five-gallon can of coffee steamin' on the cook fire for the riders as they came and went changin' shifts. And every time the outfit moved camp, he had to load and drive the chuckwagon. That meant he had to feed, water, harness, and unharness two mules, critters as stubborn as the cooks themselves.

On cattle drives, the cook had to load the chuckwagon every morning after chuck and drive it up the trail a few miles ahead of the cowboys pushin' the herd. He had to try to find a meadow with tall grass and water for the cattle. Then he had to unload the cookin' and eatin' utensils, build another fire, and have a hot meal waiting when the herd trailed up. After the riders got outside a meal, the cook would have to dance the whole fandango over again. When he sought a site for the evening camp, it was even more important to find a bed ground near tall grass and water.

So if anybody on the range had a just call to be cranky, it was the old cook. And as I remarked prior, the cook's tent, as well as his chuckwagon, were the cook's domain, a kingdom where nobody else was welcome, no more than a skunk. I learnt that lesson the hard way as a young buck in the Judith.

It was a chilly, drizzly dawn early in the spring roundup of '83. I was ridin' back to camp after nighthawkin', tired and cold as a dead snake. Unexpected as a bartender at a camp meeting, something spooked my cow pony. Maybe he caught wind of a bear or a cougar, or maybe he heard the rattle of a diamondback.

Something caused that horse to pitch, and he unloaded me in a patch of prickly pear.

Now where in the devil can a horse wrangler go on a chilly dawn to haul off his clothes and pluck hundreds of thorns from his hide? I could see smoke risin' from the stove pipe above the cook's tent, so I knew the cranky old cook was up and had built a fire. I tell myself, "There's the only warm place on the range. Go see if you can undress and dequill yourself in there."

But the darn cook wasn't there when I called for him. He must have been gatherin' firewood or fetchin' water. Hopin' to be gone before the cook returns, I step inside, yank off my thorny damp clothes, and take to pullin' thorns like a man pluckin' goose feathers. But before I'm half done, in blows the cook.

He greets me with, "You can't perch in here naked as a jaybird. Get out!"

I began to explain, but I might as well have addressed my explanations to a sore-headed bear. He snatches a butcher knife and chases me half way across camp. Then he storms back into the tent and chucks all my clothes, thorns and all, out on the cold, damp ground. For as long as I lived, I packed a heap of scorn and distrust for cow-camp cooks.

Most other cooks I cut the trail of were just as hostile to trespassers as the cook I outran that day. If the cow camp didn't have a cook's tent, the cook was just as fussy about the chuckwagon and all the ground within spittin' distance of it. Every cook I ever saw threw dirty dishwater, potato peels, coffee grounds, and any other waste that might draw flies under the chuckwagon. And never think it was because they were too lazy to walk a few paces to dump it. It was to keep us night herders and nighthawks from sleepin' under the wagon.

Yep, a cook protectin' his domain was akin to a bear guardin' his cave. No cowboy who never cooked could understand it. But we all knew most cooks had been known to pull a knife a time or two to defend their kingdom. Most of them were willin' to lay their lives on the line in such fracases. Some Texas cowboys told me of a cook who laid his life on the line and left it there.

Said cook was known by the handle of Frenchy. He was a top hand cook, and no outfit ever liked to lose him. Like all cooks, some of the cowhands played pranks on him, but he took pranks better than most cooks. Instead of lettin' his kettle boil over and grabbin' a carvin' knife, he'd wait for a shot at pullin' a prank on the pranksters.

For instance, take the time two punchers caught a bull snake big as the rattler I just told you about. They snuck it into camp in a gunny sack, and when the cook wasn't about, they poured it onto the ground near the chuckwagon. Then they dropped the cook's wash tub over the coiled serpent and waited for the fun.

Now if you don't have a speakin' acquaintance with bull snakes, let me paint a quick word picture of them. Full grown, they're as big as your biggest rattlers or bigger, and they look just like rattlers. They even act like rattlers. They coil and lift their heads and hiss at you like rattlers, and if you come too close, they'll strike at you like a rattler. They'll even sink their fangs into you like a rattler. It hurts like the bite of a rattler, but it won't kill you. The bull snake don't pack the venom of a rattler, nor does he have rattles.

When Frenchy ambles in, he cusses a blue streak about young fools who can't leave anything alone, not even a dang washtub. As he lifts the wash tub off the ground to put it back where he wants it, he's sayin', "If I see any fingers but mine touching this wash tub, I'll cut 'em off. Plant your boots on that."

The bull snake was coiled up, hissin' and fixin' to strike, when Frenchy caught his first glimpse of it. He dropped that washtub like a hot stove lid and sprang back out of range quicker than a spooked colt, remindin' the pranksters that he was no greenhorn to rattlesnake country.

There were rules against firin' guns in cow camps. It takes a lot less than gunfire to trigger a stampede. So Frenchy tied a butcher knife to the barrel of his shotgun, clubbed the snake with that barrel a few times, and cut off its head. By the time it glimmered on him the viper was only a bull snake, the riders were laughin' like loons.

"You sons of mule thieves will get this snake in tonight's stew. Plants your moccasins on that," he growls.

The riders sized up and poked into every bite the

cook piled on their plates for a few days, but they saw no signs or smoke signals of snake meat. They surmised Frenchy had fast forgotten or forgiven that prank. Cow-camp meals didn't often include dessert, but a few days later, Frenchy dishes them up the best lookin' and smellin' pudding they'd seen in months. The way they bolted down big gobs of it was a lesson to wolves. Then all of a buck, the face of every man assumed the countenance of a man shot in the back with an arrow. They all unbuckled into the biggest debauch of spittin', gaggin', and even vomitin' ya ever saw. As they were pourin' water down their gullets, it began to glimmer on them that Frenchy had poured more salt than sugar into that pudding.

As the cattle drive pushed on, Frenchy took revenge on other pranks by cookin' red peppers into the beans and cotton into the biscuits. But every time he returned a prank, he always felt guilty as a robber and cooked something darn special.

Frenchy could take a joke of almost any brand or earmark, but there was no jokin' with him about who was boss of the cook's tent or the chuckwagon. A feisty rep from another outfit named Houston Red learnt that the day he pushed Frenchy too far.

Just to rile Frenchy up and see which way he'd jump, Red says, "Frenchy, how about rustlin' me a plate of hot chuck? I feel like surroundin' a meal."

"Hell, no," he grumbles. "The men eat when I ring the triangle in this outfit."

"I reckon I'll have to help myself then," Houston

Red bluffs as he's bluffin' a few steps toward the chuck wagon. Of course, this Texan had ridden the cattle trails enough to know better than to trespass on a cook's territory, so he'd no more have stuck a hand in that chuckwagon than he'd have stuck it in a wolf's mouth. But a riled cook don't always cogitate too clear. He snatches a carvin' knife, cusses like a mule skinner, and steps two paces toward Houston Red, who hops two paces backward like Frenchy's a rattlesnake.

"Hold on, Frenchy! You know I wasn't really gonna ransack your chuckwagon," he tries as the locoed cocinero takes two more steps toward the retreatin' cattleman, flailin' that knife in the air like he's swattin' horseflies.

No Texas cowhand I ever met would scoot back from a knife more than once or twice before doing what Houston Red had to do. He pulled his Peacemaker and aimed it at Frenchy's brisket, allowin' the persuasive nature of the implement might cause the cook to take another look at the cards in his hand and maybe fold.

But the ragin' cook kept trailin' him, hackin' away at the air like a man choppin' vines. Red shot once at the ground, but Frenchy gave that report no more heed than he'd give the chirp of a robin. He lunged forward with that carvin' knife like a steer tryin' to horn a horse, and as Red lunged backward, he fired a round into the cocinero's brisket.

That same play cut loose three more times. I didn't want to believe them Texans at first, but now I can credit it, knowin' more about the nature of cow-camp cooks. Frenchy made three more plays at stabbin' Red in the belly, the odd card in that deck bein' he took three more bullets in the chest. On his fifth lunge, he heard the metal click of Red's hammer slammin' loud against an empty chamber. That sent Frenchy chargin' in with that knife like a bull. Before it dawned on the Texan that he'd shot his last full cartridge, he was receivin' orders on high to tune his harp and stand in with the heavenly chorus.

It was hard to say who won that fight, because they both hit the ground in one thump, deader than Julius Caesar. But as long as you didn't track into their domain, most pranks on cooks didn't pan out as bad as Houston Red's. Sid Willis, barkeep of the Mint Saloon, told me the two good ones I'm shufflin' to deal out to you now.

For a couple years, Sid rode for the N-Bar-B outfit near Miles City. He said the L-X outfit once drove in a herd of longhorns to ship by rail to Chicago. They were camped two or three miles from town, waitin' for the railroad to round up more cattle cars. The trail boss Jim Drummond let the cowhands take turns guardin' the herd and goin' into town to get roostered up.

About midnight, a few L-X riders detached themselves from a saloon while they could still ride and lit out for camp. As they trotted by the next saloon, they spotted their old camp cook, Alex Fitzgerald, tryin' to mount a gentle horse, but havin' more trouble than a one-armed green hand tryin' to mount a stick-of-dynamite bronc.

"He's drunker than forty fiddlers," a rider said. "Let's help him mount up."

"Havin' a little trouble with the gravity, Alex?" they asked him.

"The dang ground won't hold still."

Two riders hefted him into the saddle and flanked him on each side to keep him from fallin' off as they rode easy toward camp. Old Alex soon passed out, so they laid him across his saddle like a sack of bran and plodded along till they trailed up on a cemetery surrounded by a prim picket fence.

"What would a drunk cook think wakin' up on somebody's grave?" a rider wondered.

"Cookie can't read," another put up. "He'd think he's the corpse."

"It might scare his orneriness plumb out of him," a cowboy hoped.

They toted Alex inside the bone yard and laid him atop some nice soft grass that was covering an unfamiliar cadaver in the grave beneath him. They laughed like a tree full of catbirds as they trotted back to camp to sleep off their load of joy juice.

They woke that morning to the boom of Jim Drummond's deep voice askin', "Anybody seen Alex?"

"He was too drunk to ride last night, boss. He's resting…uh…a short distance up the road."

"Go round him up. We'll need to surround some chuck."

When the riders rode up on the cemetery, they

removed their hats and entered on foot. They were ready to say, "Up and at it, Cookie. The boss says the herders need to get outside some breakfast." But as I expounded a lope back on the trail, the cook's always the first man up and the last man to bed down in any outfit. So it didn't surprise anybody to see old Alex workin' on standin' up, stretchin' like a wakened hound, yawnin', and rubbin' his eyes. When his eyes focus on the tall marble tombstones that surround him, he spooks like a deer. Then he looks down at the grave he's treadin' on, looks at the tombstone he can't read, and solemn as a deacon, he removes his hat.

"I'll be saved in Glory!" the riders heard him spout, jubilant as a drunkard at a barn raisin'. "It's resurrection day! And wouldn't you know the loyal cook would be the first one up."

Another outfit that once camped near Miles City had a cook branded Flapjack, as good a dough wrangler as ever poured dirty dishwater under a chuckwagon. He was another cocinero who could take a ribbin' without gettin' his back up, but you can bet your spurs and quirt he'd soon surprise the jesters with a slick prank of his own.

One day, the riders caught wind there'd be a public dance in Miles City that evening. That opened up the corral gate to saddle Flapjack with some good old cow-camp ribbin'. Some riders came as close to the cook's tent as safety might advise as Flapjack was cookin' and spoke loud words meant for the cook to hear.

"Trouble with these dances," a rider antes up, "is there's always ten fellers to every girl."

"That's why we gotta get there early enough to throw a loop on 'em," another rider chips in.

"I'm sure glad I don't have to hanker around here washin' utensils and scrubbin' pots and pans," a third rider stacks in. "Flapjack will be two hours late for the hoedig."

"Every heifer will be roped, tied down, and branded before Flapjack prances in."

"It won't matter. Them prairie flowers won't dance with no crusty old cook anyway."

Flapjack let on he didn't hear them and prepared a meal like they hadn't seen in weeks. On the trail, it's always a plate of sow belly beans and biscuits. But on this gay occasion, he cooked up a tasty dish of roast beef and scalloped potatoes. After weeks of trail food, it smelled like a royal feast to all the riders. They downed it like a pack of wolves, spruced up for the first time in weeks, and lit out for that shindig in town.

"Do a good job on them pots and pans, Flapjack. We like 'em shiny as a maiden's eyes," they riled him as they trailed out, leavin' him alone as a preacher on pay day.

The riders blew into the dance in time to throw their rope around every unbranded filly in the herd of calico. Trouble was, they found none of them young mares very halter broke. Oh, they all shook their hooves on the dance floor with every cowhand once, but only once. After that, they'd prance away from any rider who tossed his loop at 'em. Soon all the riders from that outfit were ridin' the bench like a row of wall flowers.

Flapjack blew in almost two hours after the riders, but that didn't put a cork on his fun. He danced with every unbranded heifer there, not just once, but six or seven times. His feet never stopped shakin' the planks of the dance floor until daybreak. He jigged like a young water bug on a pond until the band played out. He was even thinkin' of askin' to see the school marm home.

But then his luck took a turn to the south. As folks were leavin' the dance hall, the trail boss ambled over to bid his riders a good night.

"You all smell like you had supper with the coyotes," he shot at them when he caught wind of their breath. "What was in the pan, a dead skunk?"

Quiet as a band of ghosts, the riders all looked at each other, solemn as a tree full of owls. Then they all looked at Flapjack, who looked as comfortable with their silence as a horse thief at a hangin'. The cook finally broke the silence with, "Well, goodnight, saddle pals. I'm hopin' to see the school marm home."

Four brawny bronc riders seized hold of the escapin' cook, and they weren't slow about escortin' him to the water trough.

"Put me down, you smelly polecats!" Flapjack growled on his journey to the trough. "Give me one of you shorthorns at a time, and I'll whoop you till you won't know each other from last summer's corpses.

You young whippersnappers ain't nothin' but a passel of kids. I'd rather slop hogs than feed you any day. Put me down, I said!"

His tough talk didn't save him from the trough. It took only four or five dunkings to get his confession. As the riders surmised, he'd cooked an overabundance of garlic into them scalloped potatoes.

"You're sentenced to a chappin' of forty thousand lashes," the riders holdin' Flapjack pronounced. They weren't slow about layin' him spread-eagle over that trough and preparin' him for the ritual.

As I heretofore explained, a chappin' is a spankin' with chaps on the bare rump that a cowboy renders to a sheepherder or some other deserving party. Now if this candidate had been a sheepherder or a grave robber, all the riders in the outfit would have been chewin' each other's manes for the honor of swingin' them chaps. But as long as a cowboy's anatomy requires food, he don't want to be on the cussin' side of his cook. The long and the short of it is, nobody had the sand to take them chaps and wallop Flapjack's rump, not even the tough bronc riders holdin' him down.

"Don't expect to enjoy the taste of your coffee and porridge in the morning," Flapjack warned as they cut him loose.

Sid Willis said Flapjack wouldn't have kicked much about a good chappin', but he sure begrudged gettin' wet. He lit out madder than a rained-on rooster. But at morning chuck, he dealt 'em the best breakfast they'd eaten in weeks. That's how quick most horseplay between the cowhands and the cook became forgotten and forgiven. But you can bet your six-gun and throw in your belt and cartridges, both Flapjack and the cowhands still held some high cards to play on each other later.

Remember, never argue with a skunk, a mule, or a cook.

Your friend, C. M. Russell

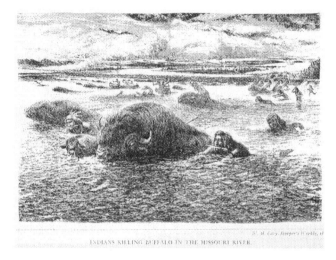

INDIANS KILLING BUFFALO IN THE MISSOURI RIVER

2012 in the moon of the melting snow

The Rise and Fall of the Blackfeet

I was never more than a green hand with a pen. A man who paints word pictures is a far better artist than we who use oil paint or water colors. Paintin' word pictures seemed like harder work to me than turnin' a night stampede. When I wrote the Rawhide Rawlins yarns, I stacked in the words, but my wife rode herd on the pen.

New pilgrims to this side of the divide sometimes ask me why I never wrote an autobiography. I always answer, "Because I deemed a lot of other people more worthy of my word pictures than me." Of course, the real reason is I was such a lame hand with a pen, havin' had so little schoolin' as a colt.

These new pilgrims tell me since my cash-in in '26, a dozen pen sharps have wasted their time, ink, and paper writin' my biographies. They say a lot of disagreement has ridden the ranges of them biographies. I'm told a few of my later biographers have branded some of the tales of my earlier biographers "The Russell Legend."

Now the question follows, like a lariat follows a loose pony, who do you believe when them biographers lock horns? My steer to you is to believe the ones who knew me. My later biographers relied plumb too heavy on early Montana journalism. Too many misdeals, misfires, and plumb silly notions, if not damn lies, rode the ranges of them early newspapers, especially in their stories about cowboys.

I'm told that one of the "legends" these new pen sharps have taken aim at is my six-month stay with the Blood Indians in Alberta. They put up I didn't honestly live with the tribe and almost become a squaw man. They wrote I camped in a shack near by with two other cowboys and just visited the Bloods from time to time.

When these smart fellers come saunterin' across the Big Divide, I'll rope, throw, and hogtie 'em long enough to shoot a few questions their way. How could I have painted so much detail into them Indians and their clothes, teepees, horses, camps, travels, huntin' grounds, and huntin' parties if I just visited them now and again? How could I have learned so much of their lingo you can still read in my letters? How could I have learned so many of their legends? And did you ever try to learn Indian sign language? It's no easier than learnin' a spoken foreign tongue. Ya can't learn it by visiting some Indians a few times. You have to live among 'em. And if you don't believe I spoke Indian sign like I was a born-again Blood Indian, just ask Joe de Yong when you cross the Big Divide. For years, we spoke nothin' but sign with each other in Great Falls, 'cause he was deafer than forty fence posts.

New pilgrims to my side of the divide say folks who doubt my half-year stay with the Bloods point to two pieces of writing to back their play. One was a Helena newspaper spoutin' I was back in Helena in late September of '88. The other was the memoirs of my friend Con Price who recalled me wranglin' horses for the Judith fall roundup of '88. Tell me, how can any man, cowboy artist or otherwise, be in two places at once?

That Helena newspaper also wrote I was fixin' to study art in Europe. I never yearned to study art in Europe, no more than I yearned to study likker prohibition in China. That newspaper was just shootin' from the hip, printin' hearsay. As for Con Price, he couldn't do nothin' wrong at ropin' a steer, ridin' a bronc, or cuttin' cows from a herd, but I wouldn't trust his aging memory to recall the dates of happenings and mishaps, no more than I'd trust my own.

My memory ain't cinched on as tight as it once was, but I hazily recall workin' the Judith roundup that fall of '88, and then I lit out to winter in Helena. But that don't prove I didn't live six months with the Blood Indians. The idea I went to Alberta the summer of '88 and returned the spring of '89 came from my wife, Nancy, when she unfolded my life's story to that writer Daniel Conway. Every biographer since then has thought of '88-'89 as the year I either did or did not throw in with the Blood Indians. But if my memory's shootin' straight—and I ain't plumb sure it is—it was the winter of '87-'88 that I became a Blood Indian.

The winter of '86-'87 was the worst winter Montana ever saw. Nine out of ten of the longhorns in the Judith froze to death or starved, which means there were only one tenth as many head of cattle as normal to gather durin' the '87 spring roundup. The work was over by mid May, almost two months earlier than most years, so I lit out for Helena and threw in with Phil Weinard and Long Green Stillwell. We soon lined out for the Blood country of Alberta, a two-week ride of almost four hundred miles, and there were no roads or bridges in '87.

Phil took a job in Alberta runnin' a ranch. Like the newer biographers wrote, Long Green and I camped in a cabin for a month or two, huntin', fishin', and visitin' the Indians. Come August, Long Green lit out alone for Montana, Phil rode east to marry a gal, and contrary to them pen sharps' words, I threw in with the Blood Indians for half a year. When you cross the Big Divide, ask Chief Black Eagle or my friends Sleeping Thunder or Medicine Whip. Be sure to refer to me as Ah-Wah-Cous.

The Maker was tellin' me to paint Montana before the nesters plowed it all under, so I left the Blood Indians and returned to the Judith for the '88 spring roundup. But I'll stand here today and back up my words with promises, poker chips, money, or bullets that my life among the Bloods is true as a sermon, and it left me all Indian under the hide. And I'd bet my saddle hoss all these biographers' doubts stem from my wife tellin' Conway the wrong year.

If I hadn't lived with the Bloods, I couldn't have soaked up enough sign talk to understand the many stories they unloaded on me. The story that carved the deepest trails in my memory is one I later branded "The Rise and Fall of the Blackfeet." When you cross the Big Divide, I'll unload it on you in sign language, which makes any story a far sight better. But today, I must be content with hen scratchin' it down in word pictures.

In the beginning, Napi, the Creator, also called Old Man, floated on a log with a frog, a fish, a lizard, and a turtle. Napi sent them one at a time diving deep into the water to see what they could find at the bottom. The first three dove and returned with nothing, for they could not reach the bottom, but the turtle dove and rose with a gob of mud. Napi rolled it around in his hands, and from that ball of mud grew the Earth.

Old Man walked about this Earth he created, but

he saw nothing good, so he created the river the white men later named the Yellowstone. Then he walked north, creating as he went the mountains and prairies, the rivers and streams, the timber and brush, and the birds and the animals. He walked north once more, creating more of these wonders everywhere he passed.

After Napi created the Milk River, he felt tired. He lay on his back and stretched out his limbs. The shape of his body was formed in the stones, and you can still see his shape there today. It is still called "The Sleeping Giant."

After Old Man rested, he walked farther north, where he stumbled over many rocks and fell on his knees. As he rose to his feet, his knees raised two big buttes. Old Man named them "The Knees." The buttes are called that to this day.

Napi grew angry at the rocks that made him fall. He scooped them up in his mighty arms and carried them farther north. With those rocks, he built the Sweet Grass Hills. Then he covered the plains with grass to feed his animals, and he put cottonwoods in the ground near the rivers. Then he created some sacred grounds that would grow roots and berries.

Napi created a big horn sheep on the prairie, but it did not travel well. He took it by the horns and put it in the mountains. It traveled with ease among the peaks where few creatures dare to tread. While in the mountains, Napi created the antelope, but it stumbled and fell over the rocks and on the hillsides. He put it on the plains and it ran swifter than the wind.

Then Old Man made a woman and a son child of clay. He molded them into human shape and said, "You must become people."

Napi looked at the forms after one sun, and he saw very little change in the clay. After two suns, he saw a little more change. After three suns, he saw even more change. After four suns, they were changed into people. Old Man told them to rise and walk with him to see his creation. As they walked along a river, the woman asked, "Will we live forever?"

"I have not thought about that," Napi answered. "Let us decide now. I will throw this buffalo chip into the river. If it sinks, you will some day die forever. If it floats, you will some day die for only four suns. Then you will live forever."

It floated. The woman should have been happy, but she was foolish. Her heart was on the ground about having to be dead four long suns. She asked Napi for another chance. Picking up a stone, she said, "Let us say if this stone sinks, we will be dead forever, and if it floats, we will live forever without being dead four suns."

"You have so chosen," Old Man answered. When they saw the stone sink, they knew all people must some day die forever.

One mournful day, the child died. The woman begged Napi to change the law of death back to how the buffalo chip had decided. He told her, "What has been made a law must always remain a law. All people must some day die and remain dead forever."

Then Old Man created more people in the manner he'd created the first woman and child. He created many women first, and then many men. In the beginning, women and men lived apart from each other, for the men feared the women, not understanding their ways. But Napi told the men, "Do not fear the women; take them as your wives."

In the beginning, Napi's people were poor, naked, and hungry. But Old Man pitied them and was good to them. He showed them what plants, roots, and berries to eat and which birds and animals were created for food. He taught them the power of herbs and told them which ones to eat for each sickness.

Napi's people had no horns, claws, or fangs. Nor could they run as fast as most animals. So the buffalo always chased the people, killed them with their horns and hooves, and ate them. Old Man declared, "This will not do. The buffalo shall no longer eat my people. My people shall eat the buffalo."

Napi cut a branch from a berry tree and peeled off its twigs, leaves, and bark. He bent it enough to tie a leather thong from one end to the other, and named it the bow. He carved a long, straight shaft of wood and attached four feathers to one end, but when he shot the shaft with the bow, it did not fly well. He tried using three feathers, and the arrow flew straight. Old Man tried many different stones as arrowheads, and he found stones of black or white flint served best.

Soon a buffalo saw the men and charged. Napi showed them how easily an arrow can pierce a beast's heart and kill it. Then he gave the people knives and taught them how to cut up the buffalo. He told them to use the hides to make clothes and lodges, and to use all the other parts of the animal to make tools, weapons, pouches, and bow strings.

"It is not healthy to eat raw meat," Old Man told his people. "I shall teach you how to prepare meat."

With a flint arrow head, Napi drilled a hole in a log of hard wood. Then he cut fire sticks from soft wood and taught his people to make fire by rubbing them in the hole. He taught them how to cook and smoke meat, and how to make a kettle by hallowing out a large, soft stone with a smaller, harder one.

Then Old Man told his people, "Before I leave you, there is one thing more you must know. When animals appear to you in your sleep and tell you what to do, you must obey them. And if you are ever alone and in danger, cry out loud for help. Whatever animal appears, be it a bear, a wolf, an eagle, or a buffalo, listen to him and obey him."

Napi left his people and again walked north. After he created the Porcupine Mountains, he began to miss his people, so he molded many human forms from mud. He blew his breath upon them, and they became live people.

"What are we to eat?" his new people asked him.

Napi made many clay figures of buffalo. He blew

his breath over them and they came to life and ran away. "There is your food," Old Man told them.

"But how can we catch them and kill them?" his new people asked him.

Napi led them to a cliff and had them stack many large piles of rock. He told them, "Hide behind the rocks as I lead the buffalo your way. When they pass you, rise up shouting and wave your arms. Frighten them into running toward the cliff."

Napi's new people obeyed, and that day they became the first people to run buffalo over a pishkin. Napi taught them how to make knives from sharp, thin stones, and told them, "Go cut up their flesh with these knives. Do not cut up the hides, for you must use them with long poles to make shelters."

Some of the buffalo were still alive, but they could not run or fight because of their broken legs. Old Man taught his people to cut strips of green hide and use it to tie stones to the ends of heavy sticks or bones. With these large mauls, they broke the skulls of the living, injured buffalo. Then Napi left his new people and again walked north.

When Napi reached the land where the Bow River meets the Elbow River, he made many more people from mud. He taught them everything he'd taught his other people, left them, and walked north again. Next he created the Red Deer River, and near it he created a hill which he lay upon to sleep. The form of his body is seen there yet, and the hill is still called "The Hill Where the Old Man Sleeps."

When Old Man woke, he walked north once more. He said, "I have worked hard creating the earth and its rivers, mountains, plains, forests, plants, animals, and my people. Now I shall have fun."

Old Man created a hill for sliding down, and like a child, he laughed all day while sliding down the hill. The marks where he slid can be seen yet, and the hill is still known as "Old Man's Sliding Ground."

With the new sun, Napi walked south to the Yellowstone River. As he passed his people, he told them, "All the land from my sliding ground to the Yellowstone River, and from the Rocky Mountains to the Red Deer River and the Saskatchewan River is your hunting ground. Only the five tribes of my people may dwell there. These are the Piegans, the Gros Ventres, the Blackfeet, the Blood, and the Sarcees. You must drive away all others who try to enter. Very bad medicine will come your way if you fail to obey."

For many generations, Napi's people obeyed his words. They became the most numerous, powerful, and feared people between the two seas. They were bold, skilled warriors, and they kept all others out of the land Old Man gave them. They lived long, bountiful lives by obeying Napi's commands.

Then from afar came men from a different Creator. Pale men with hair on their faces came to trap the mink, the beaver, and the otter for their fur. One night, a buffalo came to all Napi's chiefs and warriors in their sleep, saying, "The pale men with hair on their faces are very bad medicine. Keep them away from the land Old Man gave you."

For one or two generations, Napi's people obeyed and kept the pale men away by giving battle to those who dared enter their hunting ground. But too many of Old Man's people came to admire the pale men's magic. They had stout staffs that made thunder and could kill a buffalo at sixty paces. Napi's people longed for these weapons, and the pale men would trade them for animal hides. The hairy-faced men would also trade knives, axes, hammers, pots, pans, nails, horseshoes, and bridle bits for furs. Greed for the pale men's metal caused Napi's people to allow them to enter their hunting ground.

As the buffalo in their dreams had warned, the pale men with hair on their faces were very bad medicine. Their traders brought the smallpox that killed more than half of Old Man's people. Pale hide hunters killed the buffalo for their hides and left the meat to rot on the prairies. They slaughtered all the food Old Man had given his people, causing many thousands to starve. Pale men who spoke the words of a snake made a border through Napi's people's hunting ground, calling the south side Montana and the north side Alberta. They told Napi's people they could no longer migrate across the border, but with the buffalo gone, Old Man's people no longer had a reason to migrate.

Napi's people were ordered to live on reservations and learn the pale men's ways. Their children were put in boarding schools and forced to speak the pale men's tongue, to wear the pale men's clothes, and to forsake the teachings of Napi. Life on a reservation became easier to accept with the pale men's fire water that banishes reason. And now you savvy how disobeying Napi caused the fall of his great people.

May Dad Time be slow in snuffin' your lamp and may your trails be smooth plumb through.

Your friend, C. M. Russell

2012 in the moon of the first new grass

Why The Blackfeet Must Never Kill Mice

Ain't it surprisin'—and downright upliftin'—when ya find a tender streak in the heart of somebody who you thought had no heart at all?

When I was a stall-fed tenderfoot of sixteen winters, I threw in with Jake Hoover, the best white hunter, stalker, and trapper ever to make a moccasin track in the Judith, maybe in all of Montana. He savvied the habits of every wild critter like Bill Rance savvied likker. He'd see wild game where I'd see nothing—often not until he fired his Winchester—and he always dealt a quick, clean kill. Pin a patch the size of a silver dollar on a tree and he could cut it nine out of ten shots at ten rods. He could track fleas over granite—in the dark. He had more guts than you could hang on a fence. Once we were charged by four killer grizzlies. I took to a tree like a coon, but Jake stood pat and pumped off four rounds calm as a man grindin' coffee. The last of them silvertips dropped not twenty feet from his front sights.

I met Jake in 1880, only a year or two after the white hide hunters had slaughtered the buffalo. They must have scared off most other game too, for wild meat was scarce in the Judith as clean socks in a bunkhouse. Yet Jake was such a top hunter he made a stake sellin' wild meat to the miners of Utica. Like the Red people, his clothes and tools were made from the animals he shot. He was as good a trapper as he was a hunter, and he sold and traded mink and beaver furs in Utica. Like the cougar and the wolf, Jake lived by killin' the Creator's critters.

No, you wouldn't expect Jake's heart to be much softer than a boulder, but this gritty hunter had a soft streak in his heart big as a saddle blanket. He kept salt licks and water near his cabin for his dozen or more pet deer who were tame as tabby cats. He had all manner of critters for pets, and he didn't have to keep any of them in a cage, not even his chickens. Once he raised a pig to eat, but by the time the pig was big enough to butcher, Jake didn't have the heart to slay it.

It remained a pet. Jake told me, "Never name a critter you intend to eat."

My good friend Frank Bird Linderman became a state senator, an author, and a famous collector of Indian folk stories later in life, but he came to Montana broke as the rest of us when he was a ruttin' buck, and he threw in with a white trapper named Black George. Like any trapper, Black George made his livin' by killin' critters. But that wasn't as far as his death-dealin' tendencies went. Black George boasted he'd outlived a dozen or more men in powder burnin' contests in Texas. He also boasted, "I've drank enough whiskey to float a keel boat and shot enough lead into buffaloes to sink a man-of-war."

One day, Frank was rustlin' some chuck for himself and Black George. He was fryin' the meat of a critter they'd trapped and skinned and was fixin' to bake some biscuits. He opened the flour sack and saw a goose-feather nest housin' half a dozen baby mice. Frank placed the nest on the ground and raised an ax, fixin' to cash in the uninvited rodents' chips.

"Stop! Don't do it!" he heard Black George shout.

"I'm just gettin' rid of some mice," Frank told him.

"Don't kill 'em. They're just little babies. They haven't had a chance to live yet. How can anybody kill innocent babies?"

Years later, after Frank became known as an Indian-story sharp, he told me the Blackfeet believed they must never kill mice. I wish I could reel out this legend as pretty as Linderman told it. Whenever he whirled his verbal loop, he was always sure to fasten. But as I remarked prior, I'm a lame hand with a pen, and my memory has grown a little wobbly in the knees. But I'll try my best to unfold this tale as Frank told it.

In the beginning, Napi, the Creator, who is often called Old Man, created the Earth. Then he created his bird-people, his animal-people, and last of all, his men and women. For a long time, his animal-people and his bird-people were greater than his men and women. They had been on Napi's Earth longer, so they were wiser. Most animal-people could easily outrun men and women, and those that couldn't run fast could climb, swim, or dig into the ground much better than men and women. Bird-people were even greater than animal-people, for they could soar above the animals' heads.

Both the bear and the beaver wanted to be chief of Napi's people, and for many moons they quarreled over it. Then all the other birds and animals began to quarrel about it. Some said the swiftest should be chief. Some said the chief should be the strongest. Some argued the wisest should be chief. Some said the chief should be the largest beast, and some argued he should be the bird who can fly the highest.

Then rabbit came to Old Man and told him of the quarreling. Napi came to them one night unseen and listened to them quarrel. Shortly before daylight, he shouted, "Stop! I have grown weary of this quarreling. We will settle this now for all times."

Napi pulled from his robe a small, polished bone, and held it in the firelight for all his people to see. "Do you see this bone in my right hand?" he asked them.

"Yes, Old Man," they answered.

"Watch the bone and watch my hands," he told them. He began to sing as he passed the bone from hand to hand, rapid as the rabbit runs and as smooth as the eagle flies. Then he stopped and held his arms straight out with his hands shut tight.

"Which hand holds the bone, bear?" Napi asked him.

"The left hand," guessed the bear.

Old Man opened his left hand and the bear saw it was empty. He opened his right hand, and everyone saw the bone. Napi's people laughed long and loud at the bear.

Old Man passed the bone from hand to hand again. Then he held his arms out again with his fists closed and asked the beaver, "Which hand holds the bone?"

"The right hand," guessed the beaver.

When Napi opened his right hand, all could see it did not hold the bone. Then he opened his left hand and all saw the bone, and every animal and bird laughed long and loud at the beaver.

Then Napi told his people, "I will teach you to play this game. When all have learned it, you must all play it with one another until you find who is the most clever. He will be chief under me forever."

Napi's animal-people and bird-people learned the game fast, and soon they all played it, one against another. The bear won against many of Old Man's people, but the beaver at last beat the bear. Then the beaver held the bone for a long time, but he was at last beaten by the buffalo. But it was the mouse with his small, quick hands, who finally defeated the buffalo and all the other people Old Man had created.

Napi told all his people, "The mouse has proven himself the most clever. He will be chief over my people forever."

The mouse spoke solemnly. "My brothers, what is mine to keep is mine to give. I am too small to be your chief, and I am not warlike. I do not like having enemies. Therefore, I will grant my right to be chief to the one Napi created most like himself, if he will promise never to be my enemy."

From then on, man became greater and wiser than all animals and birds, and has since been chief of all people under Napi. And from then on, Blackfeet men and women have known they must never kill the mice-people.

When I first came to Montana in 1880, the prairie was dotted with ghost-white buffalo skulls. Mice had been living in those skulls ever since the mouse beat the buffalo at the bone game. The Blackfeet were still playing the bone game among themselves and singing the song Old Man sang so long ago.

Here's hopin' that in life's game you win health, wealth, and many birthdays before you're called to cash in.

Your friend, C. M. Russell

2012 in the moon the buffalo calves are red

Two Yarns of Frontier Justice

The spring of '89 was the last roundup I worked in the Judith. The nesters and the sheepherders were takin' the grassland and the cattle bosses were throwin' their herds up on the Milk River. We spent the whole summer pointin' 'em north.

We well savvied that within a few years, we'd see the grass of Montana's highline plowed under by a bevy of sodbusters, same as in the Judith. Already a few scattered ranches and farms were sproutin' up along the Milk River. But in '89, the lid was still off in Blaine County. There was no bob wire yet and dang little law. This was the only period of true freedom America ever knew. Anything went except murder, cattle rustlin', and hoss stealin'. No lawmen were needed to hang hoss thieves and rustlers. Frontier people graciously accepted that responsibility.

But there wasn't much thievery on the highline. These were known as the days nobody owned a key except the key that wound your clock. Although there was little law, there was a strong code of honor among cattlemen. Part of that code was to allow any traveler passin' by your spread to push his feet under your table and get outside a meal. Of course, most settlers welcomed travelers as a source of news from other counties. Even if nobody was home, the latchstring was always out for a rider. He knew he could always track into a stranger's house, build a fire, and cook a meal, and if the weather was terrible, he could camp down for the night.

But there were three rules the traveler had to heed. First, he must never insult the host by leavin' pay for the grub. Second, he must cut as much firewood as he burnt. Third, he must wash all the dishes he used, includin' pots and pans and coffee pots. Violation of that third rule was the most likely way to raise a rancher's dander.

By now, you've probably surmised them memories I just unfolded are trailin' up to a yarn. This yarn was handed down from the very first cattle ranchers in the Woody Island district up near the Alberta border, some thirty-five miles north of Harlem. It's been told so many times it must be true by now.

The fall of '89, a rough lookin' rounder who went by the handle of Bull Creek Miller blew into the Woody Island country. He was surly as a badger and snappy as a wolf, so he didn't make many friends durin' his stay. From the six notches on his gun, other cowhands knew better than to make him the goat of any pranks. But he proved to be a good roper and rider, so a few ranchers hired him off and on when they needed another hand with brandin', roundin' up, or movin' a herd. He said he'd been punchin' cattle in Canada, although everybody packed some suspicion he was wanted by the Dominion law. But part of that Code of the Old West was to never ask a man about his past or ask his birth-given name.

Bull Creek Miller honored Blaine County with his society for some six months. During that time, five or six ranchers became deficient a string of top saddle horses. To those ranchers, it was plain as plowed ground a gang of hoss thieves was stealin' stock at night and runnin' 'em across the Canadian Border. The odd card in the deck was this: every time a rancher's horses were rustled, Miller had recently worked for him. Finally, the thieves made off with a twenty-horse remuda they borrowed from a small cattle outfit, and Miller vanished the same night.

By now, the Blaine County ranchers had their bellies full of this hoss stealin'. They formed a small vigilance committee and rode north on a lope, hopin' to recover that stolen remuda and hopin' the occasion might afford them the opportunity to socialize some with Bull Creek Miller. Soon they trailed up on a rancher named Hodgins.

"My top saddle horse, the sorrel gelding, was stolen last night," he told the posse. "I'd bet a pinto Miller knows something about this. I'm ridin' toward the border hopin' to trail up on him."

Hodgins threw in with the posse and they pushed the scenery behind them at a good gait toward the Alberta line. In two hours, they reached Lone Pine Coulee, branded as such by reason of one big, solitary pine tree growin' in the sage-brush soil. It was there they cut the trail of Bull Creek Miller. No, he wasn't leadin' a string of stolen mounts. He wasn't even ridin' Hodgins' sorrel gelding. He was on foot—somewhere no cowboy ever chose to be—limpin' like a stove-up bronc fighter, his hide so scratched up he looked like he'd just lost an argument with a bobcat.

"So, my old sorrel piled you, did he?" Hodgins anted up. "He never did like the smell of a horse thief."

"Miller, it seems to us you've been abusin' our hospitality," stacked in the roundup boss of the vigilantes. "We fear it would be ruinous to the county to cut you loose to join your partners on the other side of the border."

Setting up a vigilante court took no longer than it takes four men to down a pint. Hodgins opened the ball with, "Did you steal my sorrel gelding?"

"Well, I sorta borrowed it," Miller confessed. "But he threw me so high, I darn near froze up there. And if you think I look lame and cut up, you should see the ground I hit. Takin' into account the damage to my anatomy, and considerin' that horse is most likely home by now, I'd say we're more than square on this deal."

"Have you been stealin' horses from the rest of us durin' these past six months?" another rancher chips in.

"Why, no," he first tried to hand them. But it was plain as a pike staff the posse couldn't believe he didn't steal horses, no more than they could believe he didn't drink whiskey. Miller added, "I just tipped a few fellows off who needed some horses in the worst way. It's in the Code of the West, ya know, to never deny a stranger in need, same as you never deny a hungry man a nosebag when he comes to your door."

Those words brought a light of recollection to Hodgins' face, sorta like the look of a man who just remembered it's his wife's birthday. "Say, did you surround a meal in my cabin before you rode off with that sorrel?"

"Sure. Nobody was home, so I rustled some chuck. That's within the Code of the West, you know."

"Can you read?" Hodgins asked him.

"A little."

"Didn't you see the sign on the wall?"

"I seen it, but I didn't pay it no heed."

"That's where you missed the ford, Miller,"

Hodgins told him. "We maybe could've overlooked your tippin' them hoss thieves off, but the way you defiled my cabin plumb cinches the matter."

Hodgins pointed to the lone pine tree, and the posse escorted Bull Creek Miller to it, not forgettin' to bring along a lariat. That night, the coyotes on the barren bench lands sang Bull Creek Miller's requiem.

Darkness was fallin' on the prairie as the posse rode up on Hodgins' cabin. They were glad to see the stolen gelding was back, waitin' for some oats. Hodgins built a fire, cooked the riders some beans and biscuits, and let them camp over night on his dirt floor. At sunrise, he cooked them a breakfast of flapjacks and bacon. As they got outside the meal, they saw in the new light of day the sign on the wall Hodgins had asked Miller about. It was a little grimy from the smoke of a thousand burnt flapjacks, but the posse could still read its words:

> If you are hungry, grab a plate
> You have my best of wishes
> But just before you pull your freight
> Be sure to wash the dishes

Very little law was needed in Montana when the lid was off, because when crime lowered its ugly horns, territorial folks had their ways of knockin' them off. The land was open, the grass was tall, people helped one another, the times were good, and most folks were happy. But three things ruined the country forever: civilization, eastern-style law, and the sodbusters.

Richard Bird Baker

New pilgrims to my side of the divide tell me if a man abuses or neglects a horse these days, this first thing a citizen does is send for the law. Both the horse and his master are locked up until the latter pays a fat fine. But in Montana before the lid was on, citizens themselves found a cure for such neglect. That's how the cards once fell to a rancher over by Billings. Herb Roberts once told me the neglectful party's name. Today, my memory's tryin' to rope onto that handle, but it can't quite fasten. So for now, I'll just counter-brand the cattleman "Buck."

Buck would often leave his ranch hands to ride herd on the spread's daily duties and ride into town to get roostered up. He'd snub his horse to a hitchin' post, saunter into a waterin' hole, and drink until his roll was gone, which often took days. Trouble was, he'd forget about his poor hoss tied outside and never feed or water it. For years, other cowboys pitied the poor cavayo, and they fed and watered it, but they finally waxed plumb tired of playin' Buck's hand for him. Some of them decided Buck needed a lesson in horse sense.

One afternoon, they found Buck in a saloon too drunk to hit the ground with his hat in forty throws. They escorted him out back of the waterin' hole and dressed him in old squaw clothes. Then they braided his shaggy hair and tied some turkey feathers to it. They wrapped an Indian blanket around him, war-painted his face, and strapped a big wooden doll on his back to serve as a papoose. Then they paraded him through the streets of Billings on his neglected horse until everybody in town who wasn't in jail had their fill of laughter. When the prank was played out, they swatted Buck's horse on the rump and told it, "Take this inebriate home."

Buck woke up late the next morning, still none too sober, and still harnessed in the get-up of a squaw. He couldn't rightly remember the proceedings from yesterday afternoon, so he asked his cowhands how it came to pass that he was attired in this irregular fashion. As they unfolded the events of the prank, it set them to laughin' like a pack of hyenas, but Buck couldn't see much humor in it. He waxed madder than a barkeep with a lead quarter.

"Wait till I get shed of this squaw harness and strap on two pistols," Buck told them. "I'll play even on this prank; you can plant your moccasins on that."

While Buck repaired to his ranch house to harness himself into a white man's ridin' outfit and strap on two Peacemakers, two of his riders allowed, "We'd better ride on ahead of Buck and inform all concerned parties Buck still ain't learned his lesson in horse etiquette, and he's fixin' to object to their teachin' with his guns."

As the riders high-tailed it for town, they stopped by a few outfits and rounded up enough cowhands to serve as a judge and a jury. The riders hid in a grove of willows along the trail, and as Buck pranced by, two top hand ropers unfurled their loops from tree limbs and roped Buck off his horse. Before Buck knew what fate had befallen him, the riders seized both his .45's. They left one of the lariats twined around Buck's flanks and brisket, dallied the loose end of that catch rope around a saddle horn, and snaked Buck into town on foot, something more humiliatin' to a cowboy than being dressed as a squaw.

Court was set up in the same saloon the pranksters found Buck in the day before, and he was promptly found guilty of failin' to learn proper horse etiquette and of conspirin' to express his objections to it with a gun.

"You are hereby sentenced to a chappin' of forty lashes," the judge decreed. The guilty party was led to the pool table and made ready to take his medicine. Four brawny cowhands held him down on the green velvet as every gent present was allowed to take a few swats at Buck's bare rump with some leather chaps donated for said purpose. It was said that hereafter, Buck took better care of his hoss when he went to town to contribute to the success of its waterin' holes.

Pranks were a big part of life in the Old West, due to a lack of entertainment. Every cow puncher had to learn to take a prank as well as pull one. If the goat of a prank was a poor sport, chappin' was the most common remedy for said disorder. And if the chappin' wasn't cure enough, the guilty party wasn't cut loose until he bought the house a round or two of drinks.

I've been told modern folks on your side of the Big Divide now hold chappin' bees to be what city folks now call "cruel and unusual punishment." But in my time, it sure pulled on the bridle of what city folks now call "inappropriate behavior." And let me say this for the men who now and then yielded a chappin'. If the victim ever needed help or money, these chappin' givers would be the first ones to offer a workin' hand, their last dime, or the shirt off their backs.

Ride easy to the end of the trail, and don't use your spurs till you hit open country.

Your friend, C. M. Russell

2012 in the moon of the heavy rains

Kid Curry and Butch Cassidy

If my memory's dealin' a square game, it was in 1889 when the Judith Basin Cattle Pool held its spring roundup camp on Crooked Creek, just north of the Moccasin Mountains. The Basin was waxin' thick with nesters turnin' the sod grass-side down, so the cattle outfits were fixin' to swim their herds across the Missouri and drive them north to Milk River country. In a few days, we'd be makin' that dreadful crossin'.

One evening right about chuck, a big sorrel stallion came buckin' into camp to beat four of a kind. I don't know what the stranger in the saddle was doin' to make that killer buck with such fury, but the way that sorrel kept archin' his back and crackin' like a whip would have thrown almost any good rider. But the young cowboy sat up straight and stuck to that saddle like he was born there, and never once did I see him grab leather. He rode that stick of dynamite down to a whisper and slid off calm as if he was quittin' a street car.

"Who's the roundup boss?" he asks us.

"I am," Frank Plunkett answers.

"I'm Kid Curry, and I need a job."

"Kid, if you can handle a lariat like you rode that sorrel, you're the man I've needed since the year of one."

The stranger mounted his sorrel and began to whirl his lariat, and I'll tell a man, he didn't spin it slow. He could throw a loop at a scamperin' steer while ridin' at a lope and fasten nine out of ten times. He could throw and hogtie a yearling in nine seconds flat. The boss hired him, no questions asked.

As I've heretofore mentioned, it was deemed bad manners, if not downright risky, to ask a man about his past. That was part of that Code of the Old West I've been tellin' you about. A stranger's reputation began the minute ya met him. As long as we knew the Kid, nobody knew much about his past.

For all of his short life, the Kid's past pursued him like a band of Pinkertons. Allow me to meander from the trail of his deeds and misdeals in the Milk River territory just long enough to unload on you the peaks of his life before we met him. Mind you, all this history wasn't rounded up and made known to us until years down the trail.

His baptismal name wasn't Kid Curry; it was Harvey Logan, but we didn't know that until the law wanted him. He and his three brothers were born in Iowa somewhere, but when their Ma died when Harvey was nine, his Pa moved the family to Missouri to raise horses. When their Pa died, the Logan brothers trailed the oldest brother Hank to Texas. They worked for a few Texas cattle outfits breakin' horses, and they became some of the best bronc tamers ya ever saw ride.

Harvey Logan threw in with a cattle drive pushin' a herd to Pueblo, Colorado, where he got in a brawl in a saloon. Nobody knows quite what happened, but some suspect one of Harvey's adversaries didn't survive the fracas. My guess is those suspicions weren't wrong. Harvey would never have run from a live man, but he spent most of his life runnin' from dead ones. But as I heretofore explained, you didn't ask a new rider about his past.

Harvey lit out for Wyoming, and on that ride north, he shucked his birth-given name and lifted the name Curry from his best friend in Texas, a cowhand named Flat-nose George Curry. He soon found a job workin' for a cattle outfit, and he wrote his three brothers to ride north and throw in with him. When they arrived, they all changed their sir name to Curry.

Hank was the oldest brother and the one the Kid

and his brothers Lonny and Johnny always looked up to as their leader. Soon Hank put up, "Instead of always workin' for other ranchers, why don't we start our own ranch?"

Somebody told the Curry brothers there was still cattle land to homestead in northern Montana, so they trailed up to the Milk River area to see how the grass and water looked. They knew they'd need to earn a stake to buy tools and other supplies, so they decided to work the rest of the spring roundup. Knowin' the herds were almost gathered, they figgered they'd have a better shot at findin' work if they all rode out alone and roped at different cattle outfits. And that's how the cards were stacked in the deck when Kid Curry came buckin' into our camp on that cyclone of a sorrel.

For five days, Curry helped us gather in the last of the strays, and in the end, we built up a herd of maybe two and a half thousand head. We pushed that herd into the Missouri River at Clagett near the mouth of the Judith River. As you can well fathom, swimmin' a herd across that river in the high waters of late spring is more dangerous than cussin' a cow-camp cook. The Missouri had claimed many a good rider, to say nothin' of cattle. The crossin' took more guts than you can hang on a fence.

Whatever Kid Curry may have lacked in good sense, he more than made up for in guts. Years later, Butch Cassidy was known to say, "Kid Curry has more guts than any man I've ever met. If I had the choice of only one outlaw who ever lived to back me in a showdown, I'd choose Kid Curry."

We saw our first glimpse of the Kid's courage during that '89 crossin' of the Missouri. My good friend Jim Thornhill was crossin' a stone's throw upstream from Curry, and that high, swift, spring current swept Jim off his horse. Jim couldn't swim, and he called for help as the current washed him downstream. Kid Curry saw Jim splashin' toward him, plunged out of his saddle, and caught Jim's wrists. The Kid pushed Jim's hands to the saddle horn and said, "Hold on."

Now a horse is pretty much a land animal, same as a man, so the Kid feared his hoss might not be able to swim carryin' the weight of two wet cowboys. He left it up to his hoss to pull Jim out of the river, grabbed hold of a cow's tail, and let the cow tug him to shore. The odd card in that deck was Kid Curry couldn't swim either.

We spent that whole summer driving herds from the Judith to the Milk River country. That fall, I threw in with the fall roundup of Robert Coburn's outfit, the Circle C, north of the Missouri near the Little Rockies. Many of my best friends worked that roundup with me, includin' Con Price, Kid Amby Cheney, Sid Willis, Jim Thornhill, Pete Vann, Horace and Charlie Brewster, John Mathewson, Bob and Charlie Stuart, Billy Rowe, and the four Curry brothers.

It was during that roundup the Kid and I came to know each other darn well, and after he became a wanted man, I always boasted, "Kid Curry is a friend of mine." Sure, he could wax a little ornery when he was drinkin', but when he was sober, he showed the same good-natured sense of humor as any other cowboy, and he'd ride to the end of the trail for any man who was his friend.

Before I lope any farther down the trail of Kid Curry's wranglin's, let me stray long enough to tell you about one of the greatest cattle bosses I ever met, the owner of the Circle C outfit, Robert Coburn. Coburn was one of the first settlers in Northern Montana to start a cattle ranch. His ranch was fully on its feet by 1877 when Chief Joseph and his Nez Perce fled by on their famous break for Canada. By then, the whole tribe was ragged and hungry, and Coburn fed them all the beef they could eat and gave them all the meat they could carry.

Later, Coburn moved his Circle C outfit farther north near the Fort Belknap Indian Reservation. When the terrible winter of '86-'87 hit, Coburn, like all Montana cattlemen, lost most of his stock. Unable to feed his steers, he turned them loose to let them try to survive, and they all became gaunt as gutted snowbirds. During the worst of the weather, a large number of Gros Ventres and Assiniboines came to Coburn beggin' for food.

The buffalo herds that had fed these people for thousands of winters had been slaughtered, and the wagons bringin' government food rations were blocked by deep snow. Robert told the Indians they could eat all his starvin' cattle they could kill. When times got better for ranchers, Coburn always told his cook to feed any hungry Indians passin' by. And that's the brand of man Robert Coburn was.

Robert Coburn had four strong sons, all good riders and top cattle hands. One November day, his oldest son Bob was ridin' a few miles from home when his horse stepped in a badger hole and fell, breakin' a front leg. Kid Curry found Bob unconscious under his horse with a broken jaw and a bloody, cracked head just as a killer blizzard pounced on the land. Curry shot Bob's horse in the head, rolled it off Bob, hefted Bob onto his horse, and rode double through the blizzard to the Coburn ranch. He carried Bob inside the warm cabin and lit out in that blizzard to fetch a doctor who lived forty miles away. The snow was a foot deep by the time the Kid found the doctor, and the doc was none too sober. For those two reasons, the doc refused to return with Curry at first, but the persuasive nature of the Kid's .44 convinced the doc to hitch up the buckboard and ride back with Curry to patch Bob up. Bob never forgot what the Kid did for him.

After fall roundup on the Circle C, Jim Thornhill threw in with the Curry brothers, and they started a ranch near Landusky, a little town that had grown from a former gold mining camp in the Little Rockies south of Malta. They worked hard, and the oldest brother Hank was a good hand at keeping his younger brothers out of jail. In a few years, they built up a herd of four or five hundred head of cattle and a few hundred head of horses.

If Hank Curry had lived long enough to play out his hand, Kid Curry may have never become one of the West's most wanted outlaws. But that wasn't in the deck. The way the cards fell, Hank died of consumption in a few years, leavin' Jim Thornhill, Kid Curry, and his brothers Lonny and Johnny to run the ranch. Life for Kid Curry loped along at a smooth road gait for two more years. Then his destinies got crossed with those of Pike Landusky.

The town Landusky was named after its camp finder, Pike Landusky. He'd made enough money from the short-lived mines to build his home and the town's only saloon, and it was always busy. It was said Pike was mean as a bear with a sore tail. Like a range horse, he was dangerous at both ends, front or rear hooves. He always packed a gun out of sight and he always carried a gold-handled walkin' cane. Said stick was reputed to often wail away at bystanders, whether or not they were causin' trouble, and whenever trouble did show its ugly teeth, Pike was more often than not the source. It was hard to take revenge on the bully because he was a deputy sheriff and the only law within miles.

Here's how the cards were dealt to Kid Curry. About a year after I rode out for Helena, never to work the herds again, Pike Lundusky's step daughter took a shine to Curry's kid brother, Lonny, and the young cowhand tossed his loop at her. Pike told the gal not to be baitin' her hooks for any wild young cowpunchers, but to save her smiles for men who owned ranches, mines, or saloons. He forbade her to see Lonny, but the two continued to meet on the sneak almost every day.

The next time Lonny and the Kid crossed up with Landusky, the bully swore if Lonny didn't stay away from his step daughter, he'd whoop the youth till his own brothers couldn't tell him from a buckshot hide. The Kid wasn't slow to warn Pike, "You can whoop my brother after you whoop me first." That was the first time anybody saw Landusky pull in his horns.

But soon Pike hatched up some lies about the Curry brothers changin' brands on their neighbors' cattle. The nearest jail was in Fort Benton, so he sent for Sheriff Jack Buckley to come from there and arrest Lonny and the Kid. The two lawmen ordered the Currys into a buckboard and handcuffed them to the bracing. Buckley directed Pike to drive the wagon to Fort Benton, two hundred miles away, and he caught a train and met them at the Choteau County Jail.

It was a four-day ride to Fort Benton in good weather, and whenever Landusky felt an itch for entertainment, maybe every couple hours, he'd stop the horses and refresh himself by swattin' the Currys in the head a dozen times and by spittin' out profanities about the boys' dead mother. The Kid promised Landusky he'd kill him the first opening fate dealt him.

The judge in Fort Benton, a friend of Pike's and

almost as crooked as said deputy, had to admit there was not enough evidence to fasten a lariat on, so he cut the Currys loose. Robert Coburn paid their train fair back, and as soon as they chugged into the town named for the man who'd framed them, they high-tailed it to Pike's saloon. The Kid saunters up to Pike without a word and lams him one the chin. I'll tell ya without hedgin' a chip, the fight that ensued was a lesson to grizzlies. Both men took more of a thrashin' than a mule could take, but as the fight raged on, Pike began to get the worst of it. He finally held out his open palms and said, "You win, cowboy."

Figgerin' he'd taught Pike a lesson in manners and had won his revenge, the Kid stopped swingin'. Sneaky as a snake, Pike pulled a pistol from inside his jacket and fired at the Kid's heart. But as luck had it, the gun jammed, bein' one of them new-fangled automatics, unreliable as a woman's watch. His second shot also jammed, but Curry's .44 didn't jam. It pumped two slugs into the cavity where Landusky formed his ornery notions, and from then on, Kid Curry was always as hard to find as a clean shirt in a bunkhouse.

When Sheriff Buckley arrived from Fort Benton by train the next day, he asked if anybody knew where the Kid was hidin'. Nobody claimed to know. He said, "If you see him, tell him to turn himself in. He has witnesses on his side, and I know Pike's reputation, so I can probably let him off the hook."

Trouble was, a few men who had the eye for Pike's stepdaughter told the sheriff that Curry was the first of the two pugilists to put a gun into play. The sheriff knew then this dispute would have to go to court, and he'd have to haul the kid back to Fort Benton. He told Jim Thornhill, "Tell the Kid he'll probably have to stand trial, but the deck is stacked in his favor."

When Jim Thornhill rode out to Curry's hidin' place with the sheriff's message, the Kid told Jim he'd never get a fair trial from a judge who was once Lundusky's mining partner. He said he was lucky the judge had cut him loose once, and it was a long shot with a limb in the way that his luck would roll that way twice. He decided he'd just have to outrun the law for a spell. They decided Jim would sell the Kid's share of the stock and pay him when they meet up. For the next ten years, Jim was always there to provide the Kid and his gang with fresh horses, food, and other supplies, and to give the Kid his mail. He was the Kid's major source of news about the law and the Pinkertons.

Of course, bein' on the run from the law tends to limit ones ability to find and maintain gainful employment, so Kid Curry threw in with Black Jack Ketchum's outlaw gang. In the meantime, Lonny resumed his romance with Pike's stepdaughter and their brother Johnny sorta threw in with Mrs. Landusky, who didn't seem to be overly frettin' herself about the camp bein' shy Pike.

Blackjack Ketchum and Kid Curry soon argued over the take from a train robbery, and the Kid quit the gang. He high-tailed it back to the village of Landusky long enough to round up his brother Lonny and a fresh horse, and they loped south.

In the meantime, Sheriff Buckley grew a little weary of waitin' for the Kid to turn himself in. He decided it was time to round up a posse and scout the fugitive's trail. Trouble was, nobody in the Milk River country wanted to see the Kid arrested. They all knew the fault lay with Landusky and that the judge in Fort Benton was crooked as a coyote's hind leg. So to help the Kid escape, a corral full of the Kid's best friends—my best friends, too—threw in with that posse. Among the riders were Con Price, Pete Vann, Al Malison, Kid Cheney, Johnny Griffin, and even Boss Plunkett. They used every false move in the book to throw that sheriff off track and lead him down blind trails. In fact, they told me later, "We probably spent more time in saloons than we did on the Kid's trail."

The Kid and Lonny soon found themselves in Colorado workin' for a cattle outfit. Their plan was to save their pay, buy their own ranch, and start the game of life anew, hoping fate would shuffle the deck and deal them a better hand. But that ain't the way the cards fell. Sheriff Buckley sent a wire to every sheriff in Wyoming and Colorado, and the Kid soon caught wind a few Colorado lawmen were fixin' to ride out to make their acquaintance.

Now the question again arose, when a gent's always lopin' down the outlaw trail one jump ahead of a sheriff, what does he do for a living? What would you or I do? We'd start a gang and rob banks and trains is what we'd do. Kid Curry's new gang included brother Lonny, Walt Putnam, Tom O'Day, and his old Texas friend, Flat-nose George.

Kid Curry spent most of his next ten years runnin' from the law. He sure covered a lot of territory, as I'm about to unfold. But throughout those years of ridin', robbin', and hidin' out, he was back in Montana a lot more than people realized. Folks who saw him told me their recollections, and I'll unload a few on you directly.

In the meantime, a man named Jim Winters showed Landusky's widow a deed claiming Pike had willed him the house and his land. He said he'd give her and Johnny three days to get off the property. When he returned in three days, the woman and Johnny refused to pull their freight. Hot words passed between the two parties until Johnny decided to seize hold of the intruder and show him out. Winters pulled a revolver and shot the unarmed Johnny deader than a cancelled postage stamp. He moved into Pike's house that very day, as soon as Jim Thornhill removed the corpse and buried it on the Curry's ranch. For convenience, Mrs. Landusky, who didn't seem to be frettin' herself much over the demise of Johnny, threw in with Winters.

But Kid Curry and Lonny weren't to know about Johnny's death for weeks. Their new gang rode to Wyoming and robbed a bank in Powder River. They made themselves more wanted by killin' a deputy while high-tailin' it from a posse. They blew into Deadwood, South Dakota on a lope and robbed a bank without first stakin' out the town. That mistake cost them a good man. While Tom O'Day was inside the bank pullin' off the robbery, his horse spooked and ran off, leavin' Tom afoot, a pickle no bank robber cares to be in. He was captured as the rest of the gang high-tailed it west.

The posse of cowhands that chased the Curry gang from Deadwood had as much sand and grit as Kid Curry himself. They chased the robbers all the way to Fergus County, Montana, and captured the Currys, Flat-nose George, and Walt Putnam after the Kid was shot through the wrist. They were taken back to Deadwood in a prison wagon to stand trial, but they soon overpowered the jailer, stole four fast horses, and split the breeze for Montana.

They planned to be in Montana only long enough to rob two post offices and exchange their stolen horses for fresh ones with Jim Thornhill. It was then the Kid learned Winters had shot Johnny unarmed, and that the newly-appointed deputy had declared it self defense. The Kid rode out to Winters' land and found him alone, fetchin' water. When Winters beheld the Kid approachin', his eyes bugged out like a tromped on frog's, and without a word, Winters drew his revolver. Beneath that big Montana sky, the Kid blew Winters to the northern winds with a slug between the eyes. Butch Cassidy always said Curry packed the fastest gun in the West.

Without stickin' around to see who Mrs. Landusky would throw in with next, the four rode south to

Wyoming and threw in with Butch Cassidy and the Hole in the Wall Gang. By now, Cassidy's Wild Bunch was the most famous gang runnin'. They'd gained wide fame robbin' banks and trains throughout the West, but unlike the James Gang, they didn't murder. In fact, it was said Butch Cassidy never killed a man in his life. When pursued by a posse or law men, he always shot at their horses. All the men Cassidy's gang members shot at were lawmen shootin' at them, and they always tried to side step that situation as much as an outlaw gang possibly could. Let me unload on you how.

After a bank or train robbery, the Hole in the Wall Gang would split up and meet a few weeks later in one of their three hideouts. One was the Hole in the Wall in Wyoming. Another was Robbers' Roost in Utah. The third was in Montana in the Little Rockies near Thornhill Butte, where Kid Curry had hidden after downin' Landusky. They'd lay low in one of these hideouts until the dust had settled from their last holdup, and then they'd light out on the trail of new adventures.

By the time the Currys threw in with Butch Cassidy, the Pinkertons had been chasin' him for two years. Who were the Pinkertons? There's probably nobody on your range today who remembers the Pinkertons. They were a company of private detectives who'd hire themselves out to kill or capture wanted outlaws. For the next ten years, the railroad companies would spend a baggage car of green bills to keep the Pinkertons on the trail of the Hole in the Wall Gang, and their pursuit was as relentless as the north Montana wind.

The first thing the Currys did with Butch Cassidy was rob a train near Wilcox, Wyoming. When a sheriff's posse cornered them, the sheriff was killed in the shootout. The rest of the posse pointed their horses back toward Wilcox once they realized who they were fightin'. Then that more thoroughbred and skilled posse, the Pinkertons, took to their trail and gave them another hard chase. The gang shook them and busted the breeze for the safety of the Hole in the Wall.

For the next few years, I followed the gang's pen tracks through the newspapers. Sometimes my memory seems dim as the old buffalo trails. I couldn't recollect every shootout, robbery, and narrow escape that fearless gang pulled off durin' those ten years, even if I had time. I'll just gallop through their bold career on a lope, touchin' only a few peaks of their felonies.

The gang soon left the Hole in the Wall, trailed back into Montana, and robbed a bank in Red Lodge. Then they rode north, exchanged their tired steeds for fresh horses again with Jim Thornhill, and camped awhile at their hideout near Thornhill Butte. By then, Jim Winters' nephew had come from back east somewhere to take over the land and home his uncle had gained from Pike Landusky, and Mrs. Landusky had sorta thrown in with him. After Kid Curry and the gang tracked out of Montana, folks soon noticed the nephew, his horse, and his saddle were missin'. Nobody ever saw hide, horn, or hoof of him again.

The next thing I heard was the wild bunch had robbed a train near Folsom, New Mexico. The outlaws scattered like a night stampede and met up a few weeks later at Robbers' Roost. Then they lit out for Colorado, where they robbed two more banks. A posse trailed them to Turkey Creek, and the shootout that followed made the gang even more wanted, for they downed another sheriff and a deputy. That put the Pinkertons back on their trail, so the gang split up with plans to meet in a few months at the Hole in the Wall.

Kid and Lonny Curry trailed Flat-nose George to San Antonio to winter in the sun's warmth. It was there a sheriff and a deputy recognized Lonny and George from their faces on wanted posters and tried to arrest them. In the shootout that cut loose, both Lonny and George died of lead poison. Let me tell you the last thing Kid Curry did in San Antonio. He barged into that sheriff's office and avenged the death of Lonny and George by plantin' a lead plum in both the lawmen's hearts.

As Kid Curry fled Texas through Arizona, two deputies recognized him in a saloon and tried to convince him he was under arrest. The powder burnin' contest that erupted left both deputies face down in the sawdust. Ridin' what outlaws called the hoot owl trail—travelin' by moonlight to escape the law—the Kid reached the Hole in the Wall unseen and again threw in with Butch Cassidy.

When all of Cassidy's Wild Bunch that wasn't dead or in jail had returned to the Hole in the Wall, they lit out to rob another train in Wyoming. The Pinkertons were soon on their shirt tails again and chased them plumb across Montana. Kid and Butch and the whole gang rode up to the Coburn's ranch near the Fort Belknap Reservation and, as always, the Coburn brothers swapped them fresh horses for their tired, lame ones and let them surround some roast beef, potatoes, and corn.

By now, Robert Coburn, a widower, had remarried and moved to Great Falls, leavin' his sons to ride herd on his ranch. But I'd bet a new hat Mr. Coburn would have done the same thing his oldest son Bob did next if he'd still been around. Not one hour after the Wild Bunch trailed out, the Pinkertons blew in. Bob told their cook to season and cook up some sour beans they'd been meanin' to throw to the hogs. After all, it was still within the Code of the West to feed travelers passin' by. As Bob hoped, the whole posse waxed sick in a couple hours and had to postpone their chase for a day or two, allowin' the Hole in the Wall Gang the leisure of ridin' to their hideout at Thornhill Butte without bullets tearin' up the sod around them at every jump.

Now remember, the Pinkertons were a private police outfit, and they could only kill or hogtie somebody the law already wanted. They couldn't charge people with new crimes or arrest somebody not already wanted. But these men were good bluffers and tough bullies, and they were used to gettin' what supplies and information they needed by scarin' people. So after surroundin' them sour beans, they weren't slow to demand fresh horses in exchange for their tired ones and a fistful of dollars.

By now, the four Coburn brothers had grown strong and tall as mountain pines, and they weren't green hands with a six-gun. The notches on their gun butts didn't stand for the wolves and coyotes they'd shot, but for rustlers who, like wolves and coyotes, had staked a claim on their herd. Bob had as much sand as Kid Curry, and with his brothers backin' his play, he told the Pinkerton thugs, "No, we ain't stakin' you to any horses."

Bob unloaded both barrels, tellin' them, "People like us are gonna see to it no posse ever catches up with Kid Curry, because most everybody in Montana thinks the Kid's a hero." He reminded them most folks deemed the Pinkertons lower than snakes in a wagon rut. He said only cowards would wear their badges on their undershirts, which is what the Pinkertons did when they wanted to weasel up on somebody.

In my book, what Bob Coburn told them Pinkertons rings true. Nobody respected that gang of bullies, but most everybody I knew deemed the Kid the West's new Robin Hood. I'd often hear of him givin' horses and cattle to poor ranchers and givin' money from bank and train robberies to people in need, both white people and Indians. And the Coburns and Jim Thornhill weren't the only ones who

hid, supplied, and informed the gang. Many folks did
that all over the west, especially in Montana, where
the Wild Bunch was most welcome. In fact, Cassidy
himself had worked for cattle outfits in Montana and
Wyoming from '84-'87, and like Curry, he still had a
lot of cowboy friends in the north.

The gang hid in the Little Rockies for a few months,
durin' which time they robbed two Great Northern
trains. The first wasn't carryin' much cash in its safe,
so the robbers made their way up and down the aisles
of the passenger cars wavin' pistols and sayin', "Get
your money out to lend. All of it."

Now the way the herd was grazin' that day, my
friend Brother Van, the saddlebag preacher and early
Montana's favorite psalm singer, was aboard that train,
and he handed the Kid his small pouch of dimes,
nickels, and coppers, and said, "God bless you."

"I can see by your outfit you're a sky pilot," the
Kid told him.

"I'm the Reverend William Wesley Van Orsdell,
Methodist missionary," he introduced himself. "Just
call me Brother Van."

"Brother Van? I've heard of you from Charlie
Russell," Curry told him. "I'm sort of a Methodist
myself. Put this in the offering for me next time you
hold a preachin'."

The Kid handed him a five-dollar note, returned
the preacher's coin pouch, and continued up the aisle,
minin' the other passengers' pockets.

The last robbery the wild bunch pulled off in

Montana was two months later, that famous 1901 robbery of the Great Northern Flyer near Malta. They dynamited a safe and high-tailed it with forty grand. A big sheriff's posse chased them, and a lucky long shot from a Winchester killed gang member Will Carver. A hard day's ride brought the Wild Bunch clear of the local posse, only to find themselves ridin' one or two jumps ahead of the Pinkertons once again. The gang split up with plans to meet at Robbers' Roost in a few months.

At this point, Kid Curry decided to get far enough away from the West that nobody would recognize his face from wanted posters. Once again, he hoped to start over and live a more settled life. His travels took him to far away Knoxville, Tennessee, but I'll be a prohibitionist if the Pinkertons didn't trail him way down there. Those private police tipped him off to the city police, and soon two Knoxville policemen recognized the Kid and tried to arrest him. The shootout that followed left the Knoxville Police Department shy two brave officers.

Curry fled just one jump ahead of the Pinkertons and threw in with the Hole in the Wall Gang again at Robbers' Roost. But after one or two routine bank robberies, he lined out again for Knoxville. From what I heard, he'd taken a shine to one of the painted cats he met there, and he'd saved her from that questionable profession by supplyin' her with some of the funds he'd earned through his dangerous occupation. Some say he was set on marryin' her, but the wedding wasn't in the deck. In 1902, he was finally bushwhacked, arrested, and sentenced to a life of hard labor in the Knoxville Prison. After more than a year in prison, Curry escaped with three other prisoners. They stole four fast horses and outran the Pinkertons to Wyoming, where they all threw in with Butch Cassidy at the Hole in the Wall.

Now this recitation is fixin' to embark on the mysterious and the uncanny. The last time Kid Curry was seen in Montana was in 1904, and the last person to see him was my good friend and his, Sid Willis. Late one night, Sid was closin' the Maverick Saloon—this was before he owned the Mint—and as he was lockin' the back door, he saw Kid Curry ride up. Sid let his old friend in and greeted him with, "I haven't seen you since the Bear Paw Roundup of '89. I hear tell many a man has sought your company since then."

Curry normally took a ribbin' as well as the next cowboy, but Sid said that night, the Kid seemed more troubled than a man caught rustlin' cattle. He told Sid he was in a mighty big stew and asked Sid to stake him to enough money to take a steamship to South America.

Sid knew the Kid as well as I did, and trusted him as much as everybody who knew him. Like me, Sid believed the Kid was a good man who'd been dealt a poor hand in destiny's game. Like me, he believed any other cowboy would have taken the same trails if their cards had been dealt the same way. Sid said he'd like to lend the Kid the money, but it required goin' upstairs to the office and persuadin' his business partner, Cut Bank Brown, that Curry would repay the loan as soon as he robbed a train or a bank in South America.

The Kid sat at the bar with a pint of whiskey Sid sawed off on him, and Sid went upstairs to explain the reason for this unusual visit to Cut Bank Brown. Cut Bank didn't know the Kid well like Sid and I did, so it took him a good quarter of an hour to see things Sid's way. He must have feared that if he didn't come across, Curry would dynamite his safe, same as he did with trains. When Sid came back down to the bar with a bank bag of money, Curry was gone, never to be seen again in Montana.

I was the first man Sid told of this, and we pondered over it for days. Why in the devil did the Kid disappear like that? We reckoned something about the long wait must have spooked him. But what?

Another rule of the Code of the West was you never gave away a friend or sold him out. Most often, the friendship and trust among cowboys shoots farther and truer than most other friendships, due to their so often having faced danger and hardship together. The code also held, "Never ask the law for help, and never offer it any." A cowboy would be hazed into the cutbacks if the other riders learnt he'd spilt the wrong words to the law.

But by now, Sid had been a one-term Sheriff of Valley County. We wondered, could the Kid have fancied the former lawman might feel stuck to report a wanted man to the law, even a good old friend? Of course, I knew Sid wouldn't do that. Even when he became a U.S marshal, he never turned on a pal who wasn't quite within the law, and I ain't saying how law abidin' I was. But there was a brand new invention in many offices called a telephone, and we wondered if the Kid hadn't imagined Sid talkin' to the law. But then again, it's hard to fathom Kid Curry thinkin' like that. He wouldn't have come for Sid's help if he had any doubt about Sid's loyalty. Besides, over and over, Kid Curry had shown the West he wasn't afraid of local lawmen. No, we couldn't make heads or tails of his disappearance.

News still traveled slow in 1904, and it wasn't until a few days later a new story about the Hole in the Wall Gang hit the newspapers. They wrote the gang had recently tried to rob a train in Colorado. By now, the railroad bosses had waxed impatient with the Pinkertons, and they'd hired a posse of the best lawmen in the West. The posse included an Indian scout deemed the best tracker alive. Before the Wild Bunch finished robbin' the train, this posse came boilin' out of a boxcar, already mounted on horseback and firin' Winchesters, killin' a few of Cassidy's men before the robbers realized what was afoot.

The newspapers wrote the posse tracked the outlaws day and night without rest all over Colorado until the gang's hand was forced. Half the gang died in the gunfight that followed, and half the gang escaped, includin' Butch Cassidy and the famous Sundance Kid. The papers read that Kid Curry had been badly wounded and shot himself in the head to keep from bein' captured. The papers said the Kid's body was buried in Linwood Cemetery near Glenwood Springs, Colorado.

Now here's where we ride up on the uncanny and the mysterious. The newspapers printed the date Kid Curry was killed, and Sid and I weren't slow to notice that date was almost two weeks before the Kid blew into Great Falls seekin' Sid's help.

Did we believe in ghosts? Sure, most cowboys did. Many claimed they'd rode up on one or more, sometimes without the aid of likker. At first, that was the only way we could explain the Kid's post-mortem visit and his strange disappearance from the Maverick Saloon that last night Sid saw him. But one piece in the puzzle never quite fit. Anybody who knew the Kid would have told you he'd never have given up in a fight and cashed in his own chips. We knew Kid Curry would have fought on until they killed him.

A couple weeks later, more of the story unfolded. Newspapers said the gang members who survived that last gunfight scattered like a flock of sparrows, and that Butch Cassidy and the Sundance Kid fled together. That posse of the West's best lawmen chose to trail the two gang leaders and let the others run. They stayed on their tails day and night and chased them across New Mexico and Texas. Butch and Sundance finally gave them the slip by quittin' their horses, grabbin' tree limbs, and floatin' down the Rio Grande for miles, often stayin' under water for as long as they could hold their breath. Never again would they pull another robbery on American soil.

The uncanny and the mysterious took another twist a few months later when the roundup boss for the Pinkertons who'd chased Kid Curry for ten years retired. He told the newspapers he believed the man who'd been buried as Curry had been misidentified. He held the corpse buried in Glenwood Springs wasn't Kid Curry at all, but some other member of the Wild Bunch. That gave us all a new hope the Kid was still alive and would some day wing his way back to Montana.

A few years later, the newspapers printed that Cassidy, Sundance, and one other English-speakin' gringo had robbed a bank in Argentina. We all wondered, was that third robber Kid Curry? Soon the newspapers wrote the Pinkertons had sent a posse to Argentina to corral or kill the outlaws, but they now believed the fugitives were holed up somewhere in Chile.

A year or two later, the newspapers wrote the Sundance Kid and Butch Cassidy had been chased by a company of the Bolivian army after robbin' a small-town, Bolivian bank. The soldiers surrounded them as they were hidin' in an adobe hacienda and shot the abode to flinders. The two corpses the soldiers buried were too full of holes to hold hay, let alone identify. But as no bank or train was ever again disturbed by Butch Cassidy or the Sundance Kid, folks believed they were the two deceased parties.

But the uncanny and the mysterious still hadn't played out their hands. For the rest of my stay on your side of the divide, rumors abounded that Butch Cassidy had been sighted in the United States many times. Some people believed he kept to himself and lived a long, quiet life. Some believed he changed his name and had a doctor resculpt his face so nobody could recognize him. One doctor claimed he recognized the scar from an old bullet wound he'd once doctored for the man known as Butch Cassidy. Even the outlaw's sister said he was livin' secretly in California and had visited her a few times.

I haven't ridden up on Butch Cassidy, Kid Curry, or the Sundance Kid since I crossed the Big Divide. I fear they didn't have time to square themselves with the Maker before their lamps were shot out. But to this day on the open range we're now ridin', there are still two questions that trail me and Sid Willis like Pinkertons: Who *is* buried in Kid Curry's Colorado grave? And was it Kid Curry instead of Butch Cassidy who died of lead poison with the Sundance Kid in that Bolivian shootout?

Someday you may cross the Big Divide and find yourself on the range I'm now ridin'. If you cut the trail of Kid Curry before I see him, tell him to look for the smoke of my campfire in the Shadowy Hills. Tell him a robe is spread and a pipe is lit for him. Don't forget, the latch string is out for you, too.

Your friend, C. M. Russell

New Spun Yarns From Across the Big Divide

Authors note: Below is the famous 1900 photograph of the "Fort Worth Five." From left to right are The Sundance Kid, Will Carver, Ben Kilpatrick, Kid Curry, and Butch Cassidy. In 1900, the Hole in the Wall Gang robbed the First National Bank of Winnemucca, Nevada. They fled to Fort Worth, Texas, where they dressed up and had this picture taken. They soon sent this photograph with a letter of thanks for the money they stole to the bank in Winnemucca, but their cockiness proved to be a fatal mistake. The Pinkerton Detective Agency printed this picture on hundreds of wanted posters and distributed them throughout the entire American West.

2012 in the moon the hollyhocks bloom

Wind Wagon Thomas

Yes, my old friend Sid Willis is remembered as the last person in Montana to see Kid Curry, although he still ain't sure if the Kid was a ghost or himself that night. He is also remembered as the man who owned and worked the Mint Saloon in Great Falls for more than thirty-seven years, back when that saloon held the largest collection of my oil paintings and water colors in the world. That Amon Carter Museum in Fort Worth still brands them paintings "The Mint Collection."

Many book writers have written falsely of Sid Willis. They've let it fly that Sid was the shameful mossback who sold the Mint Collection to Amon Carter, thereby deprivin' Montana of that much of my legacy. They've printed Sid gave the C. M. Russell Memorial Committee four years to buy it, grew weary of waitin', and railroaded it off to Texas. They've painted him as a selfish scoundrel and a traitor to my friendship.

I crossed the skyline in '26, twenty-nine years before Sid found his way across the Big Divide. It wasn't until Sid crossed over in '55 that I heard what became of the Mint and my collection on its walls. Sid was still sore about it when he tracked into my camp in the Shadowy Hills, and he's still none too pleased with the way word painters have smeared his renown. I think he'd be honored if I scratched down his side of the story.

When World War Two ended, Sid was seventy-eight, and as I mentioned prior, the grass in Highland Cemetery had been wavin' over me for nineteen summers. Doctor Hanley said Sid's health was on a dead card and he'd better retire. Trouble is, he had no son to take over his business. Sid and his wife Annie had a grown-up daughter named Jeanette, but the saloon business is no place for a lady, so he put the Mint up for sale.

Several businessmen who branded themselves the Mint Corporation offered to buy the Mint, but only if the sale included my art collection. They held it was an important part of the business, bringin' in all manner of travelers railroadin' through town. The sale included the saloon business, my Mint Collection, several great paintings by O. C. Seltzer, and the Charlie

Beil collection to boot. He sold the whole shebang for one hundred and fifteen grand, providin' my art would stay on the wall for all to see as long as they owned the Mint, and providin' Montanans would have first shot at buyin' the paintings back if they sold the Mint.

Sid says he don't foster many regrets, but he'll always regret not holdin' tighter to the reins of that collection. But sellin' it seemed like the thing to do at the time. No other museum wanted my art much, not even in my home town of St. Louis, and Sid sure didn't expect to live ten more years like he did.

But it's a cinch the Mint Corporation didn't buy the Mint because they yearned to become bartenders. In 1948, they sold the Mint to the Kohler brothers and put my paintings up for sale separately. The sellers kept their word and gave Montanans first shot at buyin' it, but for a hundred and twenty-five grand. The state legislature voted not to buy it, so Sid and some of my other friends in Great Falls formed the C. M. Russell Memorial Committee to raise the money. In four years, they could raise only thirteen grand, so this Mint Corporation sold the collection for a hundred and seventy-five grand to the Knoedler Gallery in New York. That outfit soon sold it to Amon Carter in Fort Worth for two hundred and twenty-five grand.

Back in Great Falls, the committee did what they could. Sid anted up one of my paintings he had at home, Josephine Trigg stacked in her collection, and a few other generous friends chipped in a few of my paintings, and startin' with that thirteen grand, they got the C. M. Russell Museum in Great Falls afloat in 1952 without the Mint Collection. Sid still regrets that loss, but never credit any of them book sharps who've written my friend Sid Willis sold The Mint Collection to an out-of-state party. I'd fight the man who says he did. That was done by George Sterling and the Mint Corporation.

But I'm chawin' at the bits to climb into the middle of this next yarn I'm cinchin' a saddle on. As I remarked prior, the question "Whatever became of Kid Curry?" trailed us like Pinkertons for years. It reminded me of the question that bushwhacked everybody in Missouri, "Whatever became of Wind Wagon Thomas?"

"Who was Wind Wagon Thomas?" Well, it don't surprise me you ain't heard tell of him. When I blew into Montana in 1880, I found nobody knew of him even then. He was a Missouri conundrum, and his story spread across that state like a prairie fire. It cut loose when I was a colt in St. Louis, swappin' school days for the lessons of the river docks. His story spilled from mouth to mouth all the way from Westport Landing to St. Louis.

Now you're wonderin', what and where was Westport Landing? It was plumb across the state of Missouri on the Missouri River. It looked a lot like Fort Benton back then, with rows of docks where steamboats and barges unloaded people and cargo. That little river town swelled enormous and was counterbranded Kansas City after I pulled my freight for Montana.

This mystery I'm fixin' to unfold fetched loose when a former sailor branded Captain Thomas blew into Westport Landing. No, I don't mean he chugged in on a train. Nor did he bump into town by stagecoach, buggy or wagon. He didn't even trot in on a horse. For the first time in my life, when I say he "blew in," I mean he honest to John blew in with the wind. He sailed up the river in a pint-sized sail boat he built. It had half a dozen of them new-fangled, triangle-shaped sails that can be turned this way and that to corral breezes comin' from any angle.

It was there in Westport Landing where Captain Thomas got his destinies tangled up with the question, "If these sails can move a boat across the water, why can't they move a wagon across the land?"

I remember Frank Bird Linderman once told me some of Lewis and Clark's men tried to turn that trick. They hoisted sails on dugout canoes tied to cottonwood carts they built, and the wind blew them over the prairie as if on a lake—for a little while, anyway. Them carts had cottonwood wheels, because that's all the explorers had to work with, and the dang wheels broke, cottonwood being soft as oatmeal mush. But if they'd had iron wagon wheels with rims and spokes, no telling how much work the wind could have saved 'em.

Anyway, Captain Thomas bought a small horse wagon, removed the sails from his boat, and rigged them to the wagon in the same fashion they were rigged to the sailboat. In other words, that wagon was rigged to run backwards. Thomas brought the wagon tongue up over the stern to serve as a helm, to be steered only by the able hands of a seasoned seaman. He first tested his wind wagon alone—not wanting anybody watchin' in case he failed to turn the trick—on the plains near Westport Landing. He found that with strong wagon springs and well-greased wheels, the wind wagon could sail almost as smooth as a river boat and faster than a horse-drawn wagon.

Soon word spread like the grace of heaven through a camp meeting that Captain Thomas was fixin' to show off a new invention he branded "the wind wagon." Thomas put up he'd sail from Westport Landing to Council Grove in one day and sail back the next day, a round trip of three hundred miles. Everybody on route waited to watch him blow by, and in Council Grove, a big crowd gathered and cheered as he blew in. The two-day trip came off the reel without a hitch. After that, he was branded "Wind Wagon Thomas."

Next, Thomas roped at the wealthiest merchants and professional sharps around Westport Landing to throw in with him to start a freight outfit that builds and runs big wind wagons. His sales pitch harped on the idea the wagons didn't need to use horses, oxen, or mules, so they didn't need to stick to routes that had streams, waterin' holes, or tall grass. He told them wind wagons didn't need to burn wood like trains, and they wouldn't have to always wait for the spring rise on the Missouri like steamboats. Wind wagons could travel faster than horse-drawn wagons and run a lot cheaper. Thomas suggested, "Let's begin by building one big wind wagon to travel the Santa Fe Trail, ropin' up trade at every stop. As we round up more and more customers, we can build more wind wagons, train more men to run them, and branch out in all directions."

Them business sharps fell for all that wind like a bevy of sheepherders. They threw in with Thomas and formed an outfit they branded the Overland Navigation Company. The investors included two saloon owners, a banker, a lawyer, a doctor, a general store owner, and the local sheriff, all convinced that wind wagons would be the way of the future, and fortune would fall to those who fastened their loop on them now while the idea was fresh out of the chute. But history has shown us how the cards often fall to folks who think they can rope and tie down the future. You might as well try to rope and tie down the wind.

These seven directors of the Overland Navigation Company staked Wind Wagon Thomas to the silver and gold needed to buy the canvas to make eight big triangle-shaped sails and to buy the biggest Conestoga wagon he could find. The wagon bed must have been a good two dozen feet long and eight or nine feet wide. Thomas took off its wheels and replaced them with wheels he built, the biggest wheels anybody ever saw. I ain't overplayin' my hand a single chip to state them wheels stood eight feet tall. They had iron rims and spokes and hard rubber tires, and between the axils and the wagon frame, big springs were fastened to smooth out the ride.

Thomas said them big wheels were needed to allow the vessel to roll at top speed and to clear big rocks, stumps, badger and prairie dog hills, and anything else in their path on the prairie. Them wheels even allowed the wind wagon to cross streams and sail over fields covered with snow. Of course, all wagons need to stay clear of mountains and forests, but this one could cross rivers and lakes, seein' how it was built to float and fixed with sails.

The bed of this new wind wagon stood a good ten feet above the ground. Ladder rungs were fastened on both sides of the wagon box for the riders to climb aboard. The tail gate could be pulled out to make room for a wooden loadin' ramp used to roll, pull, or carry cargo aboard. Like the small wind wagon Thomas invented, the wagon tongue was brought up over the stern to use as a helm, and from there the Captain would steer the wagon as it rolled backwards. Eight big triangle-shaped sails were rigged to the masts, ready to be pointed at whatever angle would best corral the wind.

It took Wind Wagon Thomas a few months to build them wheels, springs, and sails. When he finished, the Overland Navigation Company invited everybody in Missouri to watch the christening of the new wind wagon. The newspapers printed the Board of Directors would all climb aboard the wind wagon and ride around the plains east of the landing for a spell as the good captain tested the vessel's maneuverability. Everybody within forty miles who wasn't in jail trailed into Westport Landing like dry cattle to a waterin' hole.

To make a bigger splash with the spectators, two yoke of oxen were used to pull the wind wagon out onto the open plain. Once the oxen were unhitched and away from the wagon, Wind Wagon Thomas climbed the ladder and took the helm, followed by the seven members of the Board of Directors who took their seats on the three benches facing the direction the wagon would travel. But when one investor, Dr. Parker, took note of how high up the wagon bed stood above the ground, and how a wagon tongue was used as a helm, either a touch of cold feet or a sniff of pending misfortune headed off his plan. He said, "I think I'll just follow along on my saddle horse."

There was a good breeze blowin' from the West. Wind Wagon set his sails to them, released the hand brake that held the wheels, and that wagon took to foggin' it across the plains like it was late to a dance. It was a cinch to them investors that this wind wagon was puttin' the landscape behind it at a much faster clip than a horse wagon could, and they weren't slow about tellin' each other that.

"It holds over horses and mules like four kings and an ace," a bartender boasted.

"With these huge wheels and those big springs, it's sure a smoother ride than a buckboard," the sheriff chipped in.

"It's the way of the future," the merchant put up.

"We'll have so much business, we'll need to build hundreds of these," stacked in the banker.

"Somebody better tell all them mule skinners and jerkline drivers they'd better learn to sail a wind wagon," chipped in the other bartender.

That Board of Directors had more fun than a barrel of money as they blew hither and yon across the prairie for a dozen miles. The doctor on horseback was soon left in the drag, so he pointed his horse's muzzle back toward the crowd.

"I'll advertise in every newspaper between here and Santa Fe," the lawyer put up.

"Say we're in business and ready to move freight as of now," the banker raised him.

That's about the time Wind Wagon Thomas boasted, "Watch me run her in reverse and against the wind!" He set the sails at such angles they couldn't hold no more wind than a whisper, and the vessel coasted to a stop smooth as a calf's ear. Of course, no sailboats can sail straight into the wind. They have to sorta zig zag through it, like switchbacks on a mountain, always sailin' at an angle to the wind. Thomas rigged the sails to corral the wind just right, loosened the hand brake, and the wagon began rollin' backwards at an angle to the wind. In a minute, the wagon was rollin' backwards almost as fast as it had sailed forward.

In the meanwhile, Dr. Parker, returnin' to the landing on his saddle horse, hears the loud clamor of them giant wheels. He looks over his shoulder and beholds the wind wagon on his tail, comin' faster than buckshot. He spurs his pony, tugs to the left on the reins, whoops, "Yah!" and that spooked cayoose bucks out of the wagon's path not one jump too soon. The good doctor's hat blew off when that horse spooked, and one of them eight-foot wheels rendered that sombrero flatter than a corn tortilla, but the doc reckoned losin' a hat beats losin' a horse.

"If you're trying to intimidate us by sailing rearward at this speed, I believe you've succeeded," the lawyer anted up.

"I'd prefer to return to traveling in the direction we're sitting," the merchant put up.

"I'm beginning to feel a little seasick from not facing the way we're going," the banker chipped in.

"Me too," a barkeep raised him. "I'm about to heave up everything but my socks."

"Certainly, gentlemen," Wind Wagon smiled. "I simply wished for you to realize how versatile this vessel—"

That's all the words Wind Wagon has time to spit out. Straight at them, fast as a Montana norther, charges a spinnin' whirlwind. Thomas figgers the only shot he's got is to turn that wagon plumb around and outrun the twister. He pushes the wagon tongue of a stern plumb across the wagon bed, causin' the vessel to turn in a big, smooth half moon, but before he has time to move the wagon tongue back and straighten the wheels, that whirlwind pounces on the wind wagon like a hen hawk pounces on a field mouse.

Now mind you, this ain't a tornado. If it was, that

land vessel would have become an air vessel, soarin' at a height that's a lesson to eagles. It was just one of them mid-western whirlwinds. But even those little twisters have their share of muscle. That whirlwind takes to blowin' that wagon round and round backwards in a circle not much bigger than a saloon and almost as fast as the cyclone was spinnin'. If you ever saw a fox chasin' its tail backwards, you could sorta comprehend the curious path of the wind wagon.

Now the passengers didn't see the whirlwind comin', so they didn't know what was causin' this vessel to twirl like a top spinnin' backwards. They thought this new excitement stemmed from Thomas still wantin' to show off his vessel's acrobatics. But by now, as you can fathom, they weren't overly impressed by Thomas' shenanigans, no more than they'd be impressed by spinnin' off a cliff.

Weren't they scared, you ask me? Why, a rabbit in a den of coyotes is calm as a cucumber compared to these folks. But the Code of the West I've been rilin' on about orders a man to never show his fear.

"Mr. Thomas, we do not find your show-off antics amusing," barked the banker.

"We demand you control this vessel responsibly like you were doing earlier," demanded the lawyer.

"Thomas, I'll throw you in jail," threatened the sheriff.

In a few minutes, the whirl wind blew itself out, but the prevailin' wind from the west still blew strong. Thomas tried to move the helm back into the center of the wagon bed to straighten out the wagon's course, but the iron rods that connect the wagon tongue to the wheels had been bent like horseshoes. He could no more steer that wind wagon than he could steer an avalanche. The wagon took to goin' around and around in a circle, maybe a mile around, with all the passengers still ridin' backwards.

Next, Wind Wagon Thomas tried to rig the sails so they'd corral no wind, thereby causin' the vessel to roll to a stop. But the whirlwind had broken the rods that crank the sails. Thomas could no more change the direction of them big sails than he could change the direction of the wind.

When the Board of Directors all tumbled to what was afoot, they all entertained the idea of abandoning ship. But the dang wagon was movin' too fast to disembark, even from the lowest rung of the ladder. It would have been akin to quittin' a movin' train. The captive riders were stuck with circlin' backwards for maybe she's four hours.

Finally, the wind slowed down enough for them to hop off, one by one, from the bottom rung of the ladder, most of them tumblin' to their knees, skinnin' their hands and soilin' their Sunday clothes they wore for the newspaper photographs. But a seasoned sea captain never abandons his ship. Wind Wagon Thomas stayed on board to play out his hand. As the wind wagon shed the weight of them six investors, it changed its course and it came to rest against a big cottonwood.

The next day, the Board of Directors of the

Overland Navigation Company wasn't slow to send for Wind Wagon Thomas. They all sat around a long table as the lawyer read aloud this resolution:

"We the undersigned do formally conclude our business transactions with Captain Thomas. All of our plans to build a fleet of wind wagons, to train more navigators, and to expand our markets are hereby dissolved."

The letter was signed by all seven partners. It was even rumored the sheriff gave Wind Wagon forty-eight hours to get out of town.

The next day, our inventor hoisted the sails on his small wind wagon and blew out of Westport Landing, blowin' west on the Santa Fe trail. Nobody in Missouri ever saw horn, hide, or hoof of him again.

A few years later, shortly before I left Missouri to make Montana my home, word of Wind Wagon reached us, news that had traveled from Indian camp to Indian camp across the West. It was said a band of Arapahos had tracked up on Thomas, stuck on the prairie plumb out of wind. For four days, there wasn't enough wind to blow out a candle. The Arapahos took him to their camp where they fed and sheltered him. I hear they got a big kick out of the eccentric inventor, who somewhere had learnt enough Indian sign language to swap yarns. The Indians said some of them yarns were windy enough to fill Thomas' sails. After four days of windy stories, the wind blew in and Wind Wagon Thomas and his wind wagon blew windward. The Arapahos never caught wind of him again. And I'm not just tellin' a windy.

The fiasco of that wind-wagon demonstration sets my memory to grazin' on another fiasco that fetched loose in Glendive in 1911. Mame read in "The Great Falls Leader" that on the Fourth of July, a New York outfit branded the Curtis Aviation Company would sail a flyin' machine. It wrote the world's most famous flyin' machine jockey would ride in the contraption as it flies around and around the fair grounds.

Mame insisted we line out for Glendive on the train, so we found ourselves at that celebration with thousands of other folks. That's the straight goods. They say it was the biggest Independence Day roundup ever held in eastern Montana. All day long there was some spectacle afoot: a baseball game, a foot race, a few horse races, a couple concerts, a vaudeville show, and a speech by a congressman and the mayor.

But we'd been through that whole herd before. Everybody was there to see, for our first time, a man soarin' in a flyin' horseless carriage. Very few automobiles were sputterin' about in Montana yet, and they'd been invadin' the scenery for only a few years. The horseless carriage was still something we couldn't quite fathom, to say nothin' of a flyin' machine.

The flyin' machine's show was to take place at high noon. That way, the sun would never be in the jockey's eyes as he circles around the fair grounds. But by third drink time in the morning, it was posted that the flight would cut loose later in the afternoon.

The handbill read that two days prior, the New York outfit had wired they could not play out their hand. The celebration committee had roped onto another flyin' machine and a jockey in Chicago, and they were expected to fly in soon.

About first drink time in the afternoon, the flyin' carriage landed in a nearby meadow, and out bounded its owner, Miss Cosey Smith, its mechanic, Eugene Griffin, and the jockey—they called him a pilot—Felix Schmidt. They said they'd need an hour or more to refresh themselves and get outside a meal, and then they'd be back to shuffle the deck and deal out the show. Two deputies guarded the flyin' contrivance when the Chicago outfit trailed out toward the lunch counters, and everybody eyed it from a dozen paces away. One thing I can remember about that day, clear as I remember the day I crossed the Big Divide, is nobody, includin' me, found that flyin' machine overly pretty. It was even uglier than a skunkwagon, which is uglier than a new-sheared sheep.

About third drink time that afternoon, the Chicago folks returned. The mechanic took to sizin' up the vessel's mechanical parts until it was almost fourth drink time. Although the crowd was chawin' at the bits to see this spectacle, they seemed to understand the air-bound fellow's health depended on the health of the flyin' horseless carriage. But when the three Chicago folks went into a lengthy pow wow, it began to make the crowd itchy. Shortly after fifth drink time, the pilot told us, "We're sorry to make you wait. We're waiting for this wind to die down."

"What wind?" someone asked.

"This is just a little breeze," another stacked in.

"You ain't seen no wind yet," chipped in another.

"It's a little more than I can safely fly in," the aviator put up.

"We raise cattle in the wind," a cattleman raised him. "We brand, roundup, and calve in the wind. Farmers plow, plant, and harvest in the wind. We do every darn thing in the wind in Montana."

"I'm hoping this breeze will soon die down a little so I can begin," the flyer calls his hand. "The take off is the most dangerous part of the flight."

"The wind don't die down here very often," they told him. "If you don't flap your wings soon, it might start blowin' great guns."

"If we were flying back to Chicago, this wind would be fine," Miss Smith told everybody, "especially since it's blowing from the west. But when we're circling a fairground, this much wind is a hazard."

By sixth drink time, the wind was pickin' up. By seventh drink time, it was blowin' even harder. By eighth drink time, about a half hour before sunset, the pilot announced, "I'm afraid we'll need to postpone this exhibition until tomorrow."

It's hard to describe—especially to a tenderfoot who's never herded cattle—the mood and sound of a big herd about to stampede. But I detected a trace of it in this herd of eastern Montana men who'd surrounded enough nosepaint to float a keel boat. Quick and loud as a rifle shot, a mounted cowboy whoops, "Yippee!" and throws the loop in his lariat around the flyin' carriage's propeller. He points his hoss toward the Yellowstone and shouts, "Let's run it into the river!"

Like a stampede of long horns, where every steer springs to its feet at once and high-tails it in the same direction, that herd of cattlemen, sheep herders, and sod busters lowered their horns and stampeded in the direction of the flyin' machine. Now them Chicago folks were braver than I am. I'd never have the sand to be up in the sky in a flyin' skunkwagon, no more than I'd ride double with the devil. But brave as they were, they sure were a lesson to jackrabbits the way they burned the trail for the train depot when the lynch mob seized the flyin' contrivance.

Now here's how the herd was grazin'. A company of the Montana State Militia was at that gatherin', returnin' from the Custer Battlefield where they'd just played the role of the U. S. Cavalry in a drama of the last stand. Matter of fact, their range boss Major Donohue played Custer. When the lynch mob had dragged the flyin' machine almost to the river, they were forced to take another look at their hole card by a company of soldiers facin' them with fixed bayonets.

The Chicago outfit never returned for the flyin' machine. An eastbound train was about to leave Glendive when the flyin' folks high-tailed it from the fairgrounds, splittin' the air like a comet. They made it on board just in time, no doubt thinkin' the invention was smashed to flinders in the swift current of the Yellowstone. The city of Glendive became the proud owner of that new invention nobody had suspected was there to stay. Folks who've trailed me across the Big Divide tell me giant flyin' machines constantly roar through your skies these days. Whatever became of Glendive's flyin' horseless carriage?

Keep pullin' off good things until your light goes out. May it burn long and bright without a flicker.

Your friend, C. M. Russell

2012 in the moon the mosquitoes wax thick

The Courtship of High Horse

I wasn't born a cowboy. Nor did I have to become one, like a lot of young riders who were bucked off their farms by the Civil War and landed in Texas workin' cattle. I could have been what folks today call a business executive, and that trail would've been a dang sight easier than the trails I rode. But to be a business sharp, you have to be created one, like my wife Nancy. The Creator made me a simple cowboy artist.

By now, you likely think I'm just blowin' another windy. But everything in this ink talk is the naked truth. It starts with my grandfather, who was fixin' to sell the family farm near St. Louis where the Russell's spent six generations, includin' mine. Before the land sold, lightning struck the ground and unburied a vein of coal. That farm fast became a coal mine, and in the process, they found a vein of fire-brick clay. By the time I was born, the old farm had big bee-hive kilns bakin' fire bricks and fire tiles, and a big sign out in front that read, "Parker-Russell Manufacturing Company."

My father was the secretary of the outfit. The word "secretary" don't mean the same now as it did then. When I crossed the Big Divide in '26, it meant a pretty view who rode herd on the paper work for an office boss. But in my youth, it meant the owner's son who served as roundup boss for a business outfit. Dad drank whiskey three times a day but never got drunk. He smoked cigars down to the stubs and ate what he wanted and never got fat. He and his brothers never owned slaves, but they stacked their chips with the South during the Civil War. He believed in discipline, and he wasn't slow to use a razor strap if he suspected our rumps needed warmin'.

My father planned for me and my four brothers to go to college and throw in with his growing business as executives. My sister, he was sure, would marry somebody like a governor or a congressman. His idea panned out fine for some of my brothers, but I couldn't stay in the saddle even in primary school. To halter break me, my father sent me to a military school for a spell, but I was always in a stew with the officers and spent most of the time walkin' guard.

Maybe it was my mother who convinced Dad that the Creator had sculpted me to be an artist. He sent me to an art academy for a short spell, but the instructors didn't cotton to my brand of art. I can't say I ever learned anything from any instructor. Let me stray from the main trail long enough to tell you what three people taught me the most about drawin' and paintin'. One was Karl Weimer. No, I never met him, but I sure looked close at his paintings. He's still the best. The second was Jake Hoover, the trapper. No, he wasn't an artist. He didn't know any more about art than a sow pig, but he sure knew every card in Nature's deck, and he wasn't slow to tell me when my pictures lied about the scenery, the animals, or the Indians. The third person to teach me about art was Ma Nature herself.

But I'm ridin' away from the wagons. Once I took root in the Judith, wranglin' horses in the spring and summer and flankin' herds in the fall, my father told me I had no need to be a hired hand. He said if I'd homestead some land, he'd stake me to the money to build a house, a barn, and a corral, buy ten million miles of bob wire, and start a herd. After a few years of keepin' my shoulder to the wheel, I'd be a ranch owner and my own boss. I thanked him and told him I chose to remain a cowhand.

Some folks might say a man who'd rather be a cowhand than own a ranch is missin' a few slats. It's a hard conundrum to explain to modern folks. You'd have to know the spirit of the open range to understand, the range that rolled on for miles and miles with no bob wire and no plowed ground. It was Ma Nature's open range when the land still belonged to God that held me to Montana.

After I'd been in the Judith a few years, a gent named Captain Kerr from St. Louis came to visit a rancher named Major Edgar, likewise from my hometown. Mr. Kerr saw my paintings on the wall of the Utica Saloon and asked me to paint him an oil of the Sioux doing battle with the Blackfeet. I branded it "Counting Coup," and I counterbranded it "When Sioux and Blackfeet Meet." I asked for only enough jingle to pay for the paint and a couple rounds of drinks, but he insisted on payin' me five bucks more. That's when I began to wonder, can I find enough suckers to make my livin' sellin' paintings?

The day I delivered that painting to the Edgar's ranch was the first time I fell in love. That's when I met Mr. Edgar's daughter Lolly, pretty as a pinto hoss in a rose garden and sweet and luscious as a roast apple. From the jump, she sure had this cowboy in her loop. And she took to me like honeysuckle to a front porch. Her father told her, "Don't be baiting your hooks for that wild cowboy. Save your smiles for a man who will amount to something. I know Charlie's relatives back in St. Louis, and they say he's the family's black sheep. He could have been a business executive, but he chooses to be a wild cowboy and a drunk. That ne'er-do-well will never have a roof over his head."

Of course, he wasn't all wrong. But as Lolly and I took a shine to each other, we often saw one another on the sneak. I sure had competition. Evenings I'd ride over to the ranch to sneak off with her, and I'd often see a few extra saddle horses at the hitch rack. I'd know who was courtin' her by their horses. If I didn't know a horse, I'd reckon it belonged to a rider from another outfit. If the horse was sportin' a fancy rig with silver conches on the tapaderos, I'd know it wasn't a cowboy at all, but some pretty boy from town with money to throw to the birds. I'd wait until all them Romeos were gone, and then I'd injun up to her window and do a bird whistle.

You can tap yourself, if you're courtin' a pretty filly, it's a high card in your hand to be born rich. It most often seems a man without money doesn't hold openers. He draws four to a queen and never betters. But in spite of the poor hand I was holdin', she took to me more than the other men on her string, and I'll tell you why. But first, allow me to stray from the trail once more in the interest of truthful history. A fellow who recently crossed the Big Divide told me one of these new Charlie Russell scholars wrote I used to ride up to Lolly's window like a Mexican trubador singin' her songs as I strummed a banjar. Now don't that win the jackpot? I'll tell a man, my singin' was a hybrid cross between a burro with a bad cold and a slow-turnin' windmill needin' oil. Lolly would have left me for a sheepherder if I'd turned that trick.

I didn't know as much about a banjar as a maverick

steer knows about his daddy. Whoever told that writer about my serenadin' fancies must have been confusin' me with one of them fancy-saddle pretty boys I was tellin' you about or maybe some cowboy in a bad moving-picture show. Or else he was drunker than forty fiddlers. Yes, I've been told there's still a little banjar in my log cabin studio which is now a museum. I remember where I got it. I traded a pencil and ink sketch for it, and I was fixin' to give it to my banjar-pickin' friend George Washington Bird, the architect, but I crossed the divide before I saw him again.

Now I'll tell ya as honest as Brother Van, the true reason Lolly sought my company is because she liked my story tellin'. Sure, she liked my art a little, and she loved the way I never sang and wanged away on a banjar. But it was my story tellin' that roped her in, and I'd bet my half-breed sash we would have gotten hitched.

But that wasn't in the deck. Her father trumped my hand. He wasn't about to see her fall for a shiftless cowboy with no more future than a steer, so he sent her back to St. Louis to some finishin' school. We never saw each other again, and it took years to cut her memory loose. Lookin' back, it's a cinch some of my drinkin' and tradin' paintings for the society of soiled doves was a play at forgettin' Lolly.

But I held no regrets later, for my wife Nancy was the best pardner and booster a man could ask for. If it hadn't been for her, I wouldn't have kept a roof over my head. We had an adopted son Jack, but we never had a daughter, so I can't say I savvy the tough trails ya must take when ridin' herd on a girl. But almost every man I ever met who has a daughter thinks no young man alive is fit to hold her hoss, let alone marry her. And if they've never had a son, they paint a picture of the perfect son in their noggins and expect a son-in-law to live up to it. And that ain't true for just western ranchers. It's always been that way in Europe, Asia, among the American Indians, and everywhere else in the world where girls have fathers.

This speculation has set my memory lopin' back over trails long ago plowed under to a yarn Black Elk told. Who was Black Elk? Why, he was a high card among the Ogallala Sioux. You can hear more wisdom in one old Indian yarn than in forty speeches at a Chamber of Commerce Convention. And I wish we could see him tell this in sign language, because an Indian can say more in sign than a corral full of tongues—forked or otherwise—can say in words. I'm no green hand at talkin' sign myself, but I'm still a lame hand with a pen. But I'll try to tread through the boggy crossings the best I can and paint a word picture of his yarn.

High Horse was a young Sioux brave, and the beginning of this story sounds a lot like my romance with Lolly. Like me, High Horse is caught in the loop of Dawn Shadow, the girl he finds the most beautiful in the village. His heart is boilin' over like a kettle of cowboy laundry with love for this maiden, and he thinks her glances mean she longs for him too. Trouble is, she's an only child, and her aging parents protect her like a mother bobcat protects her kittens. They watch her close and walk with her almost everywhere.

High Horse saunters about the village every day watchin' for a chance to toss his loop at her, but the elders are always near. Every day they notice High Horse stalkin' them, clearly hopin' the parents and Dawn Shadow will sooner or later take different trails. Soon her father, Elk Shoulder, tells her mother, Morning Flower, "High Horse keeps stalkin' us, always sneakin' a look at Dawn Shadow. I fear he may try to steal her in the night."

And like as not, they feared she might want to elope with the buck. So every night, the aging parents took rawhide thongs and tied her to her rawhide bed.

High Horse kept sneakin' about like a camp robber, waitin' for a shot at catchin' Dawn Shadow alone. At last he saw her goin' to the spring for water, goin' alone, for it was a few steps too far for her parents. As they walked and talked merrily, joy filled their hearts. She knew she liked this young stallion more than the others on her string, and he could read that in her eyes.

"I've long wanted you for my wife," he confessed.

"You must talk about that with my father. Please do."

High Horse owned two good horses. He approached Elk Shoulder that day and told him he wanted to marry Dawn Shadow. "I offer you two good horses for that honor," he told the old man.

Elk Shoulder waved his hand from shoulder to shoulder and said nothing.

Soon High Horse told his cousin Red Deer, "My heart is on the ground. If I cannot marry Dawn Shadow, I will die of sorrow." He sadly told Red Deer how Elk Shoulder had trumped his courtship.

Red Deer answered, "He knows she is worth more than two horses, as you know yourself. Surely he will not refuse four good horses. I will lend you my two until you capture more horses."

When High Horse offered Elk Shoulder four horses to marry his daughter, the elder again waved his hand and said, "Speak to me no more of this nonsense."

High Horse resumed his pokin' around camp looking for Dawn Shadow until he finally found her walkin' to the river to wash clothes. "My heart is on the ground for you," he told her. "If we don't marry now, I shall die of sadness. Please run away with me."

"Do you think I am a cheap squaw who would run away with a man? I want the respect of being paid for like the fine maiden I am."

Poor High Horse felt more and more love sick. He couldn't eat and looked pale as a dead fish. His cousin Red Deer told him, "We'll have to steal her and run away. I know how women think, and I can see that is what she wants you to do."

Late that night, High Horse and Red Deer cat-footed up to Elk Shoulder's teepee and listened. It sounded like all three were sleep. Silent as smoke, they crept into the teepee. The plan was for High Horse to cut the rawhide thongs as Red Deer pulled up a few tent stakes. Then the two would gag Dawn Shadow, lay her on a buffalo hide, slide her out of the tepee, lay her across a pony, and bust the breeze.

Once inside, High Horses' heart took to drummin' like a tom-tom. He feared it would wake the girl's parents, but somehow it didn't. Quiet as a cat, he began cuttin' the thongs that bound the girl to her bed. Trouble is, every time he cut one, it would pop like a horse pullin' its foot out of mud, causin' High Horse to become so shaky he accidentally poked her lightly with the point of his knife. She yipped like a startled coyote and her parents sprang up and yelled, "Who is there?"

Greased lightning is slow as a blind mule compared to the pace the two young bucks stormed out of that teepee and out of the camp. The aging man and woman tried to chase them, but they couldn't run far. Trouble is, a few younger braves woke from the shoutin' and joined the chase. It was a moonless night, so the two cousins found it easy to lose them. Nobody recognized them as they fled, but Elk Shoulder and Morning Flower figgered it must have been that silly young buck who snuck around gawkin' at their daughter, that ne'er-do-well who would never own a remuda, a stack of beaver hides or mink furs, or a war bonnet full of eagle feathers, that shiftless High Horse.

High Horse grew even more lovesick, and it pained him like an icicle through the heart. He looked worse than warmed-over death. Red Deer knew he must hatch up another scheme and said, "We will disguise you as a bad spirit. That way, if you are seen, no one will recognize you, and what is better, no one will dare chase you."

Red Deer had High Horse strip naked. First he painted his cousin solid white, and then he painted black stripes all over his body and black rings around his eyes. Taken all in all, the young brave looked as scary as any bad spirit he'd seen.

That night, they snuck back into Elk Shoulder's Teepee with the same plan. Red Deer pulled up a few tent stakes while High Horse began cuttin' the rawhide thongs that bound Dawn Shadow to the bed. Trouble is, one popped so loud Morning Flower woke with a start and said, "Who is there? Wake up, old man. Somebody is in this teepee with us."

Elk Shoulder grumbled, "Go to sleep, old woman, and don't bother me."

High Horse lay still on the ground as his cousin rolled out of the teepee silent as a shadow. Red Deer waited outside still as a stump for the old woman to fall asleep so he could help his cousin turn the trick of gaggin' Dawn Shadow and draggin' her out to his pony. As High Horse lay waitin' inside, he fell asleep himself.

As day began to break, Red Deer feared bein' seen. He took the horses back to his lodge, staked them where they could eat grass, and began to return to Elk Shoulder's teepee to wake up High Horse. But before Red Deer could return, Dawn Shadow woke in the dawn's first light, saw the sleepin' evil spirit, and screamed like a gut-shot lynx. That woke the old woman, who sent forth a screech like the squawk of forty hen hawks. That woke the old man, and when he saw the bad spirit, he took to yellin' like a pig stuck under a gate.

No herd of longhorns, eyes red and wild with panic, ever cut loose in a hastier stampede than High Horse. He hit only a few high spots in the topography as he sprang across camp and toward the river. Lookin' back over his shoulder, he caught a glimpse of half the men in camp chasin' him with bows, tomahawks, and spears. When he reached the riverbank, he hid in the trunk of a hallow tree. Sittin' still as a hidin' quail, he heard a bold brave say, "The bad spirit came out of the water, and now it has gone back in."

"Our chasing it will soon bring bad medicine to our camp," spoke another. "We must inform our chief; he may decide to move camp."

The chief wasn't slow about tellin' the tribe to break camp and move the outfit farther away from the river. That afternoon, Red Deer came to the river and whistled for High Horse. High Horse, still hidin' in the hallow tree, answered Red Deer's whistle.

"We must try the same plan a few nights from now when our people are again at ease," he told High Horse. "For now, we must wash the paint off you in the river."

After High Horse' hide was scrubbed clean and red, Red Deer said, "We have moved camp. I moved your lodge for you. Come, I will show you where it is."

But High Horse told him he did not want to return to the village. He said, "I no longer care what happens to me. It is better to die in battle than to live sick with love. I am going on the warpath alone."

"You will not go alone, my cousin, for I shall go with you."

The young warriors rode four days and came to a big camp of their enemies, the Crow Indians. In the dark, they slithered up and killed the two hoss wranglers guardin' the tribe's remuda and drove off eighty horses. Before they left, they stampeded all the other Crow horses, so the Crows wouldn't be roundin' up a posse very soon. The cousins trailed that herd three days and nights with little rest and drove the whole remuda through their tribe's new camp and over to the tall grass behind High Horse' lodge.

"Is eighty horses enough for me to marry your daughter?" High Horse asked Elk Shoulder the day after the old man saw him and Red Deer drivin' the remuda through camp.

"You may marry my daughter," Elk Shoulder told him, "but I do not want your horses."

"What do you want, then, Father?"

"I have never had a son, so I've always wanted a son-in-law who is a brave, honored warrior. Everyone in the village has heard of your triumph over the Crows. You are now honored. I shall honor you more with Dawn Shadow."

And I'll tell you something, sure as the hills. That's a quality that's stayed with the Red man until this day. More than anything, he respects courage. Show an Indian courage, and he'll show you respect.

I hope you and your people see many snows but that they will not be deep and your par fleches will always be full and your lodges warm.

Your friend, C. M. Russell

2012 in the moon the berries are ripe

Mail Order Brides

Sooner or later, we all have to face it: we were meant to live with mates. I ran with a pack of wild he-wolves for many's the winter, but at last a she-wolf led me to her cave under the rim rocks. By then, my wild friends and I were no longer pups. I'd bet my saddle and my horse Grey Eagle most of the old bunch would have married before I did, but range calico was scarcer than clean socks in a bunkhouse.

Said scarcity of she-folks gave frontier women a big edge. Those who steamboated to Fort Benton every spring rise had quite a pick from the men-folks eager to court 'em. They came ropin' for men who owned ranches, mines, banks, stores, or saloons. Cowpunchers were the lowest cards in their matrimonial deck, except for sheep wranglers. Us cowboys couldn't even afford the society of dance hall hostesses. Women in a saloon shot the price of a drink from a nickel to four bits. Just to talk to a gal, we had to spend half a day's wages buyin' her a glass of fizz water. The only toss for me and my friends was to trade some of my paintings for a little quality time with the crib gals.

I thank our Creator that right there in Cascade, Montana I cut the trail of the best wife, pardner, and booster a man could ask for. Most of my friends weren't so lucky. They'd trot twenty miles to a dance to find the cowboys outnumbered the gals twenty to one. That's the straight goods. Half the cowboys had to dance the gal's part. They'd tie a bandana around their arm or even wear one on their head like a lady's scarf. That bandana was called a "heifer brand," and when the caller whooped, "Swing that heifer," he meant swing the cowpuncher wearin' the scarf.

For most men, the only shot at gettin' wed was to order a catalog bride from one of them matrimonial outfits. Those brides usually came from the East or the South, both country and city women. They and the men chose a mate from letters and photographs. Many's the groom who drove a buckboard to the stage station expectin' to pasture a filly who's pretty as a diamond flush, only to meet a bride who looked less like her picture than I look like the Prince of Wales. But the groom didn't usually bellow too much. Chances are he wasn't a parlor ornament either. In fact, taken all in all from horn to fetlock, I'd wager blue chips to whites the ladies gambled the steepest odds when playin' a hand of catalog matrimony.

Today, my memory's canterin' back over grass-grown trails to a hot, dusty, late afternoon in Lewistown. Some of the old bunch and I'd been calfin' around in a saloon since third drink time, crookin' our elbows, paintin' our noses, and relivin' some of the pranks we'd pulled or seen pulled. As the late-afternoon shade spread over the street, we took our bottles and stepped outside onto the wooden sidewalk to cool off.

Soon the rattle of an old buckboard caught our ear, and we turned to behold ol' Hugh McIver, a sorta stove-up, strugglin' rancher and former cow-camp cook, drivin' the team. I'll swear to angels, we'd never seen Hugh lookin' so sober. How sober was he? Why, a tree full of solemn owls look drunker than fired cowhands compared to Hugh's new sober countenance. What's more, he was sportin' a clean, ironed, brown Sunday suit.

"You look plumb unnatural when you ain't holdin' a bottle," Tommy Tucker warns him as he handed over a pint.

"No whiskey tonight," he told us. "It ain't in the deck."

"Have you been to a revival meetin', Hugh?" I asked him.

"It's a far sight worse than that. I'm waitin' for the stagecoach from the Falls. It's bringin' me a corn-fed, catalog bride from Missouri."

We all congratulated him, shook his paw, and slapped him on the back, tellin' him over and over how this news calls for a drink. But he circled the wagons against our temptations and fended us off for as long as any honorable groom-to-be can be expected. It was a lesson to prohibitionists how long Hugh stood his hand.

In good weather, it took a six-hoss team two twelve-hour days to pull a stagecoach from Great Falls to Lewistown. With six stops in between, some misdeal often caused the stage to run late. That long wait helped us cowboys persuade Hugh to down just one drink, then just one more, followed by just enough to persuade him to show us the bride's pretty picture.

Bets were flyin' hither and yon as to whether she'd show up, and a few side bets were put up as to how much or how little she'd favor her picture. McIver no longer needed spurrin' to take a drink. His Irish blood was now callin' for nosepaint like it thought the wedding ceremony was over. By the time the stage rattled into town, our clean, sober groom was drunker than a fiddler. Black coffee couldn't restore his sober countenance, so a few riders tried baptizin' him in a horse trough.

Having hailed from Missouri, I was picked to step forward and greet the bride—about the same face as in the picture, maybe a few years older and a few pounds heavier. She rushes me grinnin' with her arms unfurled and plows into me like a baggage wagon, knockin' my Stetson plumb off. She squeezes me like a grizzly and tells me, "You're much more handsome and more dignified than your picture."

A few of my friends must have feared they'd lose me if they didn't head her off. They snatched hold of McIver, still drunker than a boiled owl, wetter than a carp, and cussin' like a muleskinner, and they bulldogged him over to the bride.

"Ma'am, you're mistaken," Tommy politely tells her. "That's just Charlie Russell, the cowboy drifter. No woman can tie him down. Here's Mr. McIver, the honorable groom, all roped, throwed, tied down, and ready for brandin'."

"I've heard cowboys love to pull pranks, and that's fine," she told Tommy, all the while clingin' to me like honeysuckle to a front porch. "But this one's too cruel to play on a travel-weary widow. Please take that inebriate back into the saloon where he belongs and allow me to become acquainted with my fiance."

I'll tell ya without stretchin' the truth an inch, it took a cornfield of kind, honest words to convince her the wet, cussin', drunken old mossback before her was sure enough the groom and that we were to blame for his bad first impression. We hefted him into the buckboard, and she agreed to drive him to his ranch and try to sober him up enough to make a roundup of how much of a man she'd roped up.

A few days later, we all tracked into the wedding, and nobody spoke one syllable when the preacher asked if anybody could ante up a reason the bride shouldn't wed the former cussin' cow-camp cook. At the wedding supper, Hugh joined in on a couple toasts, and then we made him stay sober as a watched Puritan for the bride. After two hours of food and fellowship, the bride and groom left sober as the church deacons. That may be one reason their marriage panned out as good as any I've seen.

As I mentioned prior, in them matrimonial letters, it wasn't rare for a woman on the marry to subtract a few years from her age and a few pounds from her weight or send an old photograph of a younger version of herself to a wife seeker. The bride-to-be usually figgered that once the groom-to-be eats a few swallows of her cookin', minor matters like age, looks, weight, and temperament won't stack up to much.

But the brides-to-be weren't the only ones who side stepped the truth a little when writin' them letters. The grooms-to-be weren't as apt to fib about their age, weight, or homely features as much as the women. It was more in their hand to exaggerate the size of their spread, the yield of their corn, or the size of their cattle herd. They might exaggerate a little the size of their bank roll or describe a house they dream of buildin' some day instead of the house they live in now. Many a catalog bride railroaded hundreds of miles expectin' to move into a two-story, Victorian farm house, only to find Prince Charming camped in a one-room cabin with a lean-to for storin' tools.

But findin' out your new wife ain't as pretty as a

spring flower or findin' out your new husband's role ain't as fat as you'd hoped were only small stumblin' blocks, ones the marriage could wind its way around. But the thing that will unsaddle a marriage quicker than a wagonload of white lies is the bride and groom findin' they don't like and dislike the same things.

My friend Henry Fowler had been a good roper and rider and had worked for Robert Coburn's outfit, the Circle C, up on the highline when I wrangled there. When the sodbusters took over the grassland, Henry followed suit and homesteaded a little spread. We all expected him to start a cattle ranch, but to our surprise, he bought a plow and took to bustin' the sod.

Henry soon realized he'd made a mistake. He didn't mind farmin', but he was of the rare breed of men who liked cows, and he missed workin' cattle. He decided to buy three milk cows and sell milk on the side.

Henry finally waxed tired of livin' alone on his remote farm in the drab boar's nest he called a cabin. Eatin' his own cooking made his disposition sour, and havin' nobody to argue with isn't healthy, so he writes to one of them matrimonial outfits in Chicago and asks 'em to rope him up a bride. He told 'em, "Advertise for an attractive, healthy, young woman."

In a few weeks, a letter came from Minnesota. A photograph showed a pretty young lady with blond hair and a sweet smile named Kate. The letter described her as a seasoned cook and housekeeper. It said she'd become orphaned at eleven and from then on, she'd worked as a hired girl for years, becomin' a top hand at cookin', cleanin', sweepin', washin' dishes and laundry, and all manner of household chores. She said she'd railroad out to Montana to get acquainted if he'd ante up the train fair and promise to pay her way back if either party decided not to take cards in a hand of holy matrimony. Henry kissed that picture and wired her the money for a ticket.

The next day, she wired back, thankin' him and tellin' him when she'd stack in. In a few days, he found himself drivin' to Malta in a wagon to round her up at the depot. On route, he found himself bushwhacked by second thoughts. "What if she sent me somebody else's picture?" he wondered. "What if she's ugly as a tar bucket, cranky as a cow-camp cook, and built like a twenty-dollar mule?"

Henry decided to station his team and wagon a stone's throw from the depot in case it seemed wise to make a hasty get-away. As he walked up to the platform, he saw a small crowd had gathered to wait for the passengers they'd come to meet. He stood at the rear of the herd and watched as the arrivin' parties descended from the train and were gathered in by friends and relatives. Finally every passenger was claimed except one woman totin' a suitcase in each hand. Henry thought, "I'll bet a stack of blues that's Kate."

But Kate didn't look like the picture she'd sent, no more than Henry looked like it himself. She appeared to be on the down side of forty and no longer slim.

She had small, narrow eyes, a nose like a hawk's beak, and a mouth that looked like it was chawin' at the bits to give somebody a good scoldin'. Henry tells himself, "That ain't the woman whose picture I've been kissin'," and he turns and makes quick tracks for the wagon. As he tries to leak out of town as quietly as a wagon can rattle, Kate chases the wagon down, tosses her two suitcases in the back, and hops aboard without Henry knowin' she's there until they arrived at his ranch house, a one-room cabin with a lean-to attached.

Henry, bein' a thoroughbred gentleman, let Kate have his bed that night and slept on the floor. He decided to wait until morning and then tell her he'd been warned by an angel in a dream to stay single and to buy her a train ticket back to Minnesota. But in the morning, the smell of a good breakfast cookin'—all those arousin' aromas he hadn't smelt since he'd left his mother—quickly changed his mind, and they were hitched in the Phillips County Courthouse that very afternoon. Henry picked up the cards fate dealt him and feebly began to play his hand as a married man.

Now as I heretofore expounded, the death knell of a marriage can be the two parties not havin' the same likes and dislikes. Henry was fond of cattle and owned three milk cows, but Kate hated all cows, slobberin', diarrhetic critters that they are, although she'd admit, she often liked to use a few jiggers of milk in her cookin', the one thing about her no man could find fault with.

Henry had witnessed only one marriage in his life, his Ma and Pa's. Ma did all the work that had to do with keepin' house, washin', cookin', keepin' chickens, and carin' for young'uns, and Pa did all the work that had to do with raisin' oats, barley, corn, hogs, and horses. It had worked out well for his parents, and that's the way he insisted it should be with him and his wife. In Henry's mind, milkin' cows was one of the house-keepin' and kitchen chores the Creator intended to be done by a wife.

Of course, Kate couldn't boast she enjoyed milkin' cows. If they weren't swattin' her in the face with their smelly, dung-matted tails, they were steppin' in her milk pail or slobberin' on her calico. The last dang straw was when the three cows each ate one of the four pumpkin pies she'd left coolin' on a window sill. She put the fourth pie in the cupboard where no critters but the roaches and mice could get near it. "When Henry returns from town," she promised herself, "he'll get this pie square in the face."

But when her husband drove the buckboard into the wagon yard with his new supplies, feed, and seed, Kate rather forgot about smackin' his face with that pie, for in tow behind the wagon was a big ol' bull. Kate opens the bettin' with, "Not another cow! You know I hate cows!"

"It's not a cow; it's a bull," Henry raises her.

"That's even worse," she ups him.

"He's even-tempered," he stacks in, "and I didn't pay one copper for him."

"You stole it," she raises him.

"I won him in a poker game," he calls her.

"Same thing. What do you want with it?"

"We'll raise us some calves. We'll butcher and eat the steers and keep the cows to start us a little dairy."

"Oh, we will, will we?" she started to say, but by then, Henry had bravely untied the lariat from the ring in the bull's nose and was coaxin' the bull into the cows' pen with an armload of fresh-cut hay. Kate remembered the pie in the cupboard and how much Henry needed it splattered in his face, but fearin' the bull might defend Henry, she fed the pie to their sow pig.

Over the next few days, Henry built the bull its own pen and coaxed it inside with an armful of hay. Whenever he felt the time right to try to mate the critters, he'd coax the cows into the bull's pen with some hay or oats. Of course, he'd always lead them back into the barn in time for Kate to do her morning milkin'. All in all, Henry took fine care of his flock, and he expected the first calf crop the comin' spring.

You can't predict many things in life, but there's one thing you can predict: sooner or later, your destinies are going to ricochet off the unexpected and go glancin' off in directions unforeseen. By this time, a few horseless carriages were beginnin' to be seen and heard sputterin' about hither and thither on the dirt roads of Montana. Henry and Kate had seen one or two in Havre, but they'd never seen one yet in Phillips County. Mighty likely, this bull had never seen or heard one either.

Richard Bird Baker

One afternoon, Henry was out fencin' his north pasture where he hoped to raise a few dozen head of cattle over the next few years. For the first time ever, one of these new inventions I still call skunkwagons came growlin' by Henry's spread, passin' not more than eight rods from his bullpen. Now a bull would have to eat twice its weight in loco weed to wax as ringy as Henry's bull waxed from the growl of that throttled skunkwagon. He took to tearin' to and fro like a buffalo in a brandin' chute, and the first time he lowered his horns, he busted out of his pen like it was made of corn husks.

The ragin' killer took to bargin' around the barn yard, chargin' everything he could see. He knocked over a waterin' trough, put his horns through a wall of the barn, and smashed a bench to smitherines. He charged a one-horse buggy and busted it to flinderations, and then he spotted the water pump. Hangin' from the pump handle was a large oaken bucket which the bull decided would make a perfect target. He pawed the soil and tossed his horns a few times, snorted, lowered his horns, and charged that bucket with the rush of a norther.

When the brute's horns hit that bucket, the bull's head hit that pump handle and busted it off the pump. When all was said and done, the dang bucket was jammed over the bull's mouth and nose and it even covered his eyes. The bail of the bucket was hooked over the critter's horns, so he couldn't shake it off his head and he couldn't see daylight. 'Course that made him madder than a cow-camp cook and sent him stormin' around all the more, knockin' about like a blind dog in a meat shop.

The first chance she had, Kate climbed up on the roof of the lean-to and yelled for Henry. He scurried back just in time to see the bull knock down two fence posts and bust into the chicken yard, blindly stampedin' to and fro among the squawkin', scatterin' hens, wings flappin' and feathers flyin' as the bull's horns tossed them this way and that.

Now as I remarked prior, Henry was once a good hand at ropin'. If this bull had been a yearling steer, Henry might have been able to rope, throw, and tie it down and remove that bucket with dignity. But no ten men can throw a bull. Henry wished there was a tree handy. He could maybe rope the bull on foot and dally the loose end on that lariat around the tree trunk. But no tree was near enough, and by now, the bull had knocked down all the available fence posts. Ropin' the brute on horse back wasn't in the deck. That locoed bull would either snap Henry's saddle cinches or put a horn through the horse's flank. It looked like the only card Henry had left to play was to shoot the critter.

"Shoot my bull?" Henry argues with himself. "That would throw down my plans to start a herd or a dairy."

Just then, the bull slams into the lean-to and Henry turns to see all the tools flyin' from the wall: the shovel, the saw, the ax, the hoe, the rake…

"The rake!" Henry tells himself. "Hook the bucket's bail with the teeth of the rake."

The way Henry turned this trick was a lesson to Mexican matadors. He'd cuss at the blinded critter, causin' it to lower its horns and charge at him. The he'd side step them horns and make a play at hookin' that bucket's bail with the teeth of the rake as the bull rumbled by. It took him a dozen—maybe two dozen—tries before he finally played in luck, hooked that handle, and jerked that bucket off the bull's head. Able to see again, the tired old bull washed off his war paint and ambled back into his busted pen. He ate a little hay from his manger, bed down directly, and fell asleep.

It took Henry the rest of that day and most of the next to repair the bullpen. Then he told Kate he was ridin' into town and would be back before dark the next day. That rode fine with her. She was used to his bein' away for two or three days at a clatter. In fact, she sometimes appreciated it. The next morning, something fetched loose that she appreciated even more. A man in a wagon rode into her barnyard just as she finished milkin' the three cows and put up, "I made a deal with Henry for his bull."

Kate felt happy as a pup with two tails as she watched the stranger tie a lariat through the bull's nose ring, twine the critter to the wagon, and lead it away. She was so glad to be shed of that bull she baked Henry two apple pies.

Just before sunset, Henry rode up and saw Kate

wavin' at him from the porch with an apple pie in one hand. "I'm sure glad you sold the bull, Henry," she greeted him.

"Sold it, nothin'," he told her. "I lost it in a poker game, same as I won it."

"Oh, Lord love a duck!" she pretended to scoff, but the naked truth is she welcomed that loss like a cowboy welcomes an invitation to split a quart.

"You should be happy I didn't win that hand," Henry piled on. "There was another bull and three more cows in the pot."

That was the last bull Henry ever brought home, so his idea of raisin' calves sorta rotted down right there. In fact, one by one, he lost two of his three milk cows by overplayin' a poker hand, and ya never saw a wife happier that her husband gambled. With each loss, Kate grew more cheerful and her cookin' grew even better.

Probably the most famous rendezvous cowboys ever had with catalog matrimony cut loose in Kansas in 1890. Here's how the cards stacked up. There was a U. S. Army outfit in the Cherokee country of the Indian Territories—now folks call it Oklahoma—branded Camp Supply. During the winter of '89-'90, that army camp hired a passel of winterin' Kansas cowhands to camp there and cut firewood.

A few years earlier, not many Kansas cowhands would have disgraced themselves by cuttin' wood. Like most cowboys anywhere, they insisted they were created to work on horseback, and only a fool would find himself on the blistering end of a saw, an ax, or a shovel. But by now, every cattleman from the Rio Grand to the Canadian Rockies knew the last of the open range would soon be fenced. If you wanted to raise cattle, you'd have to homestead some land and start a ranch.

'Course, that means buildin' a house and ropin' up a bride to cook, ride herd on the house, and care for the kids until they're big enough to help with the herdin', feedin', brandin', and calvin', to say nothin' of mendin' fences. But in 1890 in cattle country in Kansas or any other western state, a bride was harder to find than Kid Curry.

One evening, Waddy Wilkins blew into camp on a high lope as the wood-cuttin' cowpunchers were gettin' outside of some chuck and walloped, "Who can read?"

Three or four riders looked at each other and then looked around for Steve, the schooled rider who always helped them read their mail. "Where's Steve?" they ask.

The summoned party rises from the ground where he was camped twenty paces away. He dumps his plate, fork, and cup into the wash tub and ambles up to Waddy, who is pullin' a small newspaper from his saddlebag.

"Steve, would ya read us what this paper says. I think it's one of them matrimonial catalogs."

"It's called 'The Heart and Hand'," Steve told 'em. "Sure, it's a hitchin' catalog."

"Read it," a few riders urged.

"I ain't about to read every word in here, mind you. I'll just ride over the trail on a lope, hittin' the high spots. It has a long list of women who are combin' our range for a husband. It says they're all corn-fed gals, mostly from farms in states like Illinois and Iowa, but some are from big cities back east. What ya do is read what's written about these gals—or have somebody like me read it to you—and if there's one you want to marry, you write her a letter about yourself—or have somebody like me help you write it—and tell her what a great man you'll be some day. Then you ride into town to have your picture took and mail it to her with the letter."

With the help of the few cowhands who could write, every man in the outfit sent a letter to one of them catalog brides, every man except Jim Pickens. Jim had been hitched once before, and he found that matrimony often worked out like tryin' to eat off the same plate with a bear. Divorce wasn't common in the Old West, and in many places, it was unlawful. But Judge Lynch of Dodge City declared, "I married 'em, so I reckon I've a right to divorce 'em." He granted Jim's wife an alimony big enough to plug a sewer and declared them ex-man-and-wife. After that play, Jim swore he'd never again be wedded alive. He held, "The only females I'll mingle with from now on will be cows."

All the women who were set on ropin' up and brandin' a husband weren't slow about writin' back.

They all sent a picture of themselves that looked pretty as a pinto hoss with a letter declarin' how much they admired cowboys for their strength, bravery, honesty, and romantic ways. 'Course, most of them had never seen a true cowpuncher, but they'd read all about 'em in them dime novels. They'd gotten the idea proned into their heads us buckaroos are as noble and chivalrous as knights of old. Some of the gals had been married before, and they all wrote the same story about how they'd been married to the meanest sod buster alive and how they yearned for the tender hearts and handsome faces these fiction writers had painted on their heroic cowboys.

The matrimonial outfit arranged for almost three dozen of them brides to arrive at Camp Supply together on May 1st. The plan was for them to take a train from their home states to Dodge City, one hundred and twenty-five miles northwest of Camp Supply. There they'd throw in with the preacher who'd been roped into tyin' the knots, the nearest sky pilot to Camp Supply bein' in Dodge City. A mule-drawn freight wagon outfit agreed to haul the ladies to Camp Supply at five dollars a head, allowin' the preacher to ride free 'cause he and the mule skinner were both Methodists.

A couple weeks before the herd was to marry, the cowhands threw a big bachelor dinner for themselves. The main course of the meal was a thirty-two gallon barrel of snake medicine, and the dessert was a wagon-load of bottled beer. Now as I heretofore mentioned,

Jim Pickens no more hankered to marry than he hankered to herd sheep, but he adorned the grooms' dinner with his presence, bein' in no way adverse to snake medicine or bottled beer. Once every man was a few drinks down the trail, a rider puts up, "When these beautiful maidens arrive, we should welcome them with some great western entertainment."

"But these are real nice gals," another rider stacked in. "We have to wait till the gospel sharp ties the knot before we unbuckle in a debauch of entertainment."

"Not that brand of entertainment. I mean somethin' like a Wild West Show."

"That's a center shot," another rider chips in. "Let's show these eastern lilies what kind of leather cowboys are cut from."

"They've prob'ly never seen real men handle snaky livestock," the first rider stacks in. "Easterners, be they steers or heifers, couldn't have a splinter of an idea what it's like to get into the middle of a pitchin' bronc."

"Or rope, throw, and hogtie a calf," another chips in.

"Or bulldog a yearling steer," stacks in another.

"Or ride a bull," chips in another.

The cowhands hatched up all the plans that evening. There'd be a chuck wagon feed waitin' for the brides when they arrived. Then before anybody was introduced to their new mates, the cowboys would deal out this Wild West Show. There'd be a bronc ridin' contest, a shootin' contest, a trick ropin' contest, a trick ridin' contest, and steer wrestlin', calf ropin', bull ridin', and tobacco spittin' contests. These spectacles would make every bride eager as a beaver to meet the mighty man she'd come to round up.

"Now to make this contest more interestin', I think we should offer somethin' worth its weight for first prize," Jim Pickens antes up.

"Ain't a one of us here who'd doubt you'll rope onto first prize," another rider stacks in.

"There's no better all-around hand in this outfit than you, Jim," another rider sees him. "What fer a prize are you ropin' at?"

"Maybe a new saddle," Jim raises 'em.

"You're deservin' of it, Jim," the rider calls him, "but that would mean a hat-pass of forty blue chips."

"We ain't aholdin' of such dust, Jim," another rider follows suit. "We're fixin' to become married men, and we'll need to pinch our rolls to show our wives a stake."

"What kind of a dad-burned first prize can we rope onto without antein' up a few chips?" Jim grumbles.

"I've got the smartest answer to that conundrum," Waddy Wilkins bursts out. "Let's say the man who wins the most contests wins first pick of all the lovely brides."

"That sure as shootin' cuts me out of the herd!" barks Jim.

"Maybe not," chips in Steve. "You might be quick to change your mind when you see these beautiful fillies."

"You're a thoroughbred booksharp, Steve, and

I respect that," Jim raises him, "but one thing you educated fellers don't pack an ounce of savvy about is the workings of a divorced man's mind. I wouldn't wish it on any man to see him married, no more than I'd wish to see him lynched. And I'll reaffirm this here and now, and back up my words with poker chips, money, or bullets, I will never again be married alive."

A vote was held, and every jolly cowpuncher except Jim voted for Waddy's motion: the grand winner of all the contests could have his choice of all the brides who arrived. The rest of the riders would keep the bride they were arranged to marry, and the cowhand whose bride the winner mavericked would marry the bride the winner cut loose.

Steve volunteered to write the matrimonial outfit and explain that two of the brides may have to swap husbands, pending the outcome of the Wild West Show, but no woman kicked about that, one cowboy bein' as good a catch as another.

"I'll tell you all without hedgin' a chip what I'm fixin' to do," Jim Pickens boasted. "I'm gonna win every one of them contests. When it comes to ridin', ropin', throwin', or spittin', I've got all you badgers skinned to the dew claws. And when I win first prize, I ain't marryin' nobody. I'm just takin' cards in this showdown to show you rounders I'm still the best hand in the saddle. And I'm doin' this so nobody has a shot at switchin' brides. If you get hitched to a woman cranky as a cook and so ugly the flies won't land on her, you can't horse trade her, 'cause I'm winnin' the jackpot, plant your moccasins on that. And if that ain't the truth, let me be the first fool among us to be branded married." And then he lit a smoke and bowlegged off to curry his horse.

"There comes a point in a man's life when he needs a lesson in humility," Steve ponders after Jim saunters off. "I wish I was roper and rider enough to hand it to him. Ain't there no man in this outfit who can clip that bragger's horns?"

They all shook their heads, and one rider put up, "No, Jim's the high card in this deck. He's gonna shine like a wolf's tooth in that Wild West show."

It took two eight-mule teams pullin' six wagons four days to haul that corral full of brides from Dodge City to Camp Supply, but they all arrived lookin' like beautiful princesses. They were fed a royal feast of steak, potatoes, corn, and biscuits, and then Steve announced, "We have a wonderful western spectacle to welcome you with, our own Wild West Show. Any rider may enter as many events as he chooses, and whoever wins the most events wins first choice of a mate for life. I'm proud to say almost every man in the outfit has entered almost every event, so it'll be a great contest. Waddie Wilkins, myself, and Pastor Arnoldson will judge the contests. Has everybody signed up? If you can't write your name, put an X on the bottom line."

"What's this paper we're signin' say, Steve?" Jim Pickens asks.

"It just says you'll deal straight and play accordin'

to Hoyle," Steve tells him. "And it says you agree that the winner gets to pick his spouse from the whole herd of calico, and nobody can argue with the winner."

"There won't be no arguin' with the winner, 'cause I'll be the winner," boasts Jim. "And I dare any man to tell me I won't be."

"You won't be," came a voice sure of itself as Buffalo Bill's. But it wasn't a man's voice that came challenging Jim; it was a voice soft and smooth as velvet. Every gent turned and beheld one of the new brides steppin' forward, slender as a fawn and pretty as a sunflower. She had hair like coal, eyes soft, deep and black like a fawn's, lips like a rose, and skin the saddle color of a French Indian. You could see with one eye she wasn't of the thoroughbred order; she was more the draft horse type.

"What do you mean, my dear?" Steve asked her, surprised she spoke up.

"Wait till I'm harnessed into some ridin' clothes and I'll show you what I mean," she answered. "I'm enterin' this showdown."

Steve and Waddie looked at each other, and then they looked at their compadres, who couldn't have looked more surprised if they'd seen a two-headed cow or an honest politician. Waddie finally said, "This is rather irregular, madam. Ladies don't normally attempt these dangerous feats. These men are all top hands."

"This won't be the first Wild West Show I've won, but it'll be the first time I've won out my pick of grooms. I'm Alberta's Rose McBride, part Irish, part

Blood Indian, and part cougar, and I'm scoutin' for a top-hand cowboy to rope up and brand."

Steve tried politely to head her off, but Rose called out to the herd of calico, "How about it, gals? Don't it seem fair and just a woman should be allowed to enter this Wild West Show? Ain't this a free country?"

The herd of calico all shouted, "Yes, let her enter," and cheered and clapped so loud the cowpunchers feared the wives-to-be would stampede if Rose couldn't take cards in the contest. She pranced back to the wagons, and in two shakes of a hen's tail, she returned outfitted to ride.

Good folks, I don't hedge a chip when I tell ya that although every man signed up for the contests, nobody was even in it with that half-breed gal and Jim Pickens. The fight they both put up was a lesson to wolverines. First came the bronc ridin' contest. The army chipped in a killer horse that nobody could break and no man had ever stayed on more than eight seconds. Rose rode that outlaw Indian style with just a hackamore bridle and no saddle, lean and loose, rakin' the horse's flanks with her boots to make him buck harder. She rode that cyclone down to a whisper and slid off easy as quittin' a Sunday-broke mare. But Jim was unloaded after about forty seconds, although he stayed on much longer than any other man.

The cards stacked up the same way in the bull ridin' contest. Jim stayed in the middle longer than any other man before spinnin' off, but the half-breed gal hung to that stick of dynamite like she was born there. She rode until the bull was too tired to spin any more, hopped off, patted the bull on the head like a puppy, and took a bow.

I'll tell ya this without a stutter: that woman could twirl a lariat, and she didn't do it slow. In the calf ropin' contest, she roped, throwed, and tied down a calf in nine seconds flat. It took Jim eleven seconds that day, a little slower than normal for him, but he was beginnin' to feel the weight of finally meetin' his match, and by a woman yet.

That gal's trick ropin' was a lesson to Will Rogers, and the acrobatics she did on that horse's back was a lesson to Sioux warriors and circus riders to boot. Rose stayed out of the tobacco spittin' showdown and let Jim Pickins win it. Then he went on to win the steer wrestlin' contest fair and square. Jim won the shootin' contest by just a hair, 'cause the half-breed gal was no green hand at findin' her targets with lead. So the way it stacked up was Jim won three showdowns and Rose won five, which left her first prize winner in the Wild West Show.

"And which of these charming young bucks do you pick to wed, Miss Rose?" Steve asked the winner.

"I came here lookin' for a real dyed-in-the-hide cowboy, so when the preacher ties the neck knots, I reckon I'll have him neck me to Jim Pickins."

Jim's countenance turned to that of a man punched in the nose. Havin' no horse handy, he lit out hot-footin' it toward the stables like his rear's afire, kickin' jack rabbits out of his way as he burned up the trail.

But his speed played second fiddle to Rose's, who snatched up a lariat, built a loop, hopped onto the back of the nearest horse—the same one she'd ridden to a stand-still in the bronc ridin' contest—chased the bunch quitter across the prairie, whirled a loop around Jim's flanks and brisket, dallied a few turns around the saddle horn, and twined the wrinkled-horn range bull back to camp.

"We'll see what the local judge says about Mr. Pickins' marital responsibilities," Rose was sayin' as she trailed in snakin' Jim on that catch rope like an ornery steer.

The only law the Indian Territories had in 1890 was the U. S. Army. The way the herd was grazin' that day, the range boss for the cavalry and his sergeants were there watchin' the show. Rose handed him the paper Jim had signed, and the officer cast this judgment: "Pickens, you've signed on this entry form your consent to allowin' the winner first choice of a spouse. You also agreed the winner's decision is final. The winner chose you, so you'll be married here and now, or we'll lock you in the stockade for as long as this camp stands. And my congratulations to you, sir; she's a lovely bride, and not a bad cowhand for a gal."

Soon the preacher called out the name of each bride, one by one, followed by the name of her groom. When each handsome prince was united with his beautiful princess, the preacher wed the whole outfit, includin' Jim and Rose, with one big hitchin' ceremony. It was an occasion that would have softened the heart of any boulder.

I know what you're thinking. You reckon they'd be one bride short, since Pickens was so handily persuaded to wed after not orderin' a bride. But I'll tell ya why bein' short a bride wasn't in the deck. Two weeks prior, when the preacher heard the winner of the Wild West Show would win out the first pick of a spouse, he'd wired to Alberta for an extra gal—the only gal he knew of who'd already won a few wild-west contests. And now you know all there is to savvy about the famous Camp Supply matrimonial day of May 1st, 1890.

I'll tell a man, them early Montana mail order brides were made of the same leather as their husbands. They made strong, unselfish wives and mothers who shared all their mates' hardships. They deserve even more praise that us early Montana men.

Too many of the wrong things have changed, but Montana men tryin' to live away from civilization can still find it hard to round up a bride. Modern inventions have rendered a modern woman's spirit too soggy for the trails early Montana women rode. That's why these matrimonial bureaus are still dealin' their game. I hear that nowadays, a gent don't have to trust in photographs. Them matchmakers ship him off to meet the bride, usually in some Asian land where the human spirit ain't been so trampled over by man's inventions.

If you're a gent who might order a catalog bride,

let me saw you off a little steer I learnt from the Blood Indians. You prob'ly won't savvy her tongue, so see how much conversin' you can do with your eyes. And sorta cook up your own way of talkin' sign. Sometimes them two lingos can say more than words.

Most important, savvy the worst woman alive is prob'ly better than the best man. So always treat her kind and on the square. If you won't do that, I hope she pulls her picket pin and drifts to better grazin'.

I wish you tall grass and deep waterin' holes until you cross the Big Divide.

Your friend, C. M. Russell

2012 in the moon the rivers are low

John B. Stetson

Do you recall what my brand was? No, I don't mean the Lazy K brand, the ranch Con Price and I owned for a spell. I'm talkin' about the little brand I always drew in the lower left hand corner of my paintings—scholarly folks called it my trademark. Remember? Sure, the buffalo skull—I always called it the bull head.

When you cross the Big Divide, some day you might cut the trail of my old pardner of the range and pardner in crime, that old cow puncher Bill Bullard. He'll prob'ly tell ya his hunch why I took on the bull head as my brand, and you can swallow it or spit it out as you choose. I try not to swallow much of the corral dust Bill churns up, but his view on the bull head hatched from a yarn I'd admire to unload. I'll gallop through this episode on a lope, simply touchin' the high spots along the trail.

Bill was as tough a twister as ever rode up the Texas trail. Men who rubbed his fur wrong learnt quick he answered rude questions with an old-time cap and ball pistol big as a hog's leg. This play bobs up when the range boss gave Bill his first day off in weeks. He loped into Malta, pulled on the bridle at the first waterin' hole he rode up on, and told the barkeep to set every bottle in the shebang on the bar. What likker he couldn't pour under his hide there, he rolled up in his slicker and packed back to camp. He hit the bed ground snorin' like a choked bull.

Tryin' to wake Bill up to ride circle the next morning was like tryin' to wake up a tree. A cow hand could be fired for havin' likker in camp, so for Bill's sake, we weren't slow about emptyin' his bottles for him. This was durin' the years when the prairie was dotted with ghost-white buffalo skulls. It might have been the whiskey or maybe the need for a little entertainment that caused me to stuff a dang buffalo skull under Bill's head so it looked like the horns were sproutin' from the cow puncher's temples. Then I covered his neck and chest with some furry buffalo-hide chaps. Taken all in all, Bill looked a heap better as a buffalo that he ever did as a cowboy.

New Spun Yarns From Across the Big Divide

You modern folks wouldn't be slow to shoot a photograph of our new Buffalo Bill. But on the range in our times, if you wanted a picture, you had to make one. There were no oil paints or water colors in camp and probably no paper, so usin' a tool called a shoe awl, I carved Bill's new image on the big lock plate of his huge pistol. Fearin' Bill might wake up and object to this prank with some hot lead, I hid that big barker in the grub box.

Bill finally wakes up gaspin', "Whiskey!" Not findin' a smell of his scamper juice at hand, he cusses a hot path to the grub box, opens the lid, and is greeted by his own face on a buffalo—on his own gun! He waxes madder than a teased bull, curls his tail over his back, and stampedes off to find that Ornery Kid Russell, swearin', "I'll kick the seat of his britches out!"

He found me nearby in my flea trap, sleepin' off some of his missin' whiskey. The only reason I didn't get the seat of my britches kicked out is because I was sleepin' in my long johns. Bill still brags the reason I took on the bull head as my brand had something to do with that rude awakening.

But don't ya credit him none. To me, the bull head was the symbol of everything the Creator wanted me to paint. It was the symbol of the animals that were once numerous as the grass but by now were almost gone. It was the symbol of the people who followed the buffalo and lived off their meat, bones, hooves, guts, and hides, but never killed more than they needed.

It was a symbol of the land the Creator had sculpted before the grass was plowed under and bob wire closed the ranges, when the land still belonged to God. It was a symbol of the West when it was the only free country in the world.

Now if we had to point to one thing and call it the best-all-around symbol of the western cowboy, what would it be? It's a cinch it wouldn't be the buffalo skull; the big herds were all slaughtered a few years before Texans started drivin' longhorns to Montana. It wouldn't be the spur. People all over Europe and Mexico used spurs long before we did. It wouldn't even be ridin' boots. Englishmen and colonial riders had some kind of ridin' boots. Chaps? No, South American vaqueros and Mexicans wore chaps before Americans knew what longhorns were. The six shooter? Well, maybe the Colt would take second place in this bull show, but six shooters were common in both eastern and western states. No, there's nothing that can symbolize the cattle country of the West like the John B. Stetson western hat.

By the time I crossed the divide, there were many brands of ridin' boots, but to a rawhide cowboy, there was still just one true brand of hat, the Stetson. No other brand name packed such fame throughout the west, except for maybe the name Colt. No other article had such a lasting effect on the dress, habits, and lives of the western people. There were thousands of cattle brands, and a few became famous, but there's only one true brand for us cowboys as a herd, and that's the Stetson hat, the crown of the West.

The "cowboy hat," as most folks today call it, is so taken for granted it's hard to fathom the Old West, or even the new one, without a big slice of the census wearin' one. But they weren't always around. I was just a sprout when they came about, and they almost didn't come about at all. If it can't be said their existence was due to a misdeal, then I'd say it was due to a long shot with a limb in the way. Here's how it fell out.

About the time I was a wobbly colt, a frail and fragile tenderfoot named John B. Stetson was workin' in his father's hat shop in Philadelphia. The lad served as a boardin' house for any malady that drifted down the trail. The plague that most often bushwhacked hatters was branded T. B. This malady soon found John's lungs unoccupied and staked a claim on them.

A sawbones told the tenderfoot's father the lad would have a better shot at good health in a land where he could breathe warm, dry air. Mr. Stetson knew of a group of pilgrims who'd soon be ridin' horseback from St. Louis to the Pike's Peak region of Colorado. He sent his son to St. Louis by steamboat, where he threw in with the pilgrims, miners, and settlers travelin' west together. It was best for tenderfeet to travel in big packs, for the great bison herds were still about, and their stalkers, great hunting parties of Red men, still ruled the plains.

As this band of tenderfoot pilgrims tracked across Missouri and Kansas, they enjoyed warm, dry weather, but as they neared the mountains of Colorado, they were pounced on by a chilly, rainy spell. Most of the pilgrims didn't pack a tent, but since they were shootin' buffalo and deer for meat, they allowed they might as well use the animal hides to make some lean-to shelters. Of course, bein' tenderfeet, they didn't pack the savvy of a mule when it came to tannin' hides. After a week or two, them rottin' hides stunk like the devil's privy.

Now as the cards fell from the deck, it's to these smelly, untanned-hide shelters that we owe the existence of the Stetson. Here's how the cards lay. One evening after the travelers pitched camp and rustled some chuck, the stench of them shelters caused our pilgrims to eat forty paces upwind. One tenderfoot said, "This rainy spell is about to let up. Tomorrow we should leave these stinkin' hides behind."

John put up, "Well, I suppose I should have turned that fur into thick felt. It wouldn't smell, and it would scarcely leak."

"What's this you're saying about turning fur to felt, son?" an old sailor asked him.

"In my father's hat factory, we have a very old-fashioned process for converting animal hair to felt," John B. explained. "That felt is used in making sturdy hats."

Most of the travelers couldn't believe animal hair could be turned into felt, no more than they could believe corral dust could be turned into felt. So John B. took the hides from two jack rabbits they'd shot and cooked, and he did whatever hatters do to mold hair into felt. Of course, there wasn't nearly enough felt to make a lean-to, but John B. declared, "Just for fun, I'll take this felt and fashion me a hat. This hat will be the best protection against the West's harsh and varied weather ever devised." The hat he molded that day was the first John B. Stetson western hat ever to set foot in the West.

"She's a big one, John," one traveler told him. "You could tote ten gallons of water in that hat." And from then on, they were branded the "ten-gallon hat."

John explained, "The wide brim is to provide shade when it's hot and shelter from the rain, sleet, and snow. You can tilt the hat into the wind, and the brim will shield you. Its crown is almost hard enough to protect your head from hail stones, unless they come down the size of goose eggs."

John B. wore that hat everywhere he went while he was in Colorado, and soon it became the talk of the Colorado mining camps. Sure, the lad took a lot of ribbin' for that strange lid, but he was a good-natured fellow, so he laughed along with those who mocked him. But John B. was to have the last laugh, all the way to the bank.

One day, a raw-hided cattle boss saw the hat and said, "I'll give you five bucks for it."

Five silver dollars was a tidy sum in those days, so our young hatter quickly made the swap, knowin' he could shoot a couple more rabbits and hatch up another hat of the same brand. When that foreman crowned himself with the hat, it gave him what was soon to become the look of the western hero, the cowboy, the king of the plains. In fact, in a few years, no man would look like a cattleman without one.

After a year, young John B. felt healthier, so he returned to his father's business of makin' ordinary hats. But the felt-hatted cattle boss kept ridin' through his memory. "There could be a big market for them ten-gallon hats," he thought. "I just need to sink a shaft and mine it."

Cattle raisin' was just startin' to become a big business. Many cattlemen didn't wear hats at all, and those who did likely wore the same hats they wore before they took to runnin' cattle. Cattlemen came from all walks of life, and they rode into their first cattle outfits wearin' all manner of hats. For instance, Richard King, founder of the biggest ranch in Texas, had been a Civil War navy captain, and he always wore a sailor hat.

John B. roped at his father to let him make a passel of big-brimmed felt hats like the one he'd made and sold in Colorado. He branded them "The Boss of the Plains" and sent them out as free samples to hat dealers throughout the West. Soon the Stetsons had so many orders they couldn't make the hats fast enough. It was becomin' known everywhere the John B. Stetson hat was the most useful card in a cowboy's deck.

A rider could use it to pack water, oats, or corn to his hoss and water to his cook fire. He could cup the brim and use the hat to drink from if his canteen was lost or leakin'. It was perfect for fannin' a camp fire and, when duty called, for slappin' an ornery steer in the face. It served to blindfold snaky horses as a cow puncher mounted, or for swattin' the horse's rump when the rider wasn't packin' a quirt. I even used mine once to bat a Mexican over the head when he stole my father's watch. They were great for fightin' grass fires, and in mock gun fights, they made perfect targets. It was an honor to wear a bullet hole or two in the crown of your Stetson. And the darn hats lasted twenty, thirty, or more years. That's the straight goods. A Stetson might slowly take on weight or reach the point where you can smell it across camp, but it would never wear out. No matter how dirty it got, you could always wipe it off with a sponge and wear it to a dance.

In the early 1880's, the big cattle drives were at full throttle. Texas longhorns were driven to Oklahoma, Kansas, Colorado, Wyoming, Montana, and Alberta. Everybody who saw the Texas cowboys' hats wanted to buy one. Even the Texas Rangers roped onto them as part of their uniform. The Stetsons had so many orders they had to build a new hat factory, thirty feet by a hundred feet and three stories high, and they quit makin' all other kinds of hats except the Boss of the Plains.

By the time John B. crossed the Big Divide in 1900, his company was turnin' hundreds of thousands of hats out of the chute every year. By the time I crossed the skyline in '26, that factory had plans to cover thirty acres. I'm told that in three decades, they were makin' four million hats a year.

Since I crossed the Big Divide, almost everything has changed about the life of the cattlemen. Breeds of cattle have changed, ranching methods have changed, saddles have changed, and skunkwagons and bob wire have caused more change than I can fathom. Everything's changed except cowboy spirit and the John B. Stetson hat, which always was and always will be a big part of the true cowboy.

There's only one drawback to wearin' a Stetson. She's such a fine hat, some long-rope might be tempted to maverick it. I'll never forget what happened to Roy Connor's hat once when he and his outfit pushed a herd to Malta to be railroaded east.

When Roy and his outfit delivered them hides, they drew their pay and stopped into a saloon to wash the trail dust down. Roy and three friends had more sense than my friends and I had at the end of a trail drive. Instead of lappin' up nosepaint until most of their role was melted like we'd do, they just downed a couple cow swallows of scatter juice and rode back to camp. But before leavin' town, Roy told his three compadres it was time for him to buy a new hat.

Roy always prided himself on ownin' a new-lookin' Stetson. Every fall, he always bought a new one, which was no more necessary than buyin' new wind, and he gave his year-old one to a cowpuncher in need. This year, when he bought a new Stetson, some socks, and some cigarette makin's in the General

Store, the merchant told him, "Blackjack Ketchem's gang is back in this territory, robbin' stage coaches and travelers at every bend in the trail. You four cowboys could probably down most of 'em in a fair shootout. But I'd bet my last plug of tobacco they'll bushwhack you before you see 'em. You'd better make sure your money is darn hard to find."

Then the merchant unfolded some savvy the riders hadn't heard. The brand new Stetsons had a small pocket hidden in the lining of the hat's crown, and its opening mingled somehow with the stitches in the sweatband, makin' it harder to spot than a fly in a current pie. "They'll never find your cash in there," the merchant advised them.

Roy was the only rider who bought a hat that day, so his three friends all asked him to cache their rolls in the secret pocket of his new Stetson. As they rode the trail back to camp, Blackjack Ketchem's gang sure as shootin' *did* bushwhack 'em, gettin' the drop on 'em from the jump. They frisked the four cowhands from forelocks to dewclaws, but the only money they found was the metal jingle in their pants pockets.

Although Blackjack was a highwayman, he was known to have a sense of humor. When he was later hung in Clayton, New Mexico, he told the hangman, "Can't you hurry this up a bit? They eat dinner in Hades at twelve sharp, and I don't aim to miss it."

So Blackjack anted up, "That's a real John B. you're wearin', ain't it pardner?"

"I've never worn no lid 'cept a John B.," Roy bragged. "No counterfeit hats for this cowboy."

"There's nothing counterfeit about this John B. on my acorn, either," boasted Blackjack. "Since I mavericked this lid in '82, it's ridden forty million miles with me, and it's been endorsed by four bullet holes. Every man between here and the Pecos would be proud to own it. Some day, one of them big museums will fork over thousands of blue chips for this proud hat."

Blackjack then snatched the new Stetson and sloshed his old John B. on top of Roy' head. He tried on Roy's new hat and it fit like a glove, so he said, "We'll just call this a Pecos swap."

The four cowhands rode back to camp, all flat busted and wearin' old hats. I sometimes wonder how long Roy wore that ventilated sombrero, and how tall a stack a museum paid him for it.

I hope you have that good horse called health under you. He's been a fine hoss to most of us, and we often ride him too hard. So don't use your spurs till you hit level country.

Your friend, C. M. Russell

2012 in the moon of the first frost

The Hanging of Big Nose George and Stu Green

Not that I don't like bein' remembered by Montanans—in fact, I'll brag I'm *proud* to be remembered. But the barefoot truth is I'm sometimes remembered for deeds I *didn't* do. Some I wish I *had* done, but some I'm darn glad I didn't try to pull off. Every now and again, I meet a new pilgrim to this range who's saddled with the belief I rode with Stuart's Stranglers.

I wish I could brag I was a high card in that honorable vigilance committee, but I was night herdin' for the Judith Pool the summer of '84. That's when Granville Stuart and his posse almost rid the territory of rustlers, creasin' a couple dozen in gun fights and hangin' twenty-six to cottonwood trees and windmills. Oh, Tommy Tucker and I twice threw in with some former Stranglers trackin' hold-up men and half-breed horse thieves, but Mr. Stuart was no longer with them. No, I can't say I was ever a true member of that prairie-justice outfit, Stuart's Stranglers, but I respected them and their leaders, Granville Stuart and Andrew Fergus.

I've always wished they had never been branded the "Stranglers." They couldn't have had a worse handle hung on them. That ugly word "strangle" should be tacked on bloody lynch mobs, not honest vigilance committees like Granville Stuart's.

If my memory's shootin' straight, I've already preached at you about the differences between the two tribes, so I won't ride down that trail too far. Just let me hit a few high spots of that sermon. A lynch mob is blood thirsty as a pack of wolves and has no more conscience than cattle in a stampede. They hang their man first and ask questions later. But a vigilance committee is organized around a wise leader like Mr. Stuart and always holds a fair trial before swingin' a man off. The accused always gets a chance for his ante, and he's not hung if there's a reasonable doubt about his guilt.

But there's one other big difference between a lynch mob and a fair vigilance committee I haven't unloaded on you yet. The committee's guest of honor at a necktie party dies from a broken neck, and he's out of this world and into Hades quick as a shot through the heart. But the lynch mob's victim usually dies chokin' and kickin' in a wrongly tied noose, just like the cards fell to Big Nose George.

Some people still tell me their favorite of my paintings is one I branded "The Hold-Up," sometimes called "Big Nose George." I can't say it's one of *my* favorites, but it's probably the best one ever to hang in the Mint Saloon. The biggest fight I ever had with Mame was when she charged Sid Willis seventy-five bucks for that painting after I promised it to him for five. But he paid her dead-man's price for it, and we agreed she knew how to pull off a holdup better than Big Nose George.

I oil painted "The Hold-up" on canvas in Great Falls in 1899 in a little house we rented at 1012 Seventh Avenue North. The cellar proved to be a good place to raise ducks in the summer and make ice in the winter. I painted that stage coach robbery in the tiny dining room. Have you seen that oil? The Miles City to Deadwood stage coach is bein' held up by Big Nose George and his gang. The driver and his guard are holdin' their hands up, and all the passengers are outside the coach, reachin' for the stars. There's a Chinaman, a school marm, a preacher, a prospector, a gambler, an aging widow, and a Jewish merchant.

I hear tell some of my historians bicker over whether the people bein' robbed favored folks I knew or if they were what scholars call "stereotypes." I'd be lyin' like a peddler if I declared my memory is still sharp as a Bowie, but I recall paintin' the widow from my memory of Widow Flanagan who ran a boardin' house in Miles City. I modeled the Jewish merchant from my memory of Isaac Katz who came out west from New York to open a clothing store in Miles City. The other passengers were folks I'd seen around Miles City whose names I never knew or have long forgotten.

Anyway, in that painting, a wooden sign on a nearby tree reads, "Wanted, Dead or Alive, Big Nose George, $1,000 Reward." Two outlaws on foot are holdin' rifles on everybody while one with a six-shooter in hand is friskin' every man from forelock to dew claws. All three bandits are wearing bandanas over their faces, but a bandana can't hide the size of George's nose. Many folks have asked me how I knew what George's stature looked like, and I have to own up, I don't know, no more than I know what the wind's stature looks like. I used Con Price as a model when I painted Big Nose George, except for his nose.

The outlaw's real name was George Parrot, but nobody knew if Parrot was his baptismal name or if it was hung on him by reason of his big beak. He blew into the Rockies from Iowa and for years he was a mountain trapper. Later he became a freighter, drivin' a bull team from Cheyenne to the Black Hills, work that takes a powerful man. Nobody knows why he one day decided to change his occupation, but he threw in with a gang of horse thieves and road agents. As the gang members were killed off or corralled in some calaboose and replaced by new blood, George rose to become the gang's leader.

Big Nose George and his gang became famous a year before I came west when their play at robbin' a train near Elk Mountain, Wyoming went south on 'em. They reckoned the easiest way to rob a Union Pacific train was to derail it by uprootin' a piece of the track. Using a crow bar, they pulled out some spikes, but the tool was too short to pry out a section of the rail. They were still wranglin' with that problem when the train arrived and passed safely. Some of the section men reported that the gang had made a play at uprootin' the track, and a railroad detective and a deputy set out to track the gang. The outlaws bushwhacked the lawmen, and for the rest of their four-year career, they were hunted as murderers.

Their luck took to rollin' a little better on their next train robbery. They made off with somewhere between thirty and forty grand near Four Corners, Wyoming without a fight. Soon after that, a Miles City merchant named Morris Cahn was plannin' to travel to Bismarck with thirty-two hundred dollars. For safety, he threw in with some soldiers escortin' an army ambulance wagon headin' east. But Big Nose George's gang got the drop on the soldiers, robbed Cahn of his holdings, and lifted all the soldiers' roles to boot.

The gang rode to the Sun River country in central

Montana where some of the members decided to quit the outlaw life and work for some local ranchers. But George augered them into throwin' in with him once again to rob an army pay master carryin' the payroll from Fort Harrison to Fort Shaw. One of the gang members named Jack Campbell tracked into Johnny Devine's Saloon near the Sun River Crossing, and he surrounded a pint of tanglefoot that would make a jack rabbit spit in a wolf's eye. There was a sayin' in the Old West, "The stuff that makes you tipsy also makes you tip your hand." Jack's boastin' of past feats led him to spill the hold-up plans that were afoot. There was a bright moon, so Johnny lit out for Fort Harrison in a buggy to warn the army.

As Devine rode through Prickly Pear Canyon, Big Nose George's gang was already layin' wait to bushwhack the army paymaster. They stopped the barkeep in his tracks, robbed him of all the money, whiskey and cigars he was carryin', and cut him loose. He rattled into Fort Harrison in time to warn the army about the robbers, and they sent a large army escort with the pay master. The outlaw gang pointed their horses' muzzles toward Wyoming, allowin' they'd try to turn the same tricks there.

It was on the trail to Wyoming where two of the most wanted men in the West, Black Henry and Arapahoe Brown, threw in with George's gang. This boosted the gang's level of sand to where they decided to make a play at the Fort Fetterman payroll. By now, the stage coaches between the fort and Medicine Bow had been robbed so often the army decided to hide the cash in flour sacks and send it with a freight wagon. It's told that Big Nose George stopped that wagon, but findin' no strong box, he turned it loose.

One evening, George and Tom Rutledge ambled into a South Pass City saloon and pulled up chairs to a poker game. A gambler named Tom Albro caught Rutledge dealin' from the bottom and called him on it. Rutledge reached for his gun, but he proved to be a classic western case of too slow. Before it dawned on him that it was Albro's gun, not his, that had just roared, he was receivin' orders from Lucifer to pull up a chair, cut for deal, and embark on a game of stud poker in Hades.

Big Nose George wasn't slow about callin' that gambler out, and with a slug between his eyes, he sent Albro wingin' his way to the Everlasting. Before the corpse hit the ground, Albro's friends were boilin' out of that saloon like tree frogs from a burning aspen, spillin' lead in George's direction as he made a nine in his tail, hot-footed it to his horse, sprang into the saddle, and busted the breeze, bullets tearin' up the sod around him at every jump. The shooters tried to trail George for a few miles, but dark was fallin', and he soon gave them the slip. He rejoined his gang and they made fast tracks for Miles City, always just a few jumps ahead of a posse.

The reward for Big Nose George or his corpse had risen to two grand, and his partner, Jack Campbell, had a thousand-dollar price on his head when the two outlaws blew into Miles City with a long string of stolen horses. Two deputies pretendin' to be horse buyers gained their trust and got the drop on 'em. Campbell somehow fetched loose, but they arrested George and railroaded him back to jail in Carbon, Wyoming to stand trial.

Now here I need to slip the cogs of time for a short ride and unfold on you something that transpired two years prior. When the outlaw Dutch Charlie was arrested near Cheyenne, the sheriff corralled him in a baggage car to be railroaded back to Deadwood to stand trial. While the train was takin' on water and fuel in Carbon, Wyoming, a mob of masked men broke down the baggage car door, escorted Dutch Charlie to a telegraph pole, and hung him up to dry.

The jury in Carbon convicted George without much jaw talk, and the judge sentenced him to be hung, what we called a suspended sentence. While waitin' to be strung up, Big Nose George made a darn good play at escapin'. As a jailor was removing George's shackles, George wrestled them from the jailor's hands and hit him over the head with them. He would have grabbed the jail keys and hit the hoot-owl trail if the jailor's wife hadn't heard the ruckus and pulled on George's halter with her Colt revolver.

Now to make a long story even longer, the same lynch mob that had swung Dutch Charlie over the jump feared George might try again to excuse himself and take his leave before attendin' the necktie party to be held in his honor. They all agreed that this necktie social would be one of the few occasions that George's absence would surely dampen the joy of. To prevent another shot at that eventuality, they thought it wise to break into the jail, escort George to the same telegraph pole, and cinch him free of the ground.

With his feet shackled and his wrists bound with rope, Big Nose George was stood atop of a barrel. A half-inch rope was dangled from the horizontal rod that held the wire high up on the pole, and a poorly-tied noose was dangled around the outlaw's neck. When members of the lynch mob kicked the barrel out from under George, the dang rope broke, spillin' the robber on the ground. As everybody waited for the mob to round up a thicker rope, nobody noticed George wrigglin' his hands free from the ropes that bound his wrists.

This time, George was forced to stand on a twelve-foot ladder. When the ladder was pulled away, George lunged for the telegraph pole with his newly-freed hands, and danged if he didn't catch hold of it. Three times he managed to pull himself up a little higher on the pole before he lost his strength to the weight of the shackles and fell danglin' on the rope, kickin' as much as a shackled, chokin' man can kick.

When the lynch mob cut the corpse down and took it to Dr. John Osborne to have it pronounced dead, the doc refused to take cards in the deal, claiming the execution wasn't official. The ring leaders hung the cadaver back up on the pole and waited for the coroner to cut George down and pronounce him dead the next day.

As soon as the coroner gave his opinion that George was indeed a corpse, our good Dr. Osborne asked the coroner for a look-in at George's brain to better savvy the workings of the criminal mind. He cut the top of the cadaver's skull off, poked around in the brain a while, and wisely proclaimed, "This man wasn't too bright."

But let me unfold what beats all. The law allowed the doctor to make a mask of George's face with the skin from his chest. Then he tanned the hide from George's legs and back and made it into a pair of shoes and a medicine bag. The top of George's skull became the doctor's door stop.

What was left of George was soon buried in a whiskey barrel, and the lawmen and the lynchmen returned to their callings. And what became of Dr. John Osborne? He became governor of Wyoming in 1893.

Maybe I should feel lucky I never saw the work of a lynch mob. No, I never witnessed a man bein' hung wrong, dyin' at the end of a lariat doing the strangulation jig. In my life, I saw only one piece of human fruit, which is what they called an outlaw who cashed in his chips danglin' from a tree. The hanged man I saw was hung properly by members of an honest vigilance committee, and he cashed in abrupt and proper by reason of a broken neck. I'm alludin' to the day Stu Green was given a suspended sentence from the windmill of Utica's public water pump.

Utica was founded shortly before I blew into the Judith in 1880, and I understand it was named after a town in New York. In the l880's, the town was an active hive of commerce. Both the mining and the cattle industries were boomin', and the saloons were busy day and night, filled to the brim with cowboys, miners, gamblers, prospectors, freighters, sheepherders, painted cats, and a hold-up man or two. The streets were always busy and noisy with freight wagons, stage coaches, businessmen, gun fighters, horse thieves, cattle rustlers, hide hunters, Indians, Chinamen, and vigilantes. A lot of money changed hands in old Utica.

But the town's leaders, men of honor, dignity, and book learnin' like Granville Stuart, knew something was missin'. The town needed to promote itself as a hub of culture and intellect, and so far, Utica was as lackin' in said assets as a cow camp. The town leaders were hard put as to what to do about said lack of mental fodder until the day John Mathewson freighted into town with a ripe idea.

If my memory's sittin' square in the saddle, my old friend John Mathewson was the last jerk-line man in central Montana. Now before we trot along any further, I'll need to pull on the reins of this yarn long enough to unload on all you tenderfeet who were born in the age of the skunkwagon what a jerk-line man was. A jerk-line outfit consisted of fourteen horses, two darn big wagons, and a cart, and I'll say without hedgin' a chip, it took a powerful man to hold the reins of that jerk line, to say nothing of steerin' them seven teams. It took nine to fifteen days to drive a jerk-line outfit from Great Falls to Lewistown, and that's in good weather. Of course, once the railroad tracks were laid, the jerk-line outfit went the way of the stage coach, the steamboats, and the bison herds.

This episode takes root in '85 when John Mathewson tracks into the Utica Saloon and unloads the news of what he's seen afoot while haulin' freight in and out of Fort Benton and Helena. He tells us a roundup called a "spelling bee" has of late taken root in those modern towns, and these intellectual contests sure help create a cultural and scholarly atmosphere.

Of course, most of the Utica folks ain't heard of such a pastime, but Grandville Stuart puts up that these spellin' bees are becommin' common as picnics back east. In fact, they're already startin' to cut loose in Billings, Missoula, Cheyenne, and Douglas.

Now at the time, Utica and Reed's Fort—now you folks call it Lewistown—were rivals in every undertakin'. If one town held a rodeo, the other town would try to outhold it. If one town put on a play or a concert, the other town would try to outplay it. If one town hosted a lecturer, the other town would seek a lecturer who could outplay or outhold him. The Utica folks knew if they didn't get on the stick and rustle up a spellin' bee, Reed's Fort would soon gain that first honor.

"Let's beat 'em to the draw and host the area's first spellin' showdown," they decided. "And let's challenge 'em to come and take us on. We'll down 'em quicker than we can down likker."

"Don't shove in your chips so quick on this play," barkeep Jim Shelton warns us. "Ain't you folks heard the Bank in Reed's Fort has a new book keeper out of Chicago named Stu Green who's educated to a razor's edge? He can probably spell every word you shoot at him."

Teddy Blue puts up, "I've met that bookkeep. Put him against the brains of Granville Stuart, and he wouldn't last long as a quart of whiskey at a barn raisin'."

"Mr. Stuart will be needed to toss out the words," Jim raises him. "I've seen one of these spellin' shootouts in Denver, and I'll tell ya, it takes a darn literate gent to deal the game. He's gotta be able to pronounce every word in English, and nobody here but Mr. Stuart could turn that trick. He's the most learned booksharp in the territory."

Bill Skelton stacks in, "I hear there's a sport in Helena who can spell any syllable that lurks between the covers of a dictionary."

John Mathewson backs his play with, "Bill's shootin' straight. I've seen the pilgrim spellin' in saloons for drinks. He can spell the hind shoes off a shave-tail mule. They call him Spelling Bee Fred."

"Let's rope him up and play him on the Reed's Fort

folks. You know they'll never stop braggin' if we let 'em down us," Pete Vann stacks in.

"Do you reckon we could lure him here to take cards in this duel of intellects?" Jim Shelton wondered.

"I'll write him," Granville Stuart puts up. "I need to hire someone with good penmanship for a few weeks to make some clear copies of my latest writings."

"But what if the Reed's Fort folks take to objectin' that this Spelling Bee Fred is a ringer?"

"In that event, we retort by beltin' 'em over the heads with our gun barrels," John Mathewson stacks in. "Can they, as guests, come surgin' into Utica dictatin' terms at us?"

"That objection wouldn't be valid," Granville Stuart trumps him. "As long as this Spelling Bee Fred is workin' for me, he's legally a pro tem citizen of our community."

When Reed's Fort receives our challenge to a showdown of orthography, they promptly call our bluff, confident their bank's new bookkeeper can outspell any educated sport Utica could rope up. They not only accept the challenge; they put up the price of five hundred steers in bets that the last speller standin' would be from their camp. The spellin' bee was set to fetch loose in the Utica Saloon two weeks from Saturday evening at third drink time sharp.

Spelling Bee Fred arrived a week before said spellin' bee was to cut loose, and he promptly went to work for Granville Stuart. He amazed his boss by finishing three weeks' worth of penmanship in just one week, the day before the spellin' bee. But Granville paid him for three weeks' work, and his generosity may have helped persuade Fred to stick around for the spellin' bee.

It was nearly third drink time in the evening of the great event when a dozen buggies from Reed's Fort came bumpin' into Utica. The travelers snubbed their horses to the hitchin' rings that lined the street and sauntered into the Utica Saloon, all of them cocky as the king of spades, ready to bet and go the limit that the bookkeepin' tenderfoot in their midst could outspell Noah Webster himself.

Stuart calls the house to order by rappin' on the bar with his .44, and he tells the five dozen contestants to line up standin' along the saloon's back wall. He sets a five-gallon keg on the bar and tells the house, "This keg is filled with scraps of paper each containing one word. I'll draw a new word for every contestant, and I won't see the word till I read it. If you misspell the word, sit down."

The words fell quick and sharp like the crackin' of a rifle, and the contestants were fallin' like wormy apples in late September. I fell to the word "weather," havin' spelled it with four E's. Granville said it was the worst spell of weather he'd ever seen. Teddy Blue lasted through three volleys and was then sent reelin' like a shot buck by the word "epitaph," spellin' it with an f like it should be spelt. That caused Jim Shelton to spell "definite" with a dang "ph," ending his participation abrupt. John Mathewson was counted out next for spelling "scenery" s-e-e-n-r-y.

"In all my miles of haulin' freight," he bellyaches, "I've seen as much scenery as any man, and I should know how it's spelt. Ain't scenery what ya see? And ain't "see" spelled s-e-e? Then I put up that s-e-e-n-r-y spells "scenery." That letter C you rung into the deck is as out of place as a cow on a front porch."

"That word and every other dang word is spelled as Mr. Stuart says," Teddy Blue reminds the freighter, pointin' at him like he's a rattlesnake.

"A man has the inalienable right to spell things as he sees fit," John grumbles on, "or there's no use in callin' this a free country. If I'm compelled to spell "scenery" with a fool C, whatever was the purpose of Yorktown and Bunker Hill?"

"Dead bird!" is all Stuart had to say to convince John to repair to the bar and slop out 40 more drops of Old Jordan.

But it wasn't only the Utica men who were fallin' like October leaves. The Reed's Fort spellers were droppin' just as fast, and by fourth drink time after we started, no one was standin' but Stu Green, the bank's bookkeeper, and Spelling Bee Fred. We watched as they both spelled over two hundred words, and neither of them once stubbed his orthographic toe. Finally, the contest took a pause as barkeep Jim Shelton dealt everyone, includin' the two ace spellers, forty drops of liquid refreshment.

The spellin' bee resumed at an unbridled lope.

Granville Stuart dealt the words until it was nearly dawn, and neither party could be fooled by a silent letter, a "ph" or a "gh." The game seemed unending as a bad winter.

But then the bank's bookkeep turns shaky as a leaf in a gale and pale as soap. It's a cinch the pressure of this showdown finally has him on the brink of a stampede. Spelling Bee Fred is still calm and steady as a church as Stuart reads him the word "cylinder." Fred's about to whirl his verbal loop when Reed Fort's bookkeep whips out a Peacemaker from inside his vest, jams it into Fred's ribs, and dictates, "Spell it with an S, or I'll send you shoutin' home to glory."

That speller Fred was game as yeller wasps. Even with the cold muzzle of a pistol in his ribs, he didn't flicker. "C-y-" he began, but that's as far as he got. To the roar of a .45, Fred came slidin' from his perch, deader than Julius Caesar.

Quick as jack rabbits, a few of the Reed's Fort vigilantes grabbed hold of Stu Green and wrestled away his gun. They stood him before Granville Stuart and their leader Andrew Fergus uttered, "It's your jurisdiction, Granville. We'll back your play."

Stuart declared, "I've always held that for justice to be effective, it must be swift and certain. As chairman of our vigilance committee, I believe we have a quorum present, so we can hold a trial. All members of the Stranglers please step forward."

When the jury was all gathered in, Stuart opened

the ball with, "Green, whatever possessed you to blow out Fred's lamp thata way?"

"I had two hundred dollars bet on the contest," Stu answered.

"I'm sure that will prove of interest to your executioners, but it doesn't answer my question. Again, what was your reason for shoving him from shore?"

"I'm the leading speller in eight states and two territories. Do you think I'd abide seeing an obscure speller like him outspell me? I'd sooner die."

"Most folks don't get their sooners in this world," Stuart tells him, "but in this case, it looks like you might." Then to the vigilantes he ordered, "Members of the jury, let's repair to the storeroom to commence deliberations. Mr. Fergus, would you and your vigilance committee kindly hold onto the accused while we vote on matters concerning his future? And John, you might hasten things up if you'd prance over to the livery stable and borrow a rope."

The jury's confab took less time than the two drinks they downed, and the vote was unanimous for hanging Green. Before they adjourned, a rap jarred the door. It was Andrew Fergus, roundup boss for the Reed's Fort Stranglers.

"Sorry to disturb your deliberations, gentlemen," he apologized, "but can we borrow Mr. Stuart for a minute? We'd like him to say a final prayer over the corpse."

We raced outside and found Stu adornin' the windmill, as I remarked prior. He was hung in proper fashion and cashed in quick, just like the play should be made.

Spelling Bee Fred was buried in Helena, and Reed's Fort and Utica shared the cost of his coffin and his tombstone that read, "Here lies Spelling Bee Fred, who preferred death to the appearance of ignorance."

If you ever drift this way, don't forget my camp. There's grub and blankets for you any time.

Your friend, C. M. Russell

2012 in the moon of the falling leaves

The Cash-in of
Charlie Bowlegs

Like as not, you've heard the Old West proverb, "A man who lives by the gun dies by the gun." Of course, gunplay didn't cut loose anywhere near as often as them dime novels and cowboy motion pictures led folks to believe. But I knew a few men who killed to live at a time when quick guns meant right. They neither feared the law nor asked her for any favors. They danced and paid the fiddler, and they usually cashed in under the smoke of the same weapons they lived by. Such a gunman was my pal Charlie Bowlegs.

As my memory canters back over trails long ago plowed under, it stops to graze a moment on a card game Con Price, Charlie Bowlegs, and I happed up on once in Big Sandy. Now before I hit the trail of that yarn, let me ask, did I ever tell you how that town had its name hung on it? No? Then I'd better unload on you that slice of history while it's still within the reach of my rope.

They say the town of Big Sandy, as well as Big Sandy Creek, was named after a mule skinner named Big Sandy Lane. He hauled freight from the docks of Fort Benton to towns like Helena and Bull Hook. One rainy day, he was haulin' a load of time freight to Fort Assiniboine. What's time freight? It's what modern shippers would label, "Rush. Perishable Goods." His load was mostly bacon and hard tack for the soldiers.

Lane was behind schedule because his wheels kept cloggin' with gumbo. But because Sandy had such a persuasive way of addressin' his mules, he made the best headway possible until he reached the crick. Due to the spring thaw, its banks were full and still risin', and the crick had its back up like a mad bronc. But Big Sandy Lane wasn't a man to quit. Trouble is, no amount of cussin', shoutin', chain rattlin', and whip poppin' could persuade his mules to cross that stream.

Big Sandy commenced to cussin' till the air around him turned blue. His heated lyrics sizzled an acre of grass and caused all the cottonwoods within thirty rods to shed their leaves. He cussed the stream, the weather, his mules, his luck, and almost every other dang thing, but he didn't cuss the Lord, and I'll soon unload on you why. He cussed until that crick dried up, and he drove his wagon and mules across the dry crick bed. He reached the garrison in time to save the soldiers from hunger, and many old freighters who knew Sandy vouched for this legend. To this day, at certain seasons, that stream sinks where Sandy crossed, and it surfaces a stone's throw away. And now you savvy why that town and creek were branded Big Sandy.

As long as I'm rattlin' on about the names of towns, did you know Havre was first named Bull Hook? The Indians hung that name on the village, naming it after a nearby butte they thought was shaped like a buffalo horn. James Hill changed its name to Havre after a town in France. He claimed the new name would give the town a touch of European culture, but I don't credit it. I'd bet a stack of red chips he wanted to change the name because the town had such bad renown. Did you know that in 1916, the Law and Order League of Chicago branded it the worst den of crime between Chicago and the West Coast on Highway Two?

Now as I remarked prior, Sandy had enough sense not to cuss the Lord. In fact, nobody in central Montana dared to cuss the Omnipotent after word spread about the fate of Bart Willard.

Bart was one of these mysterious rounders who rode to Montana pushin' a Texas herd. The rumor had it he'd been a little over-free with his gun in Texas, as the notches on his six-gun's handle might imply. But as I've heretofore mentioned, it was bad manners to ask a man about his past, so nobody knew much about Bart.

Four days after delivering that herd to Lewistown, Bart Willard demonstrated just how unnecessary he was to the town's welfare. He blew into the town's new theater one evening as a young lady on stage was chirpin' a song. From the audience, Bart builds a loop in his lariat, whirls it across the stage and around the fair maiden's flanks, and reels her toward him like she's a calf to be branded.

The kettle tender, a former cow puncher named Sheriff Bill Deaton, wasn't slow about knockin' Willard from under his hat. When the Texan rounded to, Deaton demanded, "What do you think you're doin', tossin' a loop at a heifer who's not wearin' your brand?"

"The truth is, Sheriff, I fell enamored of the lady. I had a heap of sweet words I was fixin' to pour in her ear, but you've jolted them from my memory with the barrel of your field piece."

The sheriff warns him, "You'd better take the saddle off your emotions and hobble 'em out to rest some. I don't know what you do in Texas, but in this country, that's no way to get confidential with a lady. The next time you express your romantic yearnings with a lariat, you'll be takin' room and board with me for a long spell."

A few days later, Bart went to work for Granville Stuart, helpin' a half dozen of us cowhands round up some strays missed in the spring brandin'. We gathered in a herd of maybe three hundred cows and half-grown calves and set about brandin' 'em with Stuart's DHS iron. But before we finished, a thunder and lightning storm that skins anything ya ever heard takes to explodin' all around us, and every hand plumb down to the cook is tryin' to keep that bunch of cattle calm and close-herded by singin' to 'em. Suddenly a bolt of lightning sizzles a nearby cottonwood tree, followed by an explosion of thunder that almost knocks the cattle's horns off.

"Blaze away, my grey-headed Creator!" Willard shouts at the Firmament like a locoed drunk. "You've been shootin' at me for twenty years, and you ain't hit me yet. Blaze away!"

Those crazy words scare Con Price more than the lightning itself. Fearin' such blasphemy might get him picked off when the Lord shoots at Willard, he pulls his Peacemaker, points it at the Texan, and yells, "Pull your freight! Don't stand near me when you challenge the Almighty, or I'll blaze away myself, and I won't miss!"

Willard spurred away, laughin' like a loon. Before his laughter was played out, a streak of white fire shot down to earth, followed by an explosion that almost split the ground. The lightning missed Con Price, but it sure ran the devil's brand on Willard. Both he and his horse lay still, deader than General Custer. The rowels of Bart's spurs were melted, and in the middle of his hat was a hole about the size of a .44 slug.

"She was a long shot, but a center one," Con told us when we rode up.

But I've strayed from the main trail long enough. I was shufflin' to deal the fate of my itchy-trigger-finger friend Charlie Bowlegs. If my memory's saddle ain't slippin', Bowlegs rode for the T Bar L outfit. Like so many good cow hands, he'd rode up from Texas on a trail drive and stayed in Montana to work the herds. He had several notches on his pistol when he tracked in, and by now, he'd added one more, havin' proved himself to be a better shot than the disgruntled Texan who pulled a gun on him at the Sun River Crossing.

Of course, he was branded Bowlegs because that's what he was, bow-legged as a barrel hoop. He was so bow-legged he could hardly pull on his socks. You could run a yearling steer between his legs without bendin' a hair. You could have hung him upside down over a barn door for good luck. He didn't talk much, but he didn't need to. Like many quiet cowhands, he was a box of dynamite when rattled.

One fall, we drove a herd to the railroad corrals of Big Sandy, which was a right busy shippin' point at the time. After we delivered them hides, we dropped into a waterin' hole to wash that trail dust down and maybe buy some quality time with the painted cats. The saloon was full, and the poker tables were busy as the barkeeps. We ordered a quart and plunked the sole of one boot down on the brass rail, not thinkin' much of gamblin'. Soon we heard the saloon owner call out, "We've got room in this game for two more hands at stud poker."

I hadn't gambled a chip since the day I lost my horse Grey Eagle and my saddle by gamblin' drunk in Lewistown, so I chose not to take cards in the game. But Con Price and Bowlegs, thinkin' the game was on the square, pulled a chair up to the table, cut for deal, and were dealt a hand.

We didn't savvy it yet, but this waterin' hole was a deadfall. What's a deadfall? It's a saloon crooked as a coyote's hind leg. The saloon owner is in cahoots with tin-horn gamblers who can always slip an ace off the bottom. One of the cardsharps at the table with Con and Charlie Bowlegs was a Chinese gambler who'd long played cards in the saloons of Butte. He was dressed to the nines in new fancy city togs, and he was known to always pack a big roll of greens. But none of us knew yet he was in cahoots with the saloon owner, splittin' even-up the money they hornswoggled from cowboys.

The game went lopin' along for a half-dozen hands, and Con and Bowlegs didn't take a single trick. But they stayed in the game, feelin' buoyed up by the roll they'd just drawn from the boss after deliverin' that herd. Finally Bowlegs drew a pat hand at a time the jackpot was higher than King's Hill. There must have been fifty blue chips in that pot. One by one, every player folded until there was nobody but Bowlegs and the Chinaman left holdin' cards.

Con was dealin', and the next card dealt face down was to go to the Chinaman. Before that card was dealt, and before the Chinaman put his money in the pot, Bowlegs thought he caught a glimpse of the coyote stretchin' his neck to look at the back of the deck's top card, like he's tryin' to see what card he'll draw before he risks makin' a bet. As the Chinaman shoves his money to the center, Bowlegs tells Con, "Hold it! I want to cut the deck."

I have nothin' but good will toward most Chinamen, but let me unfurl some truth. In Butte, some Chinese gamblers had a reputation for being able to unseal a new deck of cards and seal it up again so ya couldn't tell it was opened. And let me tell you something about their slanted eyes. Chinamen can mark a card with a brand so tiny no white man can see it, but they can see it clear as a lantern from across the card table.

The saloon owner and the sharp-eyed gambler both bark, "Hell no!" at Bowlegs, whereupon the cowboy springs to his feet and pulls his .45. Not pointin' it at anybody in particular, he utters, "That's the way this play is gonna come off, gents."

"I'll go get the Book of Hoyle," the owner said as he took a step toward the bar.

This time, Bowlegs *did* point the muzzle of that Colt at the sidewinder, and he cocked the trigger to boot. "Stay put. I have the Book of Hoyle right here."

I looked at Con, who looked like he was fixin' to dive under the poker table. I looked at Bowlegs, and he looked unnerved as an Indian, sportin' the sickly grin of a rattlesnake about to strike. He said, "There's only one way to settle this. Con, deal my oriental friend one card. If it helps his hand, I'm takin' the pot. If it don't help his hand, he takes the pot."

Con dealt the card, and when all the cards were turned face up, the Chinaman held two pairs and Bowlegs held three of a kind. The new card would have bettered the cheater's hand to three of a kind, and higher cards than Bow Legs held.

"I protest! This is a holdup!" the losers kicked as Bowlegs raked all the chips into his hat, still holdin' the revolver on the hoss thieves. Then he shoved his hatful of chips at the deadfall owner and said, "Give me my money damn quick!"

Of course, we wore out our welcome forever in that waterin' hole, but that wasn't the first or the last saloon Charlie Bowlegs almost had to shoot his way out of. But when a man has too much spread, somebody's bound to clip his horns. One night, Bowlegs was sloshin' around in a saloon in Dupuyer. He'd been there since second drink time in the afternoon, crookin' his elbow, paintin' his nose, buyin' rounds for the house, and playin' poker.

It was along about fifth drink time in the evening when a half-breed tracked in and saw Charlie buyin' the house another round. Charlie didn't recognize the half-breed, but the breed sure recognized him. One drunk night they'd locked horns in the same saloon, and they took the dispute outside to settle it with their lead pushers. They were both too drunk to shoot the ground. The only injury that befell them was the breed suffered a small powder burn.

"When you bought that round, you forgot mine," the half-breed tells Bowlegs.

'I ain't buyin' drinks for no injun!" Bowlegs cusses him.

With this, the ball opens. The breed reaches for his six-shooter, and quick as a rattlesnake, Charlie reaches for his. Bowlegs' demise was caused by his long overcoat keepin' him from gettin' to his revolver before the half-breed blew him from his perch. He fell to the sawdust, dead as Santa Ana, just as four guns roared from the card table and four slugs slammed into the breed. Like most men who let guns speak for them, a gun spoke Bowleg's requiem.

May your days be better than the best you've had, and may your wrinkles be from laughs, not frowns. May your nights bring dreams that make you glad, and may your joys be mountains, not mounds.

Your friend, C. M. Russell

2012 in the moon of the new snows

The Demise of Wild Wolf Willy

Charlie Bowlegs wasn't the only rawhide I knew who lived by the gun and died by its revenge. Another hombre of that leather is now loomin' up into the foreground of my memory, Wild Wolf Willy. Like most of Montana's early cowboys who too often expressed their views with a gun, Willy came up the trail pushin' a herd from Texas. He never returned to that Lone Star State.

Rumors abounded that Willy was wanted in Texas for rustlin' and horse stealin', but as I've told you a bushel of times, it was not only bad manners to ask a man about his past; it was sometimes bad luck. He worked the roundups and the cattle drives when he was down to his last chip, but he was more often found playin' poker in the saloons of Billings. Some folks suspected he'd played a role in a local robbery or two, but there was no evidence a vigilance committee could fasten a rope on.

One thing *was* known about Wild Wolf: he was ornery as a corn-drunk squaw. He didn't smile or jaw with anybody, and he was always alone when he wasn't at the card tables. More than once, he let his gun do his talkin' for him over matters of card table etiquette, and neither his shootin' hand nor his trigger finger was unreasonably slow. And let me tell you how ornery he was. His earthly span was ended one night by a .45 slug entering the back of his head and exiting through an eye. When the card sharps lifted him from the sawdust-covered floor, they saw he had both guns drawn and one hammer cocked. It takes a right ornery cuss to have the left-over impulse to draw and cock pistols when he's deader than a six-card poker hand.

Wild Wolf's demise had its roots in the killin' of a Crow Indian a few weeks earlier. Here's how it stacks up. Captain Moore, a Civil War veteran and a freighter, and his nephew Clyde were drivin' two eight-mule baggage wagons to Billings from Sheridan. At sunset, they were surroundin' some beans and biscuits when they heard the locoed voices of their mules warblin' in alarm.

Now as you may savvy, a mule is a cross between

a female horse and a male jackass. Their utterances don't quite sound like either a horse or a donkey; it's somewhere in between. Sometimes their brayin' starts off soundin' sorta like a horse's whinny and winds up with a donkey's hee-haw. And let me tell you another odd card about mules. They can smell the difference between a white man and an Indian at forty rods. I don't know why, but smellin' a renegade makes a mule nervous as a cat in a room full of rockin' chairs.

When the freighters heard their mules brayin', they looked back to see a half dozen Indians fixin' to unhitch a few of the critters. Now remember, stealin' horses, a hangin' offense among white men, was always deemed an honorable pastime among Indians, and they probably felt the same way about mules, although at this time, most of them had never seen a mule or even a jackass.

Captain Moore grabs his Winchester and fires a warning shot into the air, causin' most of the Indians to scatter like a night stampede, all except one brave who turns and fires two shots at Moore, missin' him twice. When Clyde beholds the warrior unloadin' his artillery at Moore, he steps forward with his Winchester and with one shot, he stops that brave from lopin' up and down the land for good and all.

When the warriors on the run look back and see one brave is creased, they regroup, catfoot up within shootin' distance, take cover, and take to burnin' the scenery around the two freighters with their pistols and Winchesters. Moore and Clyde take cover behind a wagon and fight them off until dark. Then all grew quiet. When Indians do battle, they usually cease durin' darkness. Indians believe that if a warrior is killed at night, he will be in the dark in the hunting grounds that follow.

The two freighters took turns keepin' watch all night, and at daybreak, the stand-off resumed with both parties wastin' plenty of ammunition but with no one being hit. When the sun was two fingers from bein' straight up, the Indian agent from the Crow Reservation rode up, searchin' for these bunch quitters who had ridden off for adventures unknown, hopin' to round them up and herd them back to the reservation before they mix into trouble.

When the Indians see the agent, they stop firin' and tell him they were tryin' to avenge their fallen brother. The agent ties a white bandana to his rifle barrel, holds the flag high, and saunters up to Moore and Clyde to start a pow wow, the Indians trailin' close behind him.

The agent tells the freighters the Indians seek justice against Clyde for killin' one of their party, and Clyde insists he shot the redskin defendin' his uncle. The agent, well-gifted with a silver tongue, augers Clyde into returnin' to the Indian Agency to stand trial, claimin' the youth will likely be acquitted, since he was defendin' his uncle in said fashion. He promised the lad protection on route to and from the agency, so Clyde lay down his Winchester and rode off with the Indians and the agent in spite of Captain Moore warnin' him, "You're a goner if you go with 'em, boy. You won't last long as a keg of hard cider at a barn raisin'."

It wasn't more than two drinks down the trail that the five Indians pulled their guns on the Indian agent, sent him away, and rode off with the captain's nephew. Like Moore had warned, by fifth drink time that afternoon, Clyde was nothin' but a memory. The Crows spread him out like a fresh hide to dry on top of an ant hill and staked his wrists and ankles to the ground. In three or four hours, every bite of flesh was eaten off the young wagoner's bones.

When Captain Moore learned of his nephew's harsh demise, he was possessed by one thought: that Indian agent has lived too long. He roped at the local vigilance committee for help, explainin' the agent deserves the same fate the Indians dealt his nephew. The vigilance committee chairman allowed that since the Indian agent wears a government brand and was actin' officially, there was no opening by which the vigilantes could cut in on the deal. It was a cinch Captain Moore would have to play his own hand to play even on the agent.

Trouble is, Captain Moore savvied the agent and the Indians wouldn't be slow to recognize him if he stalked them. The thought of being staked out on an ant hill didn't overly appeal to him either. It was a cinch he needed to hire an outlaw to cash in the agent's chips for him. One night he downed a few drinks with Wild Wolf Willy and made the ornery Texan a deal.

Willy agreed to down the agent for a hundred and fifty blue chips plus a saddle horse.

I'm told a hundred and fifty bucks don't sound like much of a roll to you folks today, but remember, in the late 1880's, a cowboy worked for a dollar a day, so the Captain was antein' up five months wages. Willy took the horse and fifty dollars as a down payment, agreein' to return within a week with the agent's ears and scalp to be paid the other hundred blue chips. A week later, Captain Moore sees Willy in a saloon crookin' his elbow and paintin' his nose with rot gut whiskey.

"Did you bring me back that agent's ears and scalp like we agreed?" Moore asked Willy.

"Nope," is all the hired gun answered.

"Didn't I give you a tall stack of reds and a pony, with my noble promise of two more red stacks for those items?"

"Yep," is all he said.

"Then why haven't you come across?"

Willy looked at Moore with the cold eyes of a wolf and answered, "When I tracked up on this agent and explained my game, he offered me three hundred blues to blow your lamp out instead of his. Now the question I needs to sling your way is, do you wish to raise this gent, or do you fold?"

"What happens if I fold?"

"Then I regretfully have to play the hand the agent dealt me and send you to the discard."

"I'll need to go to the bank," Moore tells him. He

leaves and returns within two drinks' time and hands Willy four hundred and fifty more dollars.

"This stacks up to five hundred blues I'm paying you for that scalp and them ears," he reminds Willy, "a dang high price for said ornaments. Now go play out your hand."

The wolf finished his drink and lined out on the trail of the Indian agent. It was almost a week later when Moore spots Willy trackin' into another saloon. The captain trails him in and asks, "Did you fetch me those body parts you promised?"

"Nope," was all Willy said once more.

"What's the delay this time?"

"I'll be a prohibitionist if this agent party didn't outraise you again," the wolf answered, grinnin' like he's sittin' behind a fat jackpot with an ace full. "He bumped the bet to seven hundred blues and two ponies for your hair and ears. Now the question I must shoot at you is: do you reckon to see this gent, raise him, or fold?"

"I'll need to go to the bank," Moore tells him again.

The captain returns directly and paws four hundred more pesos over to the wolf. "That raises my bet to nine hundred blues," he reminds Willy. "Now it would do me and my nephew much honor if you would kindly tend to this honest and just execution you're bein' so well paid to perform." With that blessing, Wild Wolf saddled up and rode for the Crow Reservation.

This is startin' to sound like one of them circular

yarns that have no end, but eight days later, the captain trails Wild Wolf into the same saloon, shoots the same question at him, and hears the same "Nope."

"The agent ups the ante again, Captain. He sees your two hundred dollars and he raises you two hundred more. That bumps the bet to eleven hundred blues, if my arithmetic is shootin' straight. Do you want to see this bet, raise the gent, or fold?"

"I need to go to the bank again."

"You'll find me here playin' poker," the wolf told him as he pulled a chair up to the card table, sat down with his back to the door, and cut for deal, unsuspectin' as a steer of the fate that's about to come ridin' down on him. Instead of linin' out for the bank, Captain Moore walks over to his freight wagon, straps on his gun belt, and steps back into that saloon. With that shot I mentioned prior, Wild Wolf is out of that saloon and into Hades in the snappin' of a finger.

The vigilance committee hated to take cards in the game of condemnin' Captain Moore, for there wasn't one of them who didn't suspect Wild Wolf missed out on a good hangin' years ago. But justice must be relied on to play out its hand in order to be strong in the future, so they voted to use the Captain to decorate a windmill or a cottonwood.

Before they had time to roll the game of cinchin' him up, a deputy rode up and proclaimed, "You can't hang the Captain. I just received a wanted poster from Texas sayin' there's a two-hundred dollar price on Wild Wolf's head, dead or alive. Cashin' him in was legal. In fact, Texas owes the captain two hundred berries, so he's buyin' the drinks tonight."

Wild Wolf Willy proved to be just another example: if you let a gun earn your living, it'll some day write your obituaries. And what cards fell to the Indian agent? He got his just dues. He was caught stealin' government Indian rations and sellin' 'em to sodbusters. The Indians sentenced him to the same demise that claimed Captain Moore's nephew.

Keep your six-gun in your holster, your feet in the stirrups, and never let go of the reins.

Your friend, C. M. Russell

2013 in the moon the river freezes

Frozen Windies and a Cowboys' Strike

This time of year is what the Red folks called "the moon when the river freezes." Old-timers who've lately crossed the Maker's Big Divide tell me the rivers don't freeze quite as aptly as they used to. They say man's inventions have taken to turnin' tricks with the Creator's weather, makin' the world warmer than it was when I ranged there.

The idea of warmer winters sounded good to me at first, but then they told me this here "global warming," as they call it, has been raisin' havoc with the Omnipotent's critters and causin' more draughts, floods, hurricanes, and tornadoes. I told everybody ninety years ago that no good would come of man's new inventions, but I might as well have been talkin' Chinese to a pack mule. I'm still standin' pat on that belief.

Now let me unfold on you just how bad them winters were when I rode your ranges. My friend Teddy Blue Abbot told me about a time he was walkin' across the range on foot checkin' on his boss' cattle. Normally, a cowboy would rather be caught stealin' chickens than be caught on foot. But the snow was so dang deep nary a horse could turn a card or move a wheel, so Teddy was hoofin' across the prairie wearin' snowshoes. Soon a blizzard that skins anything ya ever saw pounced on him like a hawk pounces on a chicken. Although Teddy was wearin' lots of clothes, that wind cut through him like a knife, causin' him to seek shelter.

At last he tracked up on a coulee. He thought, "The wind won't be as strong down there, so maybe I'll find a few of the outfit's cows." As he drifted down the draw, he caught sight of a man frog-squattin' near a fire. He allowed to himself, "Maybe this gent will share his flames with me long enough to warm my bones." He approached the man and greeted him, but the stranger was mum as a basket of clams. When Teddy drew nigh, he saw the stranger was frozen solid as an anvil. Teddy reached his numb hands toward the bright flames, and I'm a hoss thief if every flame wasn't frozen solid as ice.

Teddy swore that yarn was true as a sermon. If

you find it hard to chew, wait'll I unload on you what happened to Ed Silverthorne during the terrible winter of '86-'87 that cost Montana cattlemen ninety per-cent of their stock. Ed was workin' for the N Bar outfit, ridin' herd on twenty-five hundred head of cattle near the Bull Mountains. One morning, the outfit came up missin' some good cattle horses, so the boss sent Ed and Johnny Gamble out in the twenty-five-below weather to search for 'em.

Near Sixteen Mile Creek, they were pounced on by a norther pushin' a blizzard so thick they couldn't see their horses' reins. As good fortune had it, they were near Peck Williams' cabin, where Peck let 'em camp down by the fire. They allowed they'd trail out soon as the storm broke, but for six hours, so much snow fell they couldn't see out the windows. The mercury in Williams' thermometer fell to sixty below.

Ed and Johnny were cooped up in that cabin for more than one full moon, and cabin fever drove them loco as coyotes. Finally, a chinook blew in from the Southwest, allowin' 'em to ride back to their outfit's camp near the Bull Mountains. The corpses of frozen cattle and horses lay all over the land almost as thick as the meltin' snow, but none of the dead horses wore the N Bar brand. When they reached camp, they had to tell their boss they couldn't find any of the outfit's horses.

In two days, the chinook blew itself out and another blizzard blew in, and the mercury in the thermometer fell a foot. The first night on the hocks of the storm, every cowboy in the outfit was kept awake by a howlin' pack of wolves not thirty rods from camp. Finally, every rider stepped outside with a rifle. They could see the wolves plain as stars because the canines' eyes were glowin' in the dark like candles. Every one of them riders pumped a wagonload of lead in the wolves' direction, but nary a wolf fell. The cowpunchers figgered the cold had somehow made their rifles shoot off course, and they retired again to try to sleep. For the rest of the night, the wolves were quiet as a band of ghosts.

Next morning, the thermometer read sixty below, and the riders could see that pack of wolves watchin' 'em from the same place they'd seen their eyes shinin' the night before. They grabbed their riffles and made tracks toward the outlaws, figgerin' they could shoot 'em as they ran. There was a bounty on wolves, and to tell the truth, I did a little wolfin' myself. But them wolves didn't run or even wiggle an ear. As the cattlemen tracked up on 'em, they saw every wolf was frozen plumb solid as an icicle and too full of bullet holes to hold hay.

Now that yarn Ed told me may have been a little on the windy side, but I believe the next thing he told me was the barefoot, unclothed truth. He said that of the twenty-five hundred head of cattle they started with, only a hundred and twenty-five head survived the winter. As I remarked prior, cattlemen everywhere lost nine out of ten cows that awful winter of '86-'87.

But those two frozen windies don't hold openers

to the one I'm cinchin' a saddle on now. One winter, Ralph Simpson was winterin' two thousand head of cattle on Cold Creek near Billings. There was a good two feet of snow on the ground, and the north wind was so cold the Box Elder and Cottonwood trees were snappin' and cracklin' loud as a battlefield. As good fortune had it, the cattle were winterin' down in some coulees out of the wind. But one day, Ralph saw the herd was missin' its lead steer, Old Baldy, a white faced Hereford.

Simpson tracked out on foot to find that big steer, and by the time he reached the north draw, that wind felt like it had kissed the North Poll at least twice. He took to stompin' his feet and slappin' his hands to his sides to make his blood flow warmer, and I'll be a coyote if he didn't hear the same sounds behind him. He turned around to find his shadow stompin' and slappin' his sides, even after Ralph stopped movin'.

Simpson thought, "Boy, he must be cold as a well digger's feet in Alberta." He took to combin' the draw callin', "Baldy! Baldy!" But there was no sign or hoof mark of the lost steer.

Ralph was wearin' long johns, two pairs of pants, three coats, one of which was sheepskin, a heavy fur-lined hat, fur-lined boots and fur-lined mittens, but he could still feel himself growin' numb with cold. "Get back to the ranch," he ordered himself, but as he tried to walk, he couldn't move an inch. Something was holdin' his coat.

Ralph looks back and sees the hands of his shadow

clingin' to his coat. The rest of his shadow is frozen to the ground. Simpson takes off his sheep-skin coat and covers the shadow with it. He draws his Bowie knife and spends maybe she's two hours whittlin' in the ice and packed snow below the shadow. By the time that shadow is cut loose, Simpson's so dang numb he falls to the ground, helpless as a frozen snake. But that shadow's so grateful he lifts Ralph from the ground, slings him over his shoulders, and packs him back to the ranch.

Simpson told me years later, "There were half a dozen riders there who packed me inside like a frozen side of beef and thawed me out, and they'll all swear this story is true as holy writ." But by then, some of them had died and the others were scattered all over tarnation. I never met any of the men Ralph said would swear to that story.

Of course, life-threatenin' weather wasn't the only danger facin' a cowboy. His life was one of constant danger, very long work days, discomfort, and hard, demandin' tasks, and all for a dollar a day. Sometimes newcomers to my side of the Big Divide ask, "Didn't cowboys ever demand higher wages for all their sacrifice? Did it ever occur to them to go on strike, like miners and factory workers sometimes had to do?"

I 'spose a fellow has to be a cowhand to understand what drew us to that open-range life. It sure wasn't the money. As I backtrack my memory's tails, I can recall hearin' of only one strike that ever cut itself loose among cowhands, and that misdeal fetched loose in '83 in the Panhandle of Texas. I heard about it from more than one Texas rider who rode up the trail with a herd and stayed to work cattle in the Judith.

Them Texans told me that three big cattle outfits once shared the same range in the Panhandle. At chuck every evening, a lot of the cowhands took to kickin' about their low wages. They figgered, "The cattle owners have their organizations. Why not cowboys?" So they formed a cowboys' labor union, and a bevy of men from all three outfits signed an ink talk to the cattle owners demandin' a rider's pay be raised from thirty to fifty dollars a month and bronc busters, cooks, cattle foremen, and range bosses be paid seventy-five bucks a month.

The letter also announced that beginnin' April First, every cowboy in the three outfits would go on strike until their wages were raised. The union somehow provided chuck-wagon grub three times a day for a month to cowboys too broke to strike— prob'ly most of 'em.

The cattle owners weren't slow to fire every rider who'd signed that letter. The rest of the riders decided to start their strike earlier than April First. For over a month, they all sat around the chuck area, drinkin', kickin', and tellin' windies. Some became restless as colts and were tempted strong to go back to work for their old wages, resultin' in more than a few fist fights among the riders. As luck had it, nobody was shot.

Ya know what caused the strike to fail? In '83, the South was still reelin' from the Civil War. There were still a lot of restless young bucks itchin' to go to Texas and become cowboys, and for dang low wages. It didn't take the cattle bosses long to ring in these greenhorns to replace the men on strike, and, of course, some of the strikin' riders returned to work for their old wages. But some left Texas for good, like my many friends who rode up the Texas Trail with a herd pointed north and stayed to cowboy in Wyoming or Montana. Of course, they weren't paid any more in the north than they were in Texas, but for the short spell the open range lasted, I never met one cowboy who was in the work just for the money.

If hosses were health, I'd comb the range and trim every band I know. You'd go to the end of a long trail with a top hoss under you.

Your friend, C. M. Russell

2013 in the moon the ice breaks

Judge Pray's Tale of a Hijacked Steamboat

$\mathbf{F}$olks who've crossed the divide in recent years tell me most folks in Montana pack the notion all my friends were former cowboys, and the only place you'd ever see me was among my old cowboy friends in the Mint, the Maverick, the Brunswick, or the Silver Dollar. Now I can't deny most of my best friends *were* the men I once worked cattle with. Former cowboys have a comradeship among 'em that can be understood only by former soldiers, the kind that comes from facin' life-threatenin' dangers together. If you're a cowboy long enough, it's a cinch you'll ride up on some occasions where the grim reaper almost catches you in his loop.

But later in life, after Mame and I were settled in Great Falls, we made many good friends who were neither former cow punchers nor frequenters of saloons. Now the four saloons I just mentioned all held collections of my paintings on their walls. The kind of men I'm fixin' to unfold on you didn't care to tarnish their reputations by bein' seen in the saloons. If they wanted to see my art, their best shot was to sneak into them saloons in the morning when they'd least likely be seen by other tea-totalers. Of course, ladies weren't allowed to enter those distinguished drinkin' establishments. However, all four saloon owners would shut the bar down for a couple hours once a week to let the ladies come in and see my art.

Prob'ly the best known among my non-cowboy friends was the town's camp finder, first mayor, and a state senator, Paris Gibson. He was a livin' example that you can hate what a man stands for but still like the gent as a person. Gibson and I didn't see eye to eye on anything. He was Mr. Progress, lurin' the railroad here to help him establish factories, smelters, dams, and all manner of businesses. I didn't want to see any of that modern, smelly industry near here, seein' how this was such good grass land for cattle and hosses. People of my time called me a conservative old fool who opposed progress. I'm told that today, the same folks would call me a tree-huggin' liberal. Whatever I was, I was the opposite of Mr. Gibson. Yet we became good friends simply because we enjoyed each other's company.

In 1896, William Jennings Bryan was runnin' for president, train hoppin' across the West givin' speeches. One day, he was scheduled to speak in Great Falls and then in Cascade, twenty-four miles up the track. In Cascade, my pals and I hatched up the best prank of our lives. Ya see, there weren't more than a wagonload of men in Cascade who wanted to hear Bryan's hootin'—of course, the ladies weren't allowed to vote in those distinguished elections—because he was a prohibitionist. Of course, we all planted our boots on the belief that no government, American or foreign, has a right to tell its citizens what they can drink. So it was devised that every man who wanted to hear the prohibitionist would have to go do so in Great Falls, and that everybody else would hide, so that nobody but one young smart aleck would be present to welcome him to town.

When Bryan blows into Cascade, he finds the streets empty as a church on pay day, except for one lazy young whippersnapper saunterin' about. Figgerin' everybody should recognize him, Bryan don't introduce himself when he asks me, "Where is everybody?"

I answered as planned, "They all took the last train to Great Falls to hear that windjammer Bryan."

No, our ideas about likker didn't exactly dovetail, but we sure enjoyed each other once we took to jawin'. I was once known as the story teller of Judith Basin, but I sure met my match when I started swappin' yarns with William Jennings Bryan. With no ladies or children present, we didn't have to keep the bridle on our language, and that tea-totaler sure knew a passel of good, off-color yarns. We slung them windies back and forth for two and a half hours before he shook my hand and boarded that train, tellin' me, "I haven't enjoyed a bull session as much as this in years." Yep, you can sometimes hate what a person stands for but enjoy the fellow himself.

Another man I didn't see eye to eye with but enjoyed as a friend was George Washington Bird. He was a city man, raised and educated in Philadelphia. Paris Gibson had hired him to survey the town site for the streets, parks, and boulevards when Great Falls was built, and by the time I met him, he was a self-taught architect who specialized in drawin' the plans for large, brick buildings. Like Gibson, he believed in lurin' more industry, more business, and more people to the new town, the opposite of what I stood for.

I still drank when I met him, but Bird didn't drink or enter any saloons. He wasn't a prohibitionist; he believed in drinkin' whiskey to fight a cold or the flu. But when he wasn't ill, you couldn't get him to take a drink with a gun. Instead of rollin' Bull Durham like a cowboy, he rolled Prince Albert tobacco. Instead of watchin' rodeos and horse races, he loved baseball. We were opposites, but I always enjoyed swappin' yarns with him, even though he always wanted us to stick to clean and decent stories.

If my memory's not wobbly in the feet, it was on a warm summer's eve when I met Mr. Bird. Mame and I were takin' an after-supper walk up Third Avenue North when we tracked up on a Victorian-dressed fellow sittin' on his porch plunkin' on a banjar. I croaked, "Can you play that ol' cowboy song Sam Bass? It's my favorite."

"I don't know, sir; I've never tried," he told me. Then he lit into that melody like he wrote it. He played me a few more cowboy songs I asked for, and them songs led him to spillin' yarns about his grand daddy's adventures in George Washington's army. Of course, I had a few good yarns to shoot back at him myself that evening. Yes, people made a pastime of unloadin' yarns in the days before radios and movin' pictures.

That's how Mame and I met many of our friends who didn't adorn the saloons. In those days, houses were built with porches where people would perch on warm summer evenings, tellin' yarns, playin' musical instruments or cards, knittin', readin', tendin' to young-uns, and greetin' neighbors who were out for a walk. I hear tell that nowadays, people stay in their houses, watch motion picture radios, and refrigerate themselves on summer nights, more of modern man's progress.

If my memory's dealin' a square game, we met Judge Pray while porch perchin' one warm evening. Mame was studyin' some lessons Josephine Trigg had been teachin' her about business-woman English, and I was sculptin' a clay model of a buffalo that had been fightin' me on canvas, when along ambled a pilgrim in a Victorian suit. He puts up, "I see you're sculpting an animal. Could you be the artist Charlie Russell?"

I couldn't deny I was, so he chips in, "I'm Charles Pray. I've recently relocated here from Fort Benton to practice law."

I didn't know any more about politics than a cross-eyed steer, so I didn't know yet he'd been Montana's sole congressman for three terms and had lost the election the fourth time he ran. Pray was another city man, havin' been raised in New York and educated in Chicago. After practicin' law in Chicago for a few years, he hankered to know the West, so he came out to Fort Benton in 1906 where he practiced law and played his hand as a congressman. Two years before I crossed the Big Divide, President Coolidge appointed him a U. S. District Court Judge, and I hear tell he dealt that game till 1957. Of course, he didn't frequent the saloons I sloshed around in, so I may never have known him if it weren't for that old custom called "porch perchin'."

Another way I got to know my neighbors who didn't slosh around in the saloons was by way of what we called "The Fire Station Bench." A half block up the alley from my cabin, built near the alley on the southwest corner of Fifth Avenue North and Thirteenth Street, was the last of the town's fire stations to use horse-drawn fire wagons. The place was almost too colorful to paint, especially with word pictures. It was a two-story brick station with cots upstairs, a shiny brass fire pole, Dalmatian dogs, red fire wagons, curried horses, and the whole shebang.

Along the north wall of the fire station ran a full-sized horseshoe pit where the firemen pitched a game or two in their spare time. They were often joined in the sport by all manner of men from the neighborhood, includin' myself. Safely away from the bouncin' horseshoes stood a very long bench where firemen and neighbors would camp down and watch the games as they waited their turn to pitch.

Over the decades, that bench became the host to thousands of great yarns. At first, them yarns were spilt by gents waitin' their turn to pitch hoss shoes, but that bench fast became a place where neighbors would perch to gather in some windies and maybe spin a yarn or two, sorta' like a saloon with no likker. It wasn't always easy to tell the truth from the corral dust, but nobody bothered to sort out fact from fiction.

Today, my memory's canterin' back to a warm, late-summer evening when Mame and I and our wobbly son Jack were perchin' on our porch on Fourth Avenue. Jack was wearin' somebody else's brand when we first roped him into our cut, but by now, that brand had been vented, and we were ridin' paternal herd on the slick-eared tenderfoot. We'd spent most of the summer at our cabin at Lake McDonald, and we were still tryin' to town-break ourselves again, grumblin' about the ever-growin' noise and smell of more and more skunkwagons. Soon we saw Con Price ride up and snub his mount to one of the hitchin' rings in the curb. He bids a polite "Good evening" to Mame, asks, "Are ya ridin' yet, kid?" to Jack, and ambles up the alley to take cards in a game of horse shoes with the firemen.

I steer wrestled with my son for a few falls, and then I helped Mame harness him into pajamas and bed him down. When I lit out for the fire station, Mame didn't fret. Nine winters had passed since I'd last taken a drink, and she trusted me enough by now to no longer fear losin' me to likker. When I bowlegged up to the bench, I saw the friendly faces of seven firemen and my neighbors Earl Johnson, Bill DeCew, George Bird, Carl Snyder, Louis Brovan, Frank Sherer, and Gaylord Musselman. Con Price was already unloadin' a windy.

"…Charlie had just married," he was sayin', "and I was still in Cascade, workin' for an outfit breakin' horses. One night, a blacksmith and a barber surrounded too much joy juice and took to braggin' about their ridin' skills. The barber says, 'Con Price is the best rider I ever saw. He rides snaky outlaws so nobody can steal his horses. I'll bet you straight across you couldn't ride any of his broncs.'

"The blacksmith shoots back, 'I'll bet you every splinter I'm packin', four dollars, I can ride the next hoss Con rides into town. Charlie Russell here can hold the stakes.'

"But for some reason, the barber crawfishes out of the bet, sayin' he'll think it over. Now when Charlie tips me off as to the bet, I'm game as hornets to see it pulled off. Why? Because I know the winner will be buyin' a few rounds, so whoever wins or loses, I'm bound to win out a few drinks. I track into the barber shop for a haircut, and without lettin' on I know about the bet, I reassure the barber nobody but me could ever stay in the middle of any of my horses. Then I repair to the blacksmith's shop to have a shoe replaced, and I assure him all my horses are easier to ride than people think.

"Soon the bet was made the blacksmith could ride one of my horses from the blacksmith shop to the livery stable and back without being spilt. When I next ride into town, I put up the bluff I'm surprised when they stop me and ask if the blacksmith can borrow my hoss for a minute. I tell 'em, 'Why, sure,' with a smile and I dismount.

"I'll hand it to that blacksmith, he showed a lot of sand, more than most men. He climbs into the saddle like he owns the horse, takes a death grip on the reins with one hand, and clutches the saddle horn with the other. He kept that snaky stallion pacin' slow and easy, and it looked like he'd win the bet.

"But don't ya think it. Soon he rode up on a stockman named H. H. Nelson wearin' a long, canvas coat. As they passed each other, Nelson shook his coat like a cowboy shakin' out his flea trap, snappin' loose a sound like the flappin' of a big hawk's wings. My bronc buried its head, arched its back, and sprang into the atmosphere, hittin' the blacksmith in the eye with the saddle horn. The bronc's next jump sent the blacksmith spinnin' in the sky for a good forty flips. He saw more astronomy that day than any ten men ever saw before. He orbited once around Jupiter, took a squint at Mars, passed a dozen comets, and drank from the Big Dipper. As he busted the ground, a sudden eclipse came over him and blotted out his view. The barber helped him to his feet as I caught my horse.

"'I lost this bet,' the blacksmith admitted when he rounded to, 'but I want to make another one. Let's play it double or nothin' I'll whoop that sidewinder H. H. Nelson the next time he comes to town.'"

Con got his grins and chuckles and then the bridle was off to George Bird, who retold the yarn of his grandad bein' held prisoner of war by the British, escapin', and throwin' in with George Washington's army. Then it fell to Carl Snyder, who unloaded an episode of a failed attempt to rob his drug store in Stockett. Next, Frank Sherer unloaded on us the woes of bein' a German in Montana now that Uncle Sam was at war with that Kaiser. All those gents were good hands at pitchin' yarns, corral dust or otherwise, but the man who took the jackpot that night was Judge Pray.

Earl Johnson was shufflin' to deal us an off-color story when he beholds Mr. Pray and his wife Edith amblin' up to the bench. "I'd better hold this one by the collar till there's no ladies within earshot," Earl whispers.

"Anybody who wants to swear or spit has to do it in the alley till she's gone," a fireman reminds us.

Charles Pray introduces Edith to what fellows she hasn't met and tells us they'd just been dinin' at the Club Restaurant to observe their seventh wedding anniversary. The question bobbed up as to where they met, and the questions rolled around to, "How did it come about that you were born in Fort Benton, Mrs. Pray?"

She answered, "My husband loves to answer that question. May he?"

Everybody nodded as the Prays took a seat on the bench and Charles Pray filled his pipe. "That birth wouldn't have taken place, gentlemen," Pray lit out, "if it weren't for the occurrences I'm about to unfold. The saga begins a few short years after the Civil War when a youth of seventeen named Hans Wackerlin chose to leave Missouri for the wilds of Montana, just as you did as a youth, Mr. Russell. He boarded the steamboat Richmond, bound for Fort Benton, in St. Charles, Missouri, totally unaware that he was about to embark on the voyage of his life.

"As Hans boarded, a man who introduced himself as Captain Miller attempted to charge the lad one hundred thirty dollars for the passage. The youth's complaining about the high fare grew into quite an altercation, gentlemen, and resulted in Hans cocking the lever of his rifle and aiming it at Miller's heart. The captain soon saw the error of his ways and reduced that fee by fifty percent.

"'Just out of curiosity, let's see how well you

can shoot,' Miller challenged him. 'Can you hit that cottonwood tree across the river?'

"'I'll shoot off the lowest limb,' the youth bragged as he squeezed the trigger. Before the roar of the rifle had faded away, everyone could see the lad had done as he predicted. Miller and all his associates who managed the Richmond were so impressed with the youth's courage, valor, and marksmanship, gentlemen, they promptly asked him to become an associate in their commercial endeavor. Knowing nothing of this operation's history, Hans proudly accepted their offer.

"Now allow me to pause in this recitation to inform you of the kind of enterprise in which Hans had so naively engaged himself. Mr. Russell, being from Missouri, you most likely remember hearing about Quantrill's Raiders. Yes, I mean the private army William Clarke Quantrill amassed in the Missouri-Kansas border country. They were pro-Confederate forces who regularly ambushed Union patrols and convoys and they succeeded in driving thousands of pro-Union, abolitionist civilians from Missouri. When the James-Younger Gang later emerged, many of their members were veterans of Quantrill's Raiders.

"The confederacy welcomed their assistance at first, but ultimately, this militia went too far. Their infamous raid on Lawrence, Kansas, left a quarter of the town burned to the ground and one hundred fifty civilians dead. The confederacy not only condemned them with words; they, like the Union forces, sent soldiers to try to kill or capture the marauders. Many of them fled to Mexico and became mercenary soldiers for Maximilian. Of course, that dictator was soon killed by the Juaristas, and when the patriots recaptured Mexico, the former members of Quantrill's Raiders fled to Texas, where they took up the exciting occupation of robbing banks under the capable leadership of Langford Peale.

"They did quite well with their new enterprise, and before long, they'd amassed a fortune in stolen money. However, their endeavors soon became somewhat stressed, due to a decision on Peale's part to leave without notice and abscond with all the money. Of course, his former partners, now flat broke and always fighting the law, somewhat resented Peale's hasty decision. No, let's say those who weren't killed by the law became obsessed with taking revenge on Peale.

"Somehow, word reached the outlaws that Langford Peale was in Helena, Montana, living like a king. The gang outran the Texas law to the Red River, where they stormed aboard a docked steamboat, held the Negro deck hands at gunpoint, and steamed downstream toward the Mississippi. When they reached the Big Muddy, they pointed the boat's bow north toward St. Louis.

"All the deck hands were former slaves, so they were already accustomed to being impressed servants. The first thing the outlaws did was to change the vessel's name to "The Richmond" and to direct the servants to paint the new name on the boat. To earn some money, they began taking on freight as they boated northward. In fact, they did quite well for themselves, and they quickly realized their new enterprise was far more lucrative than robbing banks.

"They reached St. Louis early in May and took on a large cargo of mining equipment bound for Fort Benton. It weighed three hundred tons and the pirates charged sixty-five thousand dollars to deliver it. Thirty passengers boarded there at a hundred and thirty dollars per head, and the outlaws continued to wonder why they'd ever wasted their time robbing banks. And this, gentlemen, is how affairs stood on the good riverboat The Richmond when Hans Wackerlin joined its operation.

"Hans told me later the outlaws treated the passengers fairly well, although a voyage up the Missouri in the late eighteen sixties was never pleasurable. He said the travelers complained of only one thing: at every stop, the crew would disembark, hit the saloons, and blast their tonsils. Sometimes the passengers had to wait two or three days for the crew to sober up enough to resume the voyage.

"Shortly after leaving St. Charles, the outlaws hired a troop of traveling minstrels to serenade them as far as the next town. Once on the river, the outlaws pressed the singers and musicians into being deckhands. They were coerced into rolling barrels and toting bales all day and giving concerts every evening. Once the minstrels had learned the work of a deckhand, the pirates threw all the Negro deckhands overboard.

"For the first time, these marauders were earning big money and enjoying life to the utmost, and some of them argued they should continue running that steamboat for life. Others continually reminded their associates of their two pressing obligations: the recovery of their money from Peale and the termination of his earthly span.

"Many folks don't remember this, but at the mouth of the Marias River, about a dozen miles downstream from Fort Benton, was another steamboat landing. The outlaws decided to dock the Richmond there and send a couple men scouting out Fort Benton to make sure no posse was waiting for them. The scouts returned with word the town was safe, but also with the bad news that Peale had been killed in a gunfight in Helena.

"On July 28th, the Richmond landed in Fort Benton where the impressed deck hands were ordered to unload three hundred and sixteen tons of cargo. The outlaws sent a few men to Helena to verify that Peale was indeed firmly planted, and the rest of the gang went on a debauch until that town had no more liquor. It was in Fort Benton where the captive minstrels and Hans Wackerlin escaped from the inebriated pirates.

"When the scouts returned from Helena, all satisfied that Peale was indeed dead and buried, the outlaws had to realign their plans. The occupation of robbing banks and stagecoaches didn't seem to pay as well as boating freight, and it sure involved more risk, so the gang decided to continue serving as a shipping firm. They hired eight or nine Chinese workers as deckhands, who, of course, soon became impressed slaves, and they freighted out for St. Louis, stopping to pick up passengers and cargo at every opportunity along the way.

"But their luck took to rolling rather muddy in Sioux City, gentlemen, where they were surprised by a company of federal troops waiting to arrest them. Some were killed in the gun fighting that ensued, and some escaped on horseback to be killed later in failed robbery attempts in Wyoming and Idaho. But Hans Wackerlin stayed in Fort Benton and eventually became a successful merchant who married and raised a family, including this lovely lady with whom I celebrate seven years of marriage. And now you gentlemen know why Edith was born in Fort Benton."

This being said, the Pray's bid us good night and strolled home. Then Earl Johnson rekindled the off-color tale he'd kept the lid on until the lady left. When you cross the Big Divide, remind me to unload it on you.

Remember, the trail to my lodge is not grass grown. My robe will be spread and my pipe will lay stem toward you.

Your friend, C. M. Russell

Ink Talk One Hundred Twenty-nine

2013 in the moon of the new grass

Cowboy Proverbs and Ethics

I never had much to say when somebody asked for my steer. Nor did I listen much when somebody tried to unload some steer on me. Like any young wrangler, I thought I savvied everything. By the time I was an aging fool, I knew I should have swallowed more of the wisdom my elders blew my way. But I'm glad I tossed some of their steer in the discard. Sometimes there's a big gap between advice and help.

But by the time I crossed the Big Divide, I'd rounded up a fair-sized herd of cowboy proverbs touchin' every trail in a cowboy's life. If I'd followed some of them, I might have ridden smoother trails. Others might have caused me to be bucked off. If you're one of these folks who seek advice now and then, you might sort through this pile of horse sense and see if there's anything you can cinch a saddle on. Good luck.

- Horse sense is what a jackass lacks.
- When in doubt, let your horse do your thinkin'.
- Telling a man to go to hell and makin' him do it are two different propositions.
- Talk low, talk slow, say it plain, and don't say too much.
- There's no sense talkin' unless it can improve on silence.
- All laws are useless. Good men don't need them, and bad men don't obey them.
- You can't head off a man that won't quit.
- Play your cards close to your vest.
- You have to play some hands with your eyes shut.
- Man's the only animal that can be skinned more than once.
- Saddle your hoss before you start sassin' the boss.
- It's the man that's the cowboy, not the outfit he wears. Riggin' ain't ridin'.
- The bigger a man's head, the easier it is to fill his shoes.
- Never swap horses while crossin' a river.
- A change of pastures sometimes makes the cow fatter.

- Never grumble. It makes you about as welcome as a sidewinder in a cow camp.

- The man who uses a sticky rope is bound to hang from one.

- Run when you're wrong; shoot when you're right.

- Maybe you can't make a banker out of a hoss thief, but you can sure make a hoss thief out of a banker.

- If you don't mix with worse company than animals, you're doing all right.

- Worry is like saddlin' a wobbly horse. It gives you something to do, but it don't get you anywhere.

- Any jackass can kick down a barn, but it takes a good carpenter to build one.

- Never argue with somebody stupider than you. It'll just make him mad.

- Trouble is a private thing. Don't lend it, and don't borrow it.

- There's always somebody to take the slack out of a trouble maker's rope.

- A man with too much spread is bound to get his horns clipped.

- Never trust braggers, fleas, or tenderfeet.

- Trust everybody in the game, but always cut the cards.

- Never trust a wolf for dead till you got him skinned.

- Before a stable can get clean, somebody has to get dirty.

- All corpses look pious.

- It's after a man is dead when folks dig up a heap of virtues to pile on him.

- Never take another man's bet. He wouldn't offer it if he didn't know something you don't.

- When it comes to cussin', don't swallow your tongue. Use both barrels and air out your lungs.

- God's wildest critters live in the cities.

- The stuff that makes you tipsy also makes you tip your hand.

- Some folks are like stuffed fish. They wouldn't be in a jam if they kept their mouths shut.

- A man that packs his gun loose don't run his boot heels over side-steppin' trouble.

- The man who wears his holster tied down don't do much talkin' with his mouth.

- Sometimes it's safer to pull your freight than pull your gun.

- Don't tell people your troubles. Half won't give a damn, and half will be glad you've got 'em.

- If you want to forget all your troubles, walk a mile in a brand new pair of ridin' boots.

- Always drink upstream from the herd.

- Never smack a man who's chewin' tobacco.

- Never miss a good chance to shut up.

- Go after life like it's something that's gotta be roped and tied down before it gets away.

- Wear a hat with a brim wide enough to shed the rain, shade the sun, fan a camp fire, pour water, and whip a fightin' steer in the face.

- Wanderin' around like a pony with the bridle off don't get you to the end of the trail.

- A smile from a good woman is worth more than a dozen handed out by a bartender.

- The biggest dog was once a pup.

- There's a lot more to ridin' than sittin' in a saddle and lettin' your feet hang down.

- Don't fork a saddle if you're afraid of gettin' throwed.

- If you're gonna go, go like hell. If your minds not made up, don't use your spurs.

- If you're lookin' at the dangerous end of a scatter gun, pull in your horns.

- A hard boiled egg is always yellow inside.

- If you straddle a fence, you'll never have your feet on the ground.

- Never take to sawin' on the branch that's supportin' you unless you're bein' hung from it.

- Never spit against the wind.

Richard Bird Baker

- You can't throw mud without stoopin' low and losin' ground.

- A sharp tongue will sooner or later cut its owner's throat.

- Put off sayin' things today that might get you licked tomorrow.

- The surest way to cure a toothache is to tickle a mule's heels.

- Small minds and big mouths have a way of hookin' up.

- Meet your troubles half way up the trail.

- The man who hunts trouble in a saloon is apt to pass in his chips with sawdust in his beard.

- No matter how hard the winter, spring always comes.

- Rope with a big loop. If you miss the horns, you're more likely to fasten to the feet.

- It ain't how long the ride is; it's how well you ride it.

- Life ain't in holdin' a good hand; it's in playin' a poor hand well.

- It's the little things that get tangled in your spurs and trip you.

- Wait till you get your feet in the stirrups before you spur your horse.

- Always carry more 'n one rope. You might run across more 'n one rope can handle.

- When you find yourself in over your head, don't open your mouth. Swim.

- Life is like a cow pasture. You can't pass through it without steppin' in some muck.

- Don't corner something meaner than you.

- Don't stand in the trough when you feed the pigs.

- Never play leapfrog with a bull.

- If a crooked gambler changes his name more than once a month and keeps on the move, his chances of livin' are an even break with a dumb rustler's.

- Crooked poker players most often ain't good players. Make 'em play square and they're yours.

- It's better to know the country than to be the best cowboy.

- Walkin' away don't always mean a lack of sand. A man runs from a polecat and from a bear, but the reasons ain't the same.

- Some men think the sun comes up just to hear them crow.

- It's better to keep your tongue behind your teeth and let folks wonder if you're a fool than to open your mouth and prove it.

- If you've gotta drive cattle through town, do it on a Sunday when some folks feel more prayerful and are less disposed to cuss at you.

⊰ Nothing's better than a cool drink of water, but too much can give you a bellyache.

⊰ You'll never see a wild critter feel sorry for itself.

⊰ A lot of bad luck is undeserved; but then, so is a lot of good luck.

⊰ You can always stand more than you think.

⊰ A man who wants to loan you a slicker when it ain't rainin' ain't doin' you much of a favor.

⊰ If you give a lesson in meanness to a critter or a person, don't be surprised if they learn that lesson and return it.

⊰ When a man gets caught in a woman's loop, he's as helpless as a dummy with his hands cut off.

⊰ The easiest way to eat crow is while it's still warm. The colder it gets, the harder it is to swallow.

⊰ Never spur a horse when he's swimmin'.

⊰ Swingin' a rope is all right, as long as your neck ain't in it.

⊰ The measure of a man is in his honesty and nerve.

⊰ A man can easily brag himself out of a place to lean against the bar.

⊰ When a man calls your bluff, it's time again to look at your hole card.

- Men are like matches. When they flare up, they lose their heads.

- If you want to know who's wrong in an argument, see who gets mad first.

- The man who keeps the bridle on his temper shoots the truest.

- It's rare to find a horse everyone agrees is the best in the remuda.

- The higher you climb, the more rocks you have to dodge.

- You'll sure enough get out-pointed if you pick a quarrel with a porcupine.

- Never let your yearnings get ahead of your earnings.

- The longest rope gets the maverick.

- Stick your nose into trouble and you'll find your foot in it too.

- When opportunity knocks, don't complain about the noise.

- The wood you chop yourself makes the hottest fire.

- A man who can't dance says the band can't keep a beat.

- There's no such thing as a sure thing. Let the other fellows run on the rope if they want to, but keep your money in your pocket.

- Sometimes the only way to grab a bull by the horns is to slap on the hobbles.

- Range horses are dangerous at both ends.

- Nobody is important enough to feel important.

- If you feel important, try ordering somebody else's dog around.

- A cold wet hoss with a hump on its back is dangerous.

- It's the liar who needs the best memory.

- You can't tell how fast a horse can run by its color.

- You can't tell how well a fellow can ride by the size of his spurs.

- Never tamper with the natural ignorance of a greenhorn.

- Never call a man a liar because he knows more than you.

- Empty bellies don't sweeten nobody's temper.

- A man—slam him on the scales and weigh him—is a mighty puny critter compared to so many.

- Some men follow one wagon track and some another. Some even cut new trails.

- You can't tell what a horse's gait's gonna be till it's broke.

- You can almost always judge a man by the horse he rides.

- Never draw a gun unless you're ready to go the whole hog down to the last bristle of his tail.

- There was never a horse that couldn't be rode or a man that couldn't be throwed.
- If you're lost in a blizzard, give your horse his head.
- In the dark, don't spur a horse where he don't want to go.
- Speak your mind, but ride a fast horse.
- When a man's got his health, he's got no license to bellyache.
- You can give some folks the world and they'll want the moon for a cow pasture.
- When you throw your weight around, prepare to have it thrown around by someone else.
- Only a fool would argue with a skunk, a mule, or a cook.
- Never approach a bull from the front, a horse from the rear, or a fool from any direction.
- Most men are like bob wire. They have their good points.
- He who makes an ass of himself can expect to be rode.
- Flattery is like perfume. Go ahead and smell it, but don't swallow it.
- If you follow another man's tracks, there ain't no way of knowing if the man knew where he was going.
- Love your enemies, but keep your gun oiled.
- Be mighty careful in your choice of enemies.

- If you're ridin' ahead of the herd, take a look back every now and then to make sure it's still followin' ya.

- The difference between some men and a rattlesnake is that the snake's honest enough to rattle a warning.

- The only fool bigger than the person who knows nothing is the person who knows it all.

- If you want to stay single, look for the perfect woman.

- Never interfere with something that ain't botherin' you.

- Tossin' your rope before buildin' your loop don't catch no calves.

- A woman's heart is like a camp fire. If you don't tend to it regular, you'll soon lose it.

- Solving problems is like throwin' cattle. Dig your heels in on the big one and catch the little ones around the neck.

- Every jackass loves to hear himself bray. Because one takes a whim to bray at you, why bray back at him?

- Talk is a sorry hoss to run in a race.

- No man, unless locoed, would ever put a bet on the public.

- Too many folks get calluses from pattin' their own backs.

- Riling water only makes it muddier.

- It's a mighty sorry cowhand that'll ride a sore-backed hoss.

- It takes some falls to make a good rider.

- If you must put a Spanish bit in some mouth, let it be your own.

- Bridle a horse from the side and a mule from the front.

- Shallow rivers and shallow minds freeze first.

- The bigger the mouth, the better it looks when it's shut.

- Scientific theories are like the limbs of a tree. They'll hold if you don't go cooning out too far. Overplay, and down you'll tumble, according to how you've been perchin' low or roostin' way up yonder.

- It's better to ride an ass that carries you than a horse that throws you.

- Pride is a funny thing. Too much makes a man a fool; too little makes him a coward.

- Letting the cat out of the bag is a whole lot easier than putting it back in.

- An empty wagon rattles the loudest.

- Success is the size of the hole a man leaves after he dies.

- The sun don't blister the tongue that stays behind the teeth.

- Any man concerned about his dignity should make it a point never to ride a bull.

Richard Bird Baker

- You can cover it with sugar and bake it in the oven, but a cowpie is still manure.

- If you ain't been bucked off, you ain't been on many.

- Telling some folks a secret is like using kerosene to put out a fire.

- Laid side by side, the egg of an eagle ain't in it with a goose egg. But just the same, it holds an eagle.

- Treat mule-headed men the same way you'd treat a mule you're fixin' to corral. Just leave the gate open a tad and let 'em bust in.

- The mouth is the thing most often opened by mistake.

- A horse thief is like a calf. Give him enough rope and he'll tangle himself.

- Timing has a lot to do with the success of a rain dance.

- Sometimes you find a heap of thread on mighty small spools.

- A whale would never get harpooned if it didn't spout off in public.

- Remain independent of any source of income that will deprive you of your liberty.

- No jackass ever got ahead by kickin' up his heels every night.

- A cowchip is paradise to a fly.

- Keep skunks and bankers at a distance.

- Kickin' never gets you anywhere unless you're a mule.

- The best way to cook any part of a range longhorn is to toss it in a pot of boilin' water with a horseshoe. When the horseshoe is tender, you can eat the beef.

- Don't go pesterin' around a bee tree, get all stung up, and then declare there's no sweetness in the world.

- Money is like a drunk. The tighter it gets, the louder it talks.

- Money is like a shadow. The harder you chase it, the faster it moves.

- Nature makes few mistakes.

- The biggest sores are caused by small spurs.

- Don't build a gate before you've built the corral.

- For want of a nail, a horseshoe is lost. For want of a shoe, the horse is lost. For want of a horse, the rider is lost.

- A liar is a cowboy who says he's never been throwed.

- Strange as it may break on the ears of a tenderfoot, the three scarcest things in cow country are butter, beef, and milk.

- Trying to drown your troubles in liquor only irrigates them.

- A man can learn a heap of things if he keeps his ears washed.

- When a woman starts draggin' her loop, there's always a man willing to step in.

- Every quarrel is a private one; outsiders are never welcome.

- What's good manners in one place may be bad judgment in another, same as some saloons play straights in poker and in some, straights are barred.

- It's the blockhead that always packs a chip on his shoulder.

- Some folks can make a peck of trouble fill a bushel basket.

- Working behind a plow, all you see is a mule's hind end. Workin' atop of a horse, you can see across the country as far as your eye is good.

- A good example has twice the value of good advice.

- There's no more pleasure in a bragger's company than in a wet dog's.

- It's discomfort that pans out the good and bad in men.

- There's only two things you need to be afraid of: a woman lookin' to wed and being left afoot.

- Stay shy of a man who's all gurgle and no guts.

- The rooster makes more noise than the hen that lays the eggs.

- If you dance with a grizzly, you'd better let him lead.

- It don't take a genius to spot a goat in a flock of sheep.

- Never get into fights with ugly people. They have nothing to lose.

- If wishes were horses, some folks would need a lot of hay.

- When you wallow with pigs, expect to get dirty.

- If you run with the hounds, expect to get fleas.

- When the herd turns on you and you're forced to run for it, try to look like you're leading the charge.

- If you have to climb a hill, waitin' won't shrink it.

- The easiest life is to be part of the herd. The hardest is to be apart from it.

- Don't worry about bitin' off more than you can chew. Your mouth is probably a whole lot bigger than you think.

- Life is like bustin' broncs. Sometimes you'll get throwed. The way to win out is to keep gettin' back on.

I first blew into the Montana Territory in 1880, and for my first dozen years on the range, there was an utter lack of written law. When eastern-style law finally blundered along into our destinies, it didn't dovetail with the work, life, and fate of cattle country. Men found they couldn't obey many of them new laws even if they wanted to. I'd bet my chaps and spurs that's how the Old West got its bad reputation. But the blame should be shot at the tenderfoot lawmakers who knew nothing about life on the cattle ranges, not us cowboys.

Before sure-enough law plagued us, a system of courtesy we called "The Code of the West" rode the cattle ranges. It was known and respected on every range where men raised cattle from the Rio Grande to the Blue Rockies of Canada. If a man didn't follow this code, he'd soon find himself hazed into the cutbacks. And I'll tell ya without pinchin' a chip, if your modern hives of commerce followed this code, their dealings would be honest as a church. Let me unload on you all the details of this code that my memory can fish up.

Like our Red brothers, cowboys respected nothing more than courage. You couldn't face the daily dangers of snaky horses, mad cows, prairie dog holes, swollen rivers, quicksand, bears, cougars, and rattlesnakes, to say nothing of angry renegades, blizzards, and draughts, without grit and sand. I ain't claimin' cowboys never felt fear. Real courage means bein' so scared you're shakin' in your boots but you saddle up and ride anyway. A man without courage in a cow camp was as out of place as a barkeep at a camp meeting. Cowards risked the lives of others and were soon tossed into the discard pile.

Complainers were less welcome than a skunk at

a picnic. A good cowhand not only had to expect hardship; he needed to rely on his sense of humor to shoulder it. Cowboys could turn many tricks most men couldn't, and we faced more hardships and dangers than most men. Knowin' that fact resulted in what's called "cowboy pride." It was our belief that a man on horseback is a higher card in the Creator's deck than a man on foot. Cowboys said, "We're too proud to cut hay and not quite wild enough to eat it." Others said, "We won't be caught on the blister end of no damn shovel." Because of this cowboy pride, we never wore bib overalls, because that's farmers' riggin'. We didn't wear a spur on just one foot 'cause that's the brand of a sheepherder.

Cowboy pride meant takin' pride in his work. That included stayin' loyal to the outfit you're workin' for and above all, stayin' loyal to your friends. When you rode for another man's brand, you'd try to protect his cattle like they were your own. And finishin' what you start was an important value to cattlemen. There was a saying, "When you're ridin' through hell, keep ridin'." A quitter was as welcome among cowhands as a hog caller in a library.

Square dealin' was another virtue in the Code of the West. It was held that a man was as good as his word, and his word and his handshake should be good enough to seal any deal. Petty thievery and camp robbers were almost unknown around cow camps. Sure, I've known plenty of cowboys who wouldn't spend much time lookin' for the mother if they found a slick-eared calf, and I knew a few who'd held up a stagecoach or two. But cowboys rarely stole from one another.

The Code of the West included straight talkin'. Sometimes a man can say more by talkin' less. Talk was something to keep plain and true. Get to the point, and when all is said, stop talkin'. Of course, that part of the code wasn't in play when tellin' yarns.

The long and the short of this Code of the West is: do what needs to be done, stand up for what is right, be tough but fair, and when in doubt, follow the Golden Rule. Now dozens of unwritten rules stem from this basic code. My memory is too grassed over to remember every rule, but I can probably plow up a good many. You might go rummagin' through these rules in order to better understand this critter called a cowboy.

- Never ask a man about his past or what his name was back in the states.
- Never volunteer assistance to the law or ask it for favors.
- Never ask a man the size of his spread or how many cattle he owns.
- Revere and respect all women.
- Never give away a friend or sell him out.
- Never fire a gun near a cattle herd.
- Never have whiskey in a cow camp. The work is dangerous enough sober.
- Always wake a man with words and never with touch.

- Never strike a horse when angry.
- Never ride a horse into the middle of a herd if it's a bucker.
- Never shoot a man while smilin' or shoot an unarmed man. Follow the "rattlesnake's code," which means warn somebody before killin' 'em.
- Never ambush anyone unless you have fled them and they keep pursuin' you.
- When branding your calves, brand others you round up with their mother's brand.
- In a saloon, fill all glasses to the brim and use your shootin' hand to pour.
- Keep your hands above the table in a poker game.
- Never cut another man's fence. Pull the staples, lower the wires, and replace them after your herd has crossed.
- Always leave another man's gates as you found 'em.
- Never ride or feed another's horse without permission.
- Never dismount within a hundred yards of a bedded herd.
- If a cow breaks from the herd and gets by you, it's your job to bring it back.
- Take care of your horse before yourself.
- Lend a horse only in an emergency. The wrong rider has spoilt many a horse.

- Don't change stirrup lengths on a borrowed saddle without permission.
- Keep to the trail when ridin' across a stranger's range.
- Never draw a gun on an unarmed man.
- It's a truce if an enemy accepts a drink.
- Never touch another's gun without permission.
- Take off your hat and spurs when you enter another's house.
- In a restaurant, remove your gun before sitting down at a dining table. Remove your hat if ladies are present. If you eat at a counter, leave your hat and gun on.
- As a guest, never offer to pay for a meal. As a host, never ask your guests to pay for one.
- If you ride up on a ranch house and nobody's home, it's bad manners to leave money for the grub you eat. But always wash your dishes and cut some firewood.
- Two cattle outfits covering the same territory should hold their roundups at the same time.
- If you ride up on a man from the rear, let your presence be known by a "hello" before you're within gun range. Do the same when approaching a strange camp.
- When you ride up on a stranger face to face, greet him by raising your shooting hand to your hat brim and keep it away from your gun.

But don't lift your hand if you know a rider is on a skittish horse. It might bolt. Just nod and say, "Howdy."

- When two riders pass each other on the trail, it's a violation of the "Code of the West" to look back over your shoulder. That's a sign of distrust.

- If two riders stop to talk on the trail, they should dismount and loosen their cinches and give their horses' backs some air.

- Never abuse a horse. That will spoil the horse and make it as useless for cattle work as a sow pig.

- It's an insult to offer a man help in saddlin' his hoss (unless he's hurt).

- If you get bucked off, get back on. Never let a hoss think he's won an argument.

That's all the rules I can plow up for now, so I'll turn up the box and stop dealin'. As a single-handed talker, I'm better than a green hand, but I'm mighty lame with a pen. With this long-range talk, my sights are mighty warped, and I shoot over or under every shot. But when you ride up on my camp, I'll talk with you again at short range. When you cross the Big Divide and sight the smoke of my cabin, remember, the latch string is out. A robe will be spread and a pipe will be lit for you.

Your friend, C. M. Russell

Post Thoughts

"Each of us has our trail mapped out for us before we start by an Unseen Power. That's the way we have to travel. If we could see all the bad crossings on that trail, few of us would have the nerve to tackle it. So I guess it's a good thing we can only see the spots where the sun shines on our way."   Con Price

"If the trail is smooth where you're travelin', what's the use of worryin' about the fords ahead?" C.M. Russell

"Keep ridin', boy, live till you die; just don't live to be too dang old. You'll wind up over there in that old rockin' chair, with no dreams and no cards to fold."
        Ken Overcast (from his song "Too Dang Old")

"The grass may be short and the trail may be long, and the campfire may sometimes go out, but never lose sight of your destination, for that's what this ride's all about. Chase you a rainbow and rope you a dream, ride tall where no others remain. Keep your feet in the stirrups and lookin' ahead, and never let go of the reins."
                        Jay Dean (from his song
                        "Don't Let Go of the Reins")

"Here's hoping your trail is a long one
 Plain and easy to ride
 May your dry camps be few
 And health ride with you
 To the pass on the Big Divide."

C. M. Russell